# JACK

## Max McBridge

'Uneasy lies the head that wears a crown.'
William Shakespeare

Copyright © Max McBridge 2020.

The right of Max McBridge to be identified as the author of this book has been asserted in accordance with the Copyright, Designs and Patents Act 1988.

No part of this book is to be reproduced in any form without express permission of the author. All rights reserved.

ISBN: 9798671610086

First published by McBridge Foundation 2020.

Edited by Ben Jeapes.

Photos by 📷 @sanbloo.

All present-day characters in this story are fictitious and bear no resemblance to anyone living or dead.

https://mcbridge.uk/

This book is dedicated to the people of London who
show the world that an open and inclusive city is possible.



Still more needs to be done and therefore £1 of this
book's purchase price goes directly to charities that
help to close the gap between those who can afford the
rich opportunities of this great city and those who are
increasingly left behind.

# In the Beginning

It began on Friday, August 31st 1888. The prostitute Mary Ann Nichols was found dead in a Whitechapel street by a wagoner at around three o'clock.

A dead prostitute was nothing unusual in this area of London. Murders were all too frequent. But the nature of death surprised even the most experienced crime experts. According to Dr Llewellyn, who autopsied the body a day later, the killer had grabbed the victim from behind, held her mouth shut and cut her throat with a sharp, long blade. Then he sliced open her abdomen.

The investigation into her murder was headed by Chief Inspector Frederick G. Abberline. Abberline soon found himself grappling not only with the murderer but with the British press, who had got wind of the case. Pages were filled with speculation about the killer. They gave him the nickname 'Leather Apron', because the scene of the crime was near a slaughterhouse.

Only a week later, on 8th September, Annie Chapman's body was found in a niche between a courtyard staircase and the fence of the adjacent house. It was as cruelly disfigured as the body a week ago. After the autopsy, there was no doubt that the two murders had been committed by the same person. But this time the victim was almost decapitated as the stranger had tried to break through the neck vertebrae.

Witnesses testified that the prostitute spoke to a john at 5 a.m. that morning. The man wore a hunting hat and was about forty years old. He might have been a foreigner, dressed shabbily and quite small. Annie had asked if he wanted to do it with her; the unknown man had answered this question in the affirmative. Then the two disappeared into one of the dark alleys. Two hours later, Annie was found dead by porter John Davis.

To Abberline's disappointment, none of the witnesses said they would recognise the stranger.

Inevitably, rumours began to spread. The inhabitants of Whitechapel had a brutal murderer in their midst. Further afield, people liked to be safely outraged. The murders sold newspapers so the British press did all it could to stoke the flames. Very soon the mob was making it difficult for legitimate owners of leather aprons – shoemakers, cork makers, butchers – to go about their perfectly legal business. Reports to the police soared sharply, whether based on genuine suspicion or paranoia or for the fun of it. The police searched two hundred lodging houses all over London. Not wanting to appear lazy, they also started to arrest suspicious-looking foreigners and beggars at random. An irritated Abberline estimated that about one thousand people were arrested wrongly. All it did was distract resources from the genuine investigation. He asked the overall head of London CID, Sir Robert Anderson, to put an end to them but the case had become political. The police had to be seen to be acting, and his requests fell on deaf ears.

Vigilante patrols of citizens now roamed the streets of Whitechapel between two and five in the morning.

On September 10th, Abberline thought the case was finally solved. The thirty-three-year-old Polish Jew John Pilzer was arrested by Detective Sergeant William Thicke. Five large, sharp knives were seized during the search of his room. However, when interviewed, Pilzer had a watertight alibi for the time of the crime. His brother had advised him to stay in his room because of the Leather Apron hysteria, and none of the witnesses to Annie Chapman's john recognised him.

Seven days after the arrest of Pilzer, police received the first letter from the killer. It was addressed to the Chief Constable, began 'Dear Boss', and was signed, 'Jack the Ripper'.

When Abberline read the letter he immediately began to wonder whether the killer had any connections to the police. The author of the letter indicated that there was a secret known only to him and to Sir Robert Anderson. But what was this secret? Abberline had to put this question to one side as further letters followed. In one letter, the Ripper even identified the next crime scene.

Now that they knew the scene, the Chief Inspector and experts tried to work out who might be the next victim. Despite all their planning, the Ripper beat them to it. At one o'clock in the morning on September 30th, in the pouring rain, Louis Diemschutz found a woman's body in his backyard. The post-mortem examination revealed that the victim was forty-four-year-old Elizabeth Stride. Witnesses reported that Stride, before her violent death, had had contact with a little man with a long dark coat, dark trousers and a hard felt hunter's hat.

One small ray of hope was that Louis had disturbed the Ripper and thus he had got no further than slicing her neck open. Still, it was worrying to realize that the killer had committed the murder in an extremely short period of time: only a few minutes before, PC William Smith had passed the crime scene during his patrol. Nor had the Ripper been disturbed by the thirty members of the nearby International Working Men's Educational Club, who had been singing loudly with the window open.

Just forty-five minutes later, the police found another female body. Forty-three-year-old Catherine Eddowes was lying on her back, her right leg pulled up and her face turned to the left. Her dress was pushed up over her chest. The body had been slit from the sternum to the abdomen, and the murderer had taken out the intestines and carefully laid them over her right shoulder.

The two murders led to a furious argument within the police, because Catherine Eddowes should not even have been free to become a victim of the Ripper. She had been arrested that night for drunken behaviour and disturbing the peace. However, the officer in charge at the police station had released her at one o'clock in the morning, contrary to the regulations, just under an hour before her death.

During the post-mortem examination of Catherine Eddowes, the doctor found that the left kidney had been removed with a clean cut. The kidney appeared two weeks later, in a letter sent to the head of the Whitechapel

Vigilance Committee – the vigilante committee set up by the citizens of Whitechapel. It was clear to the police that the Ripper had to have medical skills. The language and vocabulary of his letters also suggested an educated man.

Politics now began to rear its head further. The murders overlapped with the territories of the Metropolitan Police and the City Police, and the newly founded Scotland Yard was also involved. Sir Robert Anderson, personally appointed by Queen Victoria, had difficulty uniting all the departments under one leader. Meanwhile more letters came in from the Ripper, now making fun of the police and their work.

Abberline continued his work. Why did all the women have to die? There had to be another detail that connected them together, but he still had no clue what this detail might be.

On November 9th 1888, at about 10 a.m., the last murder was committed. Candle maker and tenement owner John McCarthy sent his assistant to 13 Miller's Court to collect the overdue rent from Mary Jane Kelly. The boy knocked but no one opened the door, so he looked through the window. What he saw made him run screaming to his boss, who immediately alerted the police.

Abberline was one of the first at the scene. He made sure that nobody entered the place and called the police doctor. After a quick look into the room, the doctor threw up in front of the door. Abberline came close to vomiting himself: he hadn't seen anything like it during his entire career.

On the bed lay the severely mutilated corpse of Mary Jane Kelly. The Ripper had severed her throat from one ear to the other, as deep as the front of spine. The nose and the ears were cut off and the face was slashed beyond recognition. The amputated breasts and liver were at the side of the bed, the kidneys were under the head, the spleen was to the left of the corpse and the intestines to the right. On the table Abberline found scraps of meat from the abdomen and thighs. The Ripper had apparently taken the heart with him because it could not be found. In the fireplace was a large pile of the victim's burnt garments.

Jack had done his bloody work by the light of the fire. What surprised Abberline, however, was that neither the other tenants nor passers-by seemed to have noticed anything, even though the Ripper had been in the room for over two hours before he pushed a chest of drawers against the door and escaped through a window.

Abberline's first witness was prostitute Mary Ann Cox. She had seen Mary Kelly before midnight with a john. About two hours later Cox had visited Mary in her room at Miller's Court to warm her hands. Black Mary, as Mary Kelly was also called, had been drunk and singing an Irish folk song. Cox had gone to sleep about three o'clock and Mary had quietened down.

Another witness, the unemployed night watchman George Hutchinson, had seen Mary Kelly talking to another suitor at two o'clock that morning. He had been about thirty-five years old, was not tall and wore a dark felt hat. It was clear to Abberline that Hutchinson had seen the Ripper. But he had not seen the face of the stranger, because the man had kept his head low.

Finally there came a point when Abberline had questioned every witness. Now he just had to collate all the evidence and draw his conclusions.

The truth that finally emerged was unbelievable – but the facts could not lie.

JACK

# London 1888

Darkness lay over the largest city in the world, like a black veil of mourning. A cold wind swept through the empty streets. At this time of day, London had something threatening and unfriendly about it. The inhabitants of the West End had long since retired to their villas and town residences. Rocking gently in his carriage as it clattered through the dark of St James's, Frederick Abberline felt as though he was moving through a void.

The interior of the carriage regularly filled with light from a passing gas lamp, weak and diffused through the fog, then dwindled again into darkness. Abberline looked thoughtfully at the pile of papers on his lap in the rhythmic spurts of light. They were tied with a string into a package, and the first sheet was typewritten with its file number: No. 123_08/1888 JtR. The answers were all in here. He had spent countless nights talking to witnesses, threading clues together to make a coherent picture. It was only looking back that he really realised how many doors had deliberately remained closed to him.

He had needed answers to two big questions. Had the five prostitutes known each other? And how had the Ripper so easily slipped through the police net, over and over again?

Now he had the answers to both questions.

A glance out of the window told him he was near his destination. He slipped the pile of papers into his case as the carriage drew up outside a large white terraced house.

He looked up at the house as he paid off the carriage and it moved away. With a few exceptions, all the windows were dark. Then he glanced down the dimly gaslit street towards the great bulk of St James's Palace, the seat of the heir to the British throne. In front of the main gate, two soldiers stood on sentry duty. Abberline's expression turned thoughtful as he wondered what would be the reaction if he went a bit further down the street and presented his file to the person now living there. He doubted he would get that far, he thought, with a wry and reluctant smile.

The butler who opened the black wooden door gazed at Abberline with a haughty, appraising eye.

'Chief Inspector Frederick Abberline, to see Sir Robert Anderson,' Abberline said.

The butler's impassive face creased slowly into a reluctant frown.

'Sir Robert will not want to be disturbed at this time of day, sir.'

'I'm well aware of that, but your master will not want to learn that you turned me away!'

The butler raised one eyebrow and Abberline was aware of the impression he made. His grey frock coat was somewhat worn. The black stained cylinder of his hat, on top of his dishevelled hair, only reinforced the butler's opinion.

With a slight tilt of his head, the butler indicated that Abberline should enter.

'Wait here, sir.' And with that, he walked away to fetch the chief of police.

Frederick Abberline looked around the great marble hall. On his right was a small table with an oversized mirror hanging over it. Opposite, a portrait of the house's master hung in a gold frame. A large black wooden staircase led to the upper chambers. The only light for the whole hall came from the street lamp in front of the house, through two large windows next to the door.

After a while, the butler returned, his way lit by a night light in his hand.

'If you would please follow me?'

He led Abberline along a long corridor. At the end he turned left and opened a brown wooden door. 'Sir Robert, Chief Inspector Abberline to see you.'

'He can come in!'

Abberline found himself in the director's study. The walls were decorated with old wooden shelves full of books. A heavy wooden desk stood on a large Persian carpet in the middle of the room. Sir Robert sat on a green leather armchair behind the desk. He was still wearing his evening dress, a black tailcoat and a wide bow tie with a matching shirt.

'I'm glad you could see me at such a late hour, sir,' Abberline said, 'but I wanted to be the first to inform you of the results of the Ripper investigation.'

Anderson looked intrigued and pleased.

'Very well, please sit down.' Anderson showed Abberline to a chair in front of the desk. 'Can I offer you something to drink?'

'No, thank you, sir, I'd rather get right to the point.'

'As you wish.'

'So ...' Abberline put the big package on Anderson's table. He opened it and began to read.

Half an hour later, Sir Robert whistled slowly.

'I thought this case would never be solved. You're brilliant.'

'You see why I wanted you to see it, sir. This is ... sensitive.'

'More than that, Chief Inspector.' Sir Robert shuffled slowly through the papers. 'Explosive.'

'So ... how do we make this known, sir?'

Sir Robert looked up and smiled coolly.

'We do not.'

Abberline was an experienced, street-hardened policeman. There were very few times that he was actually speechless. But for just a moment, this was one of those times.

'Sir, may I ask why you say that?'

'Of course.' Sir Robert maintained his cool smile. 'You know for yourself that this secret can never be made public. Not in these times.' He waved a hand at the pile of papers. 'This had to happen, for the sake of the country. If we had just stood by and watched, our government would have become susceptible to blackmail. We couldn't let that happen. Britain is on the brink of civil war, Chief

Inspector. We need a strong lead, or we will sink into chaos.'

'This is not the Middle Ages, sir! We are a democracy!'

'I don't appreciate that tone, Chief Inspector. What's more, you have no idea about domestic issues. You're just a police inspector. No, you can leave the thinking about these things to us. Our system has been proved by time and I will not allow it to be harmed. Take a look at these new states in Europe! All these so-called republics clinging to some kind of stability. We are the only remaining world power and that is thanks to a strong leader!'

'But, you don't seriously think the Ripper did it all on his own?' Abberline was baffled. 'There had to be people behind the scenes who knew. In Downing Street! In Parliament! We owe it to the dead – we owe it to the people of this country to state the facts. And even if these killings were justified,' he went on, 'just to argue that point, if I must – may I ask why the Ripper committed these murders so … so outrageously? The killings would have been ignored if he hadn't drawn so much attention to them by his own actions!'

'You may be right,' Anderson agreed calmly. 'I, too, found the methods of our faithful servant, let's say, not appropriate to the occasion. But as another member of our club put it so aptly: "We just didn't have him under control anymore!"'

The full implications of Anderson's frequent use of the word 'we' finally sank in.

'My God,' Abberline breathed. 'You were in on it too! You're a *policeman!* You stand for law and the truth!'

Anderson shook his head.

'Above all I stand for stability, Chief Inspector. Law and truth are subordinate to the continuity of tradition. Every man who believes firmly in something will find himself forced to defend that belief. This action involves weighing compromises, which I have done!'

'Oh, my God! Oh, my God!' Abberline clutched his head. 'Stability *starts* with law and order! To believe otherwise – you're no better than any murderer in this town, sir, except you do it here from your office, in an expensive tailor-made suit.'

Abberline glared at Sir Robert, not quite believing what he had just said. Anderson returned the look, pitiful and condescending. The room was silent apart from the ticking of the wall clock that cut through the air.

Anderson broke the silence.

'I'll overlook that outburst, Chief Inspector, because you've done an excellent job. I'll take the file so it can be finally closed and filed at Old Scotland Yard.'

'But, sir!'

'Chief Inspector Abberline, there's no need to raise your voice. I'm just thinking about your future and your health, as you should also.' Abberline swallowed as the threat sank in. Anderson continued. 'Naturally, I expect complete silence from you, for reasons of national security.'

Stunned, Abberline still stared at Sir Robert while his thoughts whirled.

But at the back of his mind, he thought, *Thank God for a policeman's suspicion.*

He hadn't wanted to believe what he had been thinking, but as an honest cop, he'd had to be open to the possibility. What had just happened had not come as a complete surprise.

It was one tiny comfort: the ace up his sleeve, if he survived the evening.

*I won't play it now*, he thought. *But when I do …*

Sir Robert rose from his chair to tug on a bell pull. 'Now, if you don't have any more questions, I'll ask you to leave.'

The wooden door to the study opened and the butler entered the room. His tone was tired and slightly acid.

'If you'd like to follow me, please.'

\*

Lost in thought, Sir Robert Anderson sat behind his desk for a while after Abberline had left. Then he tugged on the bell pull again.

'Get my coat and hat, and call my carriage. I have to go out again.'

He picked up the pile of papers in front of him and left the office.

The carriage was waiting as he left the house. He gave the coachman his destination and gazed out of the window as it lurched away into the dark, cold night of the big city. Absent-mindedly, he played with his gold ring. It was embossed with a large coat of arms that every child in England knew, framed by a compass and a set square, which together formed a hexagonal star.

Sir Robert had been thinking about the past few months. Was this way really the right way? Would the family really be protected by the club's actions?

He caught himself after a few minutes of self-doubt, dispelling the thoughts with a firm shake of his head. This was the right way and there was no reason for remorse! They were only five whores. You didn't have to mourn them. Whatever life they had, it was surely worth less than the future of a whole nation.

His destination appeared at the end of the long avenue.

# CHAPTER 1

'When my parents were kids,' James Kent remarked casually, 'they said London was black. It was all dirty. Now look at it. They really cleaned up, didn't they?'

His companion frowned.

'Eh?'

'I mean, look at it.'

James waved a hand towards the Palace of Westminster across the river. Sir Charles Barry's neo-Gothic triumph glowed golden, its many peaks and turrets bathing in the sun. London had an image as a wet and grey metropolis, but when the weather was fine, James could not think of anything more beautiful.

James and his companion sat on green metal chairs at a table, shaded from the sun beneath a red and white parasol, outside what had once been County Hall, the seat of the Greater London Council and now home to the London Aquarium, a Salvador Dalí exhibition and a large arcade. The cafe owner was scurrying back and forth between guests as he took orders, with a big grin on his face. Sunny, busy days like this in London brought him a booming business.

Bells chimed on the other side of the Thames, ringing the three-quarter hour from the soaring Victoria clock tower. It would be another quarter-hour until Big Ben itself rang out the hour to the crowds that thronged on Westminster Bridge, shuffling their way towards Parliament Square or, in the other direction, towards the attractions of the south bank – the Museum of Modern Art, the aquarium, and of course the London Eye, the hundred-metre-high Ferris wheel that stood directly beside County Hall, a few metres away from the two men.

'Parliament is gold,' James went on. 'Well, golden brown. Westminster Abbey is white. Dad always said he'd never have dreamed that when he was little. Everything was just … black.'

James was a slender, athletic man with short brown hair and deep brown eyes. He wore expensive dark blue jeans and a matching red polo shirt from the Royal Team, which he had bought for the last Cartier Queen's Cup game in Windsor. The round table hid his new sneakers.

Steve, his companion, tried to keep a smile fixed on his face. It was in danger of becoming a scowl. James scrutinized him with cool eyes. He knew exactly the effect he was having. His friend wanted to talk business and James did not, both because it was tedious at the best of times, and on this occasion he was going to have to find a nice way to say no. But it was true. The London of old wartime pictures had scrubbed off the decades of soot and grime and now it was full of colour and wonder. He was very proud of this city.

'Concentrate, James?' Steve said. Steve was James's physical opposite. Short, with a stocky rugby player's body. His eyes were blue and his blond, greasy hair lay cut short on his compact head. Unlike James, he didn't pay much attention to his appearance. His thick legs

## CHAPTER 1

were stuffed into a torn pair of jeans. He wore a checked lumberjack's shirt, which lacked the upper button and was much too tight around his massive body. Stains showed that his last meal had included ketchup and mayonnaise. 'James, I don't understand you! What's so hard about doing an old friend a favour?'

He tapped the copy of *Time Out* that lay on the table between their cups of tea.

'You don't have to do much except give a little hint in the magazine. That's it! That's all I'm asking!'

'It's not that simple, Steve,' James protested. 'Of course, I can talk to Will about your pub, and as an old friend I'll do it, but don't expect much from it. I have to turn it into an article. Give me something to work with. Make yourself interesting to the readers. Innovate! Do something fancy! Something people don't expect from a run-down dive.' He grinned. 'Maybe even change your shirt.'

Steve's face twisted in thought.

'So, so, innovation ... An event pub ... Hmm. I'm just a chef, I'm not meant to be an ideas guy. I don't do creativity. But I have to pull the money in somehow.' He paused. 'I mean, most of us don't have handy inheritances.'

If that was meant to be a dig, it worked. James refused to feel guilty about his background – why should he? It wasn't his fault. But he liked to think he paid his way, and he liked other people to think it too. At least, he liked his friends to think it.

And Steve did work hard in his pub. Just ... not imaginatively.

And so he changed to flattery.

'Sure, you do creativity. I only got through art school with your help! And isn't a good chef an artist?'

'Painting and cooking are totally different!' Steve protested.

'Well, they both require imagination, right?'

'I guess.' Steve looked at his watch. 'Okay, I've got to get going and I guess I'll get busy on working out a food theme or something that you're not too proud to put into *Time Out*. What are you doing tonight?'

'I don't have anything definite planned yet.' James picked up the *Time Out*. 'I'll take a look.' Then he saw that Steve was looking for change in his wallet. 'Hey, let me get these, right?'

Steve smiled with one corner of his mouth.

'My turn next time?'

'You're on. See ya?'

'See ya!' Steve said goodbye and headed off towards Waterloo Station.

James leafed through the *Time Out* in search of interesting evening activities. Maybe he just wasn't in that kind of mood, but today there wasn't much that appealed to him.

'Home, James,' he said to himself.

He tucked a ten-pound note on the table under a saucer and left the terrace. He crossed the overcrowded Westminster Bridge and passed Parliament Square, which was almost suffocated by the heavy traffic. The

## CHAPTER 1

statue of Winston Churchill looked darkly over towards the House of Commons. Abraham Lincoln gazed thoughtfully at the people and traffic masses below him. Tourists clustered around the feet and hooves of the Boudicca statue, posing for photos.

James could have walked up Whitehall but he decided on the slightly more scenic, less crowded route. Instead of turning right, he kept going until he reached St James's Park, then turned right up Horse Guards Road.

He soon came to Horse Guards itself, once Henry VIII's tournament court, now the parade ground where the ceremony of the changing of the guard took place every day and where once a year the Queen celebrated her official birthday. In between those two events, and thanks to the prolonged drought, it was only a dust-dry backyard of power. The southern side was dominated by the high wall of the garden of 10 Downing Street, and without moving his head James could see the backs and roofs of half a dozen ministries lining Whitehall itself.

James reached the great red-paved boulevard of the Mall and turned right towards Trafalgar Square. London's main venue for rallies and other popular gatherings was dominated by the fifty-metre-high column of Admiral Lord Nelson and overshadowed by William Wilkins's mighty National Gallery. The blue dancing fountains looked cool and relaxing on this warm day, inviting you to plunge in and cool off. Landseer's mighty bronze lion statues made it very clear they would disapprove of such activity.

A quick glance at the crowds thronging around the National Gallery's pillars and steps told James he did not feel like a bit of art browsing. Instead he strolled casually into the apartment building at the corner of the square.

After emptying the mailbox and entering his password, he took the elevator to the top floor. He pushed through his black mahogany door into the bright white hallway and dropped his keys into a silver bowl that stood on a small marble table next to the door. With a quick check on his appearance in the large mirror above the bowl, he headed across the dark wooden floor towards the kitchen.

James was a passionate hobby chef and particularly proud of his large kitchen, which was equipped with the most modern utensils. The cooking hob and oven were part of a pedestal in the middle of the room. But as he was only making lunch on this occasion, he quickly heated some pasta in a pan while he prepared his tuna and caper sauce, humming to himself quietly and keeping one eye on the panoramic window with a view of the thronging Trafalgar Square.

He took the hot noodle dish into his living room. Light colours also dominated here. All his furniture was white and the floor was black ebony. On the walls hung black and white photographs of famous women, framed in white gold. The masterpiece of his collection was, without question, his Mario Testino Diana photo from 1997.

James dropped himself on to his large, light grey sofa in front of the blank, flat-screen TV. He set the noodles down on the table and clapped his hands sharply together. The TV came on. It was just one of the apartment's utilities to

## CHAPTER 1

be wired up to a sound sensor. It was a gimmick and he knew he was not really too lazy to walk across the room and turn it on himself, but he always found it funny.

It came on in the middle of a BBC newscast and he almost clapped the TV off again, until he realised it was talking about London.

'... the exhibition relives all the questions from the case of the most famous murderer of all time. Jack the Ripper was a serial killer who murdered and mutilated five prostitutes in 1888. Still ranking as one of Scotland Yard's greatest failures, the culprit was never caught – and yet, the series of murders came to a halt as suddenly and inexplicably as they began. Why did the killer stop so abruptly? Was he caught after all, for another crime? Did he die of some other cause? To this day, the identity of the Ripper has never been proved. The highlight of the exhibition, which deals with the assumptions and theories that have been made over the years, is without doubt the alleged diary of the Ripper, which is to be auctioned off next week by Christies. The exhibition is open daily from 8 a.m. to 6 p.m. and is free of charge for all the amateur detectives out there.'

The picture switched back to the studio. With a broad grin the blonde presenter turned to her colleague who was standing in front of a map of Great Britain.

'Well, Tom, I hope it won't be a foggy night, because then you would have to avoid dark alleys.'

'Ha ha ha!' The weatherman laughed as though it were the funniest joke ever. 'No, I don't think so, but—'

*Clap.*

# JACK

The TV went blank just as the phone started to ring. James glanced at it in surprise – who used the landline nowadays? He didn't even know why he kept it connected.

'James Kent?' he said into the receiver.

The voice at the other end was old and male, sounding full of dust and importance.

'Mr Kent, my name is Lord George Anderson.'

James blinked.

'Right … And what can I do for you …? Sir. Lord. Anderson?'

'It's a little complicated and I don't want to discuss this on the phone, but in a nutshell I would like to hire your services. I am sure you are the right person for a job that is of particular importance to my family.'

James frowned.

'I'm flattered – but are you sure you have the right number? I don't do jobs for hire. I write the occasional review for *Time Out*.'

'I am aware of that, but it is your expertise as a journalist that I am after. A good journalist knows how to investigate, dig deep, weed out the truth.'

James laughed.

'You have me confused with Woodward and Bernstein. I'm a food critic. For investigative journalism, I wouldn't know where to start.'

'You are the son of the late John Kent, aren't you?'

James's jaw dropped.

'Eh … how do you know my father?'

# CHAPTER 1

'Well, he worked for me, for a while, but he was unable to finish the task I have in mind.'

Silence, while all the negative memories came welling up. His quarrel with his father and, a few years later, the death in a traffic accident. James swallowed.

'I'm sorry, sir, I can't help you. If you really knew my father, then you also know that we broke off contact before his death. Whatever he was doing when he died – I have no idea.'

'I understand. I was a very good friend of his. Think of this as helping carry out his last wishes.'

'His last wishes?' Anderson mentioning his late father had been exactly the right way to hook his interest, but if the old man was now going to lecture him on his father's last wishes – well, that wasn't worth it. 'I very much doubt they included me taking over his work,' James said shortly. 'Leave me alone, please. I don't want anything to do with my father.'

'Mr Kent, I can understand your grief, but I urge you to reconsider. Did you know that your father was on the verge of solving a particularly vexing issue of huge importance? We were going to meet and he was going to tell me everything. On the way, he tragically died. Do you want his death to be in vain?'

The bloody cheek! James was torn between hurling the phone out of the nearest window, and giving in to curiosity, Curiosity, just, won.

'What are you implying? That it wasn't an accident?' he asked tonelessly. He could feel the warmth drain out of the day at just the thought.

'Well, as I said, I don't want to discuss it on the phone. How about dinner? Give me just a few minutes and I'll try to explain it to you. If I'm wasting your time then the worst-case scenario is you get a free and very good meal.'

Every instinct was telling James to tell the old man to get out of here … But he also knew his curiosity was hooked.

'Where and when?' he asked resignedly.

'Do you know the Rules? Six o'clock this evening?'

James weighed up everything in his head. Oh, what the hell.

'Six o'clock,' he agreed, and hung up.

He looked at the phone.

What the hell was that all about?

He was already strongly minded to dial 1471, get Anderson back on the line and cancel the deal.

But as an actor friend had once told him, 'Always do the audition, James. You never know what it might lead to.'

'I guess I never do …' he murmured.

# CHAPTER 2

Feeling a little embarrassed, at six o'clock precisely James stood outside one of the oldest restaurants in London. The setting sun lit up the rooftop of Rules. The rest of Covent Garden's Maiden Lane was in shadow.

James gazed into the interior through the gold lettering on the windows.

'Well, Anderson must have money,' he thought. He knew that Charles Dickens and Charlie Chaplin had both eaten here, so he had put on his good black suit and a light grey tie. Slowly and thoughtfully he walked towards the entrance.

The door was opened before he could get there by a waiter in a black tuxedo, who asked James his name. When James announced himself, the waiter just nodded and accompanied him to a double table in a corner between a window and wall.

'Your companion will be here any minute, sir.' The waiter left him with these words.

The interior was a Victorian dream: chandeliers and stained glass skylights lit up dark wood and crimson benches. Portraits, landscapes and animal trophies hung everywhere, like in a grand English country house. But James did not have long to explore the restaurant extensively, because an old man on with a stick approached his table.

'Ah, very much the father's son, I see! George Anderson.'

James stood up and shook the man's hand.

'James Kent.' James helped the old man into his chair and sat down opposite him. The man had short grey hair and his face was hidden by a three-day beard. His dress style was classic and simple – a grey checked suit accompanied by a striped tie.

The waiter approached and half opened his mouth to ask the obvious question.

'The usual, for both of us,' Anderson said without looking around. The waiter disappeared.

'And what is "the usual"?' James asked, given that Anderson obviously expected him to enjoy it.

'Well, since I always come here around six, it means just the main course of today's special, with a matching wine. Today that would be a fillet of highland beef with wild mushrooms in a Chartreuse sauce, and I believe the wine is a dry Burgundy,' Anderson replied.

'Just the one course?' James asked, though he wasn't going to complain. 'Don't we have much time?'

Anderson fixed with him with a good-humoured but steely eye.

'I'd rather start over. Does the year 1888 mean anything to you?'

James smiled.

'On any other day, the answer would be no. But in fact I heard that date on the news just before you called. Something to do with Jack the Ripper.'

## CHAPTER 2

'That's right! It was the year of the Ripper murders. My grandfather Sir Robert Anderson was the chief of police. He was not the kind of man to accept defeat easily – but the fact is, he failed. We don't know why the murders stopped, but we do know it was not because of anything he did. And so, no one could ever be sure they wouldn't start again. The fact that he could not catch the Ripper weighed heavily, not only on him but also on our whole family. But that was not the worst stain on our honour. That was the belief that there was some kind of royal conspiracy behind the killings, and Sir Robert Anderson was involved in it. Are you familiar with this theory?'

James shrugged.

'I know hardly anything about the Ripper as it is, and I'm more interested in facts than theories – so, no. My father, on the other hand, loved things like that. That was just one difference between us. So, what does this conspiracy theory say?'

Anderson smiled without humour.

'The theory – which, let me say straight up, is utter nonsense – says that Prince Albert – not the Queen's husband, but her grandson of that name, who was nicknamed Eddy, to avoid confusion – that Albert, the Duke of Clarence, son of the Prince of Wales and Queen Victoria's favourite grandson, married a certain Annie Crook – a woman of, let's just say, the lower orders. Married, and even had a child with her. Of course, the poor thing knew nothing about her husband's royal ancestry, let alone that he was second in line to the throne. It wouldn't have been unusual for an East End salesgirl to be so ignorant. She would have had no way of recognising him. No social media in those times, not even photographs in newspapers, which she couldn't have read anyway. Not like today at all.'

James smiled out of polite interest.

'I assume the Palace wasn't so pleased about this development?'

'Quite right. The main problem was not that Eddy had married below his estate, but that he was the oldest son of the future King Edward VII and so any children of his could have become king or queen in turn. Victoria wanted to prevent this at all costs. In fact, as far as we know he didn't have any children, and he died before his father, so the throne went to his brother who reigned as George V – and George is the grandfather of our own dear Queen.'

The waiter put two wine glasses on the table and poured Anderson a little sip. On his nod, the glasses were filled to a third. After James took a sip of his own, he asked, 'And how did they fix the problem?'

'Eddy was placed under house arrest – which isn't so arduous when the house in question is a palace. Annie's fate was a little crueller but not uncommon for the time. The Palace commissioned Sir William Gull, the Queen's personal physician, to declare the girl insane, which he did without batting an eyelid.'

James pulled a face.

'So she was locked up in some asylum?'

## CHAPTER 2

'Eventually,' Anderson agreed dourly. 'But first there was a small operation – which again was quite usual for the time.'

'Operation ...' James murmured, suddenly seized with a foreboding based on everything he had ever heard about Victorian medicine.

'They liked to remove parts of the frontal lobe.'

'Jesus!'

'It was believed that you could heal people that way.'

'By turning them into zombies? That's horrible! But – okay, I can see that would have fixed the problem, from the royals' point of view. What happened to the kid? According to the theory?'

'She was given to a home and grew up in complete ignorance of her parents. But actually it did not fix the problem. There were other problems. Five of them.'

'That's a very precise number.'

'There were a precise number of witnesses at the wedding. No wedding is legal without at least one or two. These ones were friends of Annie's, in the same line of business as her. After Annie disappeared, they did their own investigating. They learned that her husband was a Prince and a member of the Royal Family. So, they decided to blackmail the Palace. Sir William Gull was once again instructed to solve the problem. Permanently.'

James sat slowly back in his chair as he took this all in.

'So, the Queen's doctor was supposed to be the Ripper? That's ridiculous. He must have been an educated man. Surely he would have thought of a more elegant solution than mutilating five women in such a disgusting way?

Not to mention a subtler way that wouldn't arouse attention? Why not just have them all lobotomised too?'

Anderson gave a thin smile.

'It's a conspiracy theory. Of course it's full of holes. The more holes there are, the more a certain mindset likes to believe it. But now my family comes into play. The police are supposed to have known about this terrible incident and covered it up.'

'And now that the Ripper is back in the media, your name is back in the game?' James guessed.

'That's right. Now, a few years ago I unearthed some clues that lit up the trail again. I asked your father to go on a search.'

Even though any talk of his father was still a sore subject, James's eyebrows shot up.

'My father was senior partner in the family law firm. Why on earth would he take on this ... what? Private investigation?'

Anderson chuckled.

'Oh, he loved the investigating, James! He told me it was the best bit of the job. Tracking down witnesses and all that. The thrill of the chase, he liked to say! And as we both know ...' Anderson coughed. 'He didn't exactly need the money, did he? He always said the firm was just a way of subsidising his hobbies.'

James grunted.

'That does sound like Dad. So, are you saying he actually found evidence of the Ripper's identity?'

Anderson gave a slow, expansive shrug.

## CHAPTER 2

'I can't say. All he said at the time was that he had solved the mystery and wanted to meet with me to explain. It never happened and so I can't tell you what he knew. The police unfortunately found no documents or other records in the car wreck. Even in his estate, as far as I know, there were no records, were there?'

'It was all handled by our solicitor – but no, he certainly never mentioned anything.'

Anderson gazed at him shrewdly.

'If I may ask – and you don't have to tell me – how did you two fall out?'

'Ach.' James pulled a face as though the dry burgundy had changed to vinegar. 'We had a difficult relationship. I guess I never was good enough for him. He worked so hard and I couldn't really see the point. Look, after his death, I received my share of the inheritance and that was that. I didn't get anything else – certainly no files or notes or anything like that. If you wanted me to look into this then I'd have to start all over again, and there are far better investigators than me. I'm not Sherlock.' He laughed without humour. 'And it's not like no one's ever tried it before.'

'I understand your concerns, but they're unfounded. I still have material from that time – the clues I gave to your father. Mainly old documents, including a diary. No, not the Ripper diary,' Anderson quickly added when he saw James's bewildered face. 'My grandfather's diary. He goes into a lot of detail about the Ripper case. I think that could help you a lot.'

The two men locked gazes over the table. James's thoughts were spinning. He could already predict that this would absolutely be a complete waste of time. He wouldn't turn up anything new. But Anderson wasn't going to take no for an answer.

James could just walk away now – turn his back on what promised to be a splendid meal – but that wouldn't change anything. A fixated old man like Lord Anderson would just keep bothering him.

The only way to convince Anderson was to fail.

James sighed.

'I'm still sceptical, but send me the documents and I'll take a look at them.'

Anderson raised his glass.

'Thank you, James. I'll bring them over tomorrow morning. To success!'

James silently returned the toast. And then, because – damn it! – he was still intrigued about one thing, he had to ask.

'Only one question remains. Why?'

'Why what, Mr Kent?'

'What's all this in aid of?'

'I told you. The media are writing about it again.'

'So spend money on a good media lawyer. You can't get them for slander because you can't slander the dead, but there are other ways.'

Anderson beamed.

'Thank you, James – you're obviously thinking this through already! The reason? Honour, quite simply.

## CHAPTER 2

I come from a very old family where honour, old-fashioned as it may be, still means something.'

'It's not just throwing good money after bad, then?'

'It's my money. Some spend their money on overpriced paintings. I spend mine on honour. Don't worry, I'll be able to afford your rate.'

They were interrupted by the waiter serving their meal. James waited until they were alone again.

'I'll try to help you,' he said, 'but please don't promise yourself too much. I'd hate to disappoint you.'

*Even though that is exactly what I will do ...* he thought.

'We've been living with this disappointment for over a hundred years now.' Anderson pushed an envelope across the table. James opened it and found a black card with an address in London's West End written in red calligraphy: INVITATION TO THE OPENING OF THE RIPPER EXHIBITION.

'There is a party tonight celebrating the auction of the Ripper diary,' said Anderson. 'You'll be expected there. That's why we only have time for the one course.'

'Who am I expected to meet?'

'Oh, sorry, I said that wrong. No, I meant, you should be there. Perhaps you will find interesting suggestions for where to begin your research.'

'Heh. Thanks. That's very nice of you, but aren't these events for celebrities?'

'Maybe you'll meet some friends?' Anderson suggested with a smile. 'I'm prepared to bet that a man who can afford to live in an apartment off Trafalgar Square knows some interesting people.'

James reminded himself that this old man was buying him dinner, and besides that was now technically his employer. So he would not just walk out. That would be rude.

'You're well informed,' he said wryly. 'All right, I'll take your assignment, but only because it arouses my journalistic curiosity. I'm not doing this for the money.'

'Quite,' Anderson chuckled. 'Working for money – how common is that?' His ironic smile showed it was a joke. Then the smile faded. 'One thing you ought to know. This could potentially be very explosive. In the very unlikely event of me bring wrong and the royal theory actually being true – well, it could bring a lot of trouble down on your head. Are you ready for that?

James frowned.

'You don't really think that?'

'What I think doesn't matter. People who think wrongly can still do a great deal of damage.'

And while James was absorbing that, Anderson tossed back the remains of his dry burgundy.

'Drink up. I'll drive you to the party.'

# CHAPTER 3

A grey Rolls Royce Phantom and a grey-uniformed chauffeur waited in front of the Rules. The man opened the rear door for them. The interior was pure luxury – precious wood and finest, handcrafted leather. At a leisurely pace they set off into the evening through the West End.

'This car is beautiful!' James couldn't hide his enthusiasm.

'Do you like it?' Anderson asked casually. Then he smiled to show that he understood. He waved a hand forward, towards the Spirit of Ecstasy atop the radiator grille. 'In my eyes, that emblem has always stood for uncompromising quality. Too bad it's not purely British anymore. I must invite you to my family seat because I have a whole collection of cars there.'

'I'd be delighted!' James said.

'When all this over, of course,' Anderson added. 'If possible, nobody should know you're working for me.'

The car soon stopped in front of a tall Georgian house, the former domicile of the Bank of New York. The chauffeur walked around the car to open the door again. James climbed out but Anderson stayed seated.

'Take care, James. I promised your father.'

'Sure, I will.' James pushed the door shut and went through the whole conversation again in his head as he watched the car pulled away, the rear lights receding into the traffic. Then he turned towards the front entrance of the building. A security guard pounced as soon as he was inside the porch. Despite James's suit, something seemed to tweak the guard's antennae that here was someone who shouldn't be.

'Your card, sir?'

'Right here.' James handed it over. The guard perused it with an obvious longing that should be a forgery, but it passed the test.

'Please go in, sir,' said the man with a forced smile. James walked on.

He found himself in a medium-sized room with Greek columns and a red carpet that led from the entrance to a door exactly opposite the entrance. To the right and left of the carpet, behind a red cord, was the press, representatives of television stations and newspapers from all over the world. They automatically went mad at the sight of a new guest, cameras clicking and flashing like crazy, until one by one they realised James was no one important and decided to keep their time and effort for someone who deserved it. James crossed the room quickly with a few large steps, anxious not to be splashed on the front covers of the glossies, glad that he was on his own and not nearly interesting enough to tickle their interest.

The next room was almost ten metres high. It also had Greek columns but these were further in and formed an inner courtyard in the centre of the room. The ceiling was decorated with bright white stucco and the floor

## CHAPTER 3

was large white marble slabs. A bar stood in one corner for the hundred or so guests who had made it so far. The walls were decorated with photos of the Ripper's victims, along with other prominent people of the time, in particular Queen Victoria. Display cases scattered artfully around the floor displayed Ripper memorabilia, mostly objects that had belonged to victims.

James took a glass of champagne from the silver tray held by a man in white tails by the door, and strolled on in to admire the exhibition.

He hadn't realised that so much had been preserved from that time. One could read the Ripper's letters, displayed behind bulletproof glass. Madame Tussauds had recreated the victims in wax, as they had been found after the Ripper had struck, each one in a glass sarcophagus.

And there was Jack himself. The Ripper stood in a glass cabinet. He was wearing a long black coat, under which a tailcoat could still be seen, and a cylindrical top hat, pulled low over his face to hide the fact that no one actually knew what he had looked like. His left hand brandished a long knife that shone in the room's lights.

James knocked back the champagne and went over to the bar at the back, to order a vodka on the rocks. Sipping on his glass, he looked around the guests. There was J.K. Rowling, with her husband. In front of a showcase, Orlando Bloom and Daniel Radcliffe were chatting together. And at the centre of that knot of people over there – Princes Charles and William, plus their respective wives.

James was so busy checking people out that he didn't even notice the tall blonde woman at his side. Only when she spoke did he look around, into her dark blue eyes:

'I never thought the Ripper would attract so many people. I'm Alice Gull.'

'James Kent, very pleased!' he replied, a bit bewildered. He wasn't usually the kind to be struck dumb by a good-looking woman – he had known a few in his time and slept with more than a couple – but this one! She had long blonde hair and a physique that competed with every model on the planet. Her elegant red dress definitely came from a famous French fashion house and she wore a matching De Beers diamond necklace around her neck.

He was also trying to remember where he had heard the name Gull before. Quite recently, where was it …?

She must have noticed his head tilt and his slightly absent frown as he tried to remember. She started to speak just as the memory came to him.

'Any relation to—'

'I'm here—'

They both cut off and waited for the other to speak. Then they laughed together. He indicated that she could go first and she changed whatever she had been about to say.

'You were going to ask if I'm any relation to Sir William Gull, Queen Victoria's personal physician, weren't you?'

## CHAPTER 3

'I have to confess I was. Which in a place like this must be the corniest question ever.' James paused. 'And are you?'

'Unfortunately!' she said heavily.

Despite all his disclaimers to Lord George Anderson, James found he did have a journalist's instincts. He wanted to know more. He wasn't going to ask himself if the same would have applied had Alice Gull been Andrew or Alistair instead.

'Do tell?' he asked, with a smile to show she was under no compulsion. She pulled a face.

'There are people who think my great-great-great-grandfather was involved in some conspiracy to do with the Ripper.'

'No!' he exclaimed, as though he hadn't been hearing precisely that less than half an hour ago. 'But, if it's a sore subject … can I ask why you're here?'

'I was invited by a friend. And what about you?'

'I'm here on business, you could say.' James decided to stretch the truth a little. 'I'm a journalist. Too bad about your friend, because … I would have loved to invite you for a drink.'

Three things could happen now, he told himself. She could decline, she could take offence, or she could accept. He had had all three happen to him at one time or another.

'That's kind, but my friend made the same offer five minutes ago … He really is just a friend, and he's not even going to be that if he doesn't tear himself away soon.'

She gestured inconspicuously at a young man chatting to Orlando Bloom and showing no sign of heading towards the bar. The face was vaguely familiar – James was reasonably certain he was the son of some lord or other.

'What a shame. All that expensive education and he doesn't know that the one thing you do not do when you offer your date a drink is get sidetracked on the way. It shows a misplaced sense of priorities.'

She blew a scornful raspberry.

'His priority is to tell all his friends that he got off with a descendant of William Gull.' Her blue eyes flashed him a challenge. 'Not that he has, or is going to. And when the diary is auctioned off in a week, and plainly shows William Gull wasn't the Ripper, my friend over there will lose interest altogether.'

James smiled, lifting his glass to his mouth. Anyone who could lose interest in Alice Gull had problems he wasn't prepared to diagnose.

And then it occurred to him.

'You know, you might not have to wait until next week.'

'Oh?'

'I said I'm a journalist? I have' – his thoughts span as he rattled out the smooth story, trying to keep it as close to the truth as possible – 'a source who'll be dropping some papers off tomorrow. He doesn't believe the William Gull conspiracy theory either and he's pretty sure what he's got will hit it on the head.'

Her eyes narrowed.

## CHAPTER 3

'Just now you had no idea there even was a William Gull conspiracy theory.'

*Shit!*

If in doubt, James told himself, give a goofy grin and come clean. Which he did.

'Okay, full journalistic disclosure, it's possible I just wanted to keep talking to you.'

She tilted her head thoughtfully.

'But these papers …'

'Are absolutely real. As real as my desire to keep talking to you.'

Alice seemed to come to a slow conclusion. She pursed her lips and nodded, once.

'I'd like to be there when you go through it all.'

James blinked.

'Really?'

'Really,' she said coolly, challenging him with her big, blue eyes to doubt it. He had absolutely no idea what to make of it. Did she want to end up in bed with him as much as he wanted to with her, or was she really offering to go through some dry and dusty records based on five minutes' acquaintance, or what? One thing he did know: he wanted to find out, just out of curiosity. Damn but that's a good way of hauling a guy in, he thought with admiration.

'Well,' he said, conjuring up a reluctant sigh, 'if you want, but I warn you, it will be very boring.'

'I don't think so.' She smiled, looking a little over his shoulder, and the warmth faded. 'And now I think my friend is waiting to drive me home. I guess I'm not getting that drink. So, when shall we meet?' Alice asked.

James thought. It suddenly struck him that Anderson hadn't given a time for when he was dropping the stuff off. He had just said, 'tomorrow morning'.

'How about ten o'clock tomorrow?'

He passed her card and saw how her eyebrows carefully didn't go up when she read the address. Nor did she ask how a journalist could afford a flat off Whitehall.

'It's a date. Well, it's been a pleasure meeting you, James Kent.'

'The pleasure was all mine. Good night!'

He watched her walk off towards her (he guessed) very soon-to-be ex-boyfriend. Her ass swung slightly back and forth, which delighted James quite a bit. How could anyone move and be so damn sexy in high heels? She left the room to run the gamut of the British press again. *Thank God I'm not rich and powerful*, he thought to himself.

And then came a voice that scraped down his nerves like broken glass.

'Hi, honey, I see you just met the suspect's granddaughter.'

James turned to see a young brown-haired woman, champagne glass in one hand, towering over him by half a head in her white high heels. James knew from experience that her Latino-like tan was entirely natural and went all the way over her body, and the short, white summer evening dress made her even more seductive.

## CHAPTER 3

'Oh, Monica, what a delightful surprise! What are you up to? Are you still spying for the Secret Service?'

She pouted.

'Oh, come on, you know I'd have to kill you if I answered that. Let's just say I'm still sleeping with the gun under my pillow But, do you know, I can still read moods and I'm getting the faintest suspicion you're not glad to see me.'

'Well, I'm worried about this friend I have,' James said. 'He was sleeping with this amazing woman on a reasonably regular basis, but it wasn't just the sex, he did actually care for her, a lot, and he thought she might actually have some kind of feelings for him in return but, do you know, it turned out she was just using him to get a better job, and then she moved abroad with work, the bitch. And now he's just learned she's back in the country. I mean, what can you do? What can I tell my friend?'

'Oh, James, I'd tell your friend that was over two years ago and it may be time to draw a line under it and move on. I can show you how. I'm in a nice little hotel right around the corner, until I can sort out something more permanent.'

James moved his face closer to hers and smiled icicles as he nodded over to the nearest glass sarcophagus.

'Right now, I'm more likely to get it up for Lizzy Stride.'

Her face twisted in disgust.

'A dead whore? Classy as always, James.'

'At least she used to be alive and never pretended she was something else.'

'Well, if you change your mind, I'm staying at Sanderson's. Room 101.'

James had to laugh.

'As in, the place where George Orwell kept the worst thing in the world?'

'Maybe you'll reconsider. Take care.' She kissed him conspiratorially and left him, no doubt fully aware of his angry glare on her back.

The party had stopped being fun, so he took a black London taxi home. Why pay a fortune at the bar when he had a bottle of Laphroaig calling his name?

# CHAPTER 4

James incorporated the hammering so successfully into his dreams that it took a moment to wake up and realise someone was outside, knocking hard on the front door. He pulled on his bathrobe and padded to the door.

Under his coat, George Anderson seemed to be wearing the same grey suit as yesterday. He held up a package wrapped in thick fabric.

'What are you doing at this godless hour?' James asked grouchily.

'Ten thirty in the morning? We have different ideas of godlessness. I can't linger, but here's the goods.'

*Ten thirty … shit!*

James's brain was catching up with the night before. A promise had been made. Ten o'clock … had she been and gone already, because he had self-medicated a bit too heavily on the Laphroaig?

'Yeah, okay. Thank you.' James took the package. 'Excuse me, but I do need to freshen up.'

Anderson gave the fondly exasperated smile of a parent confronting a teenager who is already regretting the night before.

'Have fun puzzling, my boy, and good luck.' Anderson turned towards the elevator and James closed the front door.

## JACK

Tired, he put on the kettle and went into his bathroom. It had a wooden floor with a round bathtub in the middle, two metres wide, which he loved to bathe in but that took forever to fill up with hot water. He didn't have time for that, not if there was any chance she was still coming round, so he only took a quick shower, one ear cocked for anyone at the door. Quickly James dried off, put on his bathrobe again and went to the kitchen to take the kettle off the stove. Carefully he poured the hot water over the tea leaves and slowly began to sip the tea. By now it was 11 a.m. and the beautiful blonde from the evening before was already over an hour late.

Disappointed, James let his eyes wander over the package. Carefully he loosened the knot and opened the documents. They had a smell of dust and cobwebs, and the feeling of grit rubbing against his fingers as he opened them.

He was amazed to discover that these were original files from the years 1888 to 1889. He began to read. It wasn't hard. They had had typewriters back then, a crude Courier font, and the handwriting was fairly copperplate but still easy to decipher.

It wasn't that much, and he knew most of it from television or books, but it was interesting to read an eyewitness's report. The files came from Sir Robert Anderson's personal assistant, Mr Schmitt, and gave an insight into how the then police commissioner had led the investigation. Unfortunately, Schmitt had not actually documented the results of Anderson's work – but he had made a note of the numbers of the folders where

## CHAPTER 4

they could be found. George Anderson had left his own handwritten note to say that these folders would all be in Scotland Yard's archives.

'Well, thanks,' James murmured. 'I guess I'll just mosey on over and ask for them, right?'

The sudden ringing of the doorbell disturbed his thoughts. *Why the hell couldn't Anderson have used that instead of knocking?* he thought grumpily as he went to open it.

He spent far too long staring at Alice Gull, standing on his doormat. Today she wore dark blue trousers, black flat shoes and a white blouse.

'Do you want to let me in, or should I wait here?' she asked after a moment of his just looking at her. He stood aside quickly.

'Oh, come on in! Excuse the bathrobe. Would you like something to drink?'

'Yes, thank you, I'll have a coffee.' She stepped through into the hallway and James guided her towards the living room, then darted into the kitchen to put the coffee on. While it hissed and bubbled its way through the machine, he got rid of the bathrobe and pulled on black jeans and a matching polo shirt.

Armed with coffee pot and cups, he came back into the living room. Alice was bent with interest over the open files.

'I see you've already started! That wasn't part of the deal.'

'Nor was turning up at nearly twelve,' James said righteously, as though he had been up at the crack of dawn to wait for her.

'Let's call it evens, then. What have you found so far?'

'Meh. It's all very top level. Jack the Ripper brutally murdered five women. He always struck at night – but never in the fog. That was just made-up horror movies.'

'Where do you get that insight from?' she asked in surprise. He patted the file.

'It's right here, including weather conditions. So he had to know the streets of the slum very well, which suggests a local, but the cuts on the victims pointed to an educated man with medical knowledge, and they weren't thick on the ground in Whitechapel. And that's as far as we go. The way I see it, the important documents are at Scotland Yard and it's not going to be that easy to get them.'

'Do you know which Scotland Yard?'

'Which one?' He frowned. 'There's only one. Right?'

'And its official name is New Scotland Yard,' she pointed out. 'Because there's also an old one. The original, near Whitehall.'

James's jaw hung foolishly open for a moment.

'I had forgotten that,' he confessed.

'Not the kind of thing an investigative journalist who knows London like the back of his hand would really forget, is it?'

Her blue eyes challenged him again, and he knew only the truth would work.

## CHAPTER 4

'True. But a part-time food writer for *Time Out* ... probably doesn't have much to do with Scotland Yard, new or old.'

'But you're a pretty good food writer,' she said with a smile, and he wondered how long she had known.

'And, technically, I am still a journalist. I pay my NUJ dues and I really have been hired by someone to look into this. Which is how I have these files.'

'These are the main thing, aren't they?' she agreed. She flipped slowly through a pile of dusty papers, but she didn't seem really to be reading it.

'And neither of the Scotland Yards will let us just walk in and look up the old archives,' he pointed out.

'Oh, if it's Old Scotland Yard, I can probably get us in.'

'Really?' he asked in surprise. She looked up, coolly amused, just like the night before.

'Really.'

\*

They walked down Whitehall towards Parliament, then turned left towards Northumberland Avenue and the river. Soon they stood side by side in front of the red brick building, gazing at the impressive facade, massive and Gothic in good nineteenth-century imperial fashion. It was lined with white painted windows and the building was wrapped around an inner courtyard. It looked very grand, but when you took a closer look you could see where the Old Scotland Yard building was slowly decaying.

James broke the silence.

'You know they won't just let us in, right?'

'Watch and learn,' Alice said with a mischievous grin.

*Damn, you're good*, he thought with admiration as he followed through the large arch into the courtyard. Hooking a man by his sense of curiosity was the best way of doing it, and the great thing – for her – was that it promised nothing in return.

They came to a large, dark wooden door. James held it for her and followed her in.

The room behind the door was dark, shabby and old. A man sat at a small desk with a computer that looked ten years old. He was in some kind of uniform, also old, like he had been there since the police decamped to their new premises. Behind him a wrought-iron staircase curled towards the upper rooms. The sunbeams that came through the open door illuminated the particles of dust that hung in the air.

Alice crossed the room briskly, somehow pulling authority out of the air around her. By the time she had stopped in front of the desk, her body language was screaming that this was a visiting dignitary. The man looked up from his crossword and hastily folded the newspaper away. He looked up at her with the worried attitude of a man who realises he may not have got an important memo.

'Can I help you, ma'am?'

## CHAPTER 4

'I believe you can.' She gave him a smile that cut him some slack, treating him as another professional rather than a servant, winning him over by showing him respect but making it clear who was in charge. 'Scotland Yard archives, 1888. They will be here, correct?'

'Well, yes, miss, and for some decades before and after, but I can't just ...'

Alice held out a card.

'I think this might help.'

James's eyes went wide as the man didn't just reject the card out of hand. He studied it, turned it over, and slowly handed it back, with a smile.

'Well, that does put a different complexion on it. Just for the record, ma'am, you really are supposed to phone ahead and make an appointment ...'

'I understand,' Alice said, her tone suggesting that while she understood she didn't especially care. 'Obviously, I wouldn't just spring this on you if it wasn't important.'

'Well, of course, ma'am, that goes without saying!' The old man smiled, like it was the first smile since he had forgotten how, many years ago. 'Our lad has been cleaning the files in the basement all week. He'll know exactly where to find what you're after.' The man turned and bellowed into the room behind his desk. 'Henry!'

A boy in his late teens came panting out. He had round glasses askew on his nose and long red hair.

'Yes, Mr Wallis?'

'We've two very important guests here needing access to the archives. 1888.'

The young man looked James and Alice up and down.

'Important guests, Mr Wallis?'

James couldn't help himself.

'MI5,' he joked.

Alice dug him in the ribs with her elbow and Mr Wallis grinned toothily, but the boy's eyes were circles.

'For real? MI5?'

Mr Wallis cackled.

'Just give 'em what they're after. I've verified their credentials.'

'Of course! Please, come this way!' They followed Henry into the back room. 'This is awesome! If I could tell the others – but I mean, I can't, can I, it's all secret? Oh, does James Bond really exist? Because I'm a really big fan. I mean, I know he's just a movie character but—'

'James Bond is MI6,' James said, already regretting his joke. MI5 was domestic intelligence, MI6 dealt with matters abroad. He could have saved his breath. Henry's words still came out at machine-gun speed.

'… is there someone like him? Okay, the last movie wasn't so hot but …'

Alice gave James a look that could have meant annoyance, could have meant amusement.

They were in a narrow hallway without windows that led to a small, very narrow staircase. The wall was supposed to be white but through the years the colour had crumbled away and the naked stone was emerging.

Henry continued to chat without James or Alice listening to him as they descended the wobbly stairs two floors down. At the bottom they turned left and walked

## CHAPTER 4

along an even more run-down passage. At the end they came to a door with numbers painted in flaking paint: '01/1800 – 12/1902.'

Henry pointed to the numbers with his left hand while with his right he fumbled for a bunch of keys in his pocket.

'Number before the dash is the month, numbers after are the year. So here we are, 1800 to 1902, the entire nineteenth century plus a bit.'

He pushed the door open and felt for the light switch. Neon tubes on the ceiling flickered on with a low hum. The three of them were at one end of a long room, an old cellar vault with a curved brick ceiling. It was lined with rows of moveable stacks of shelves in 1960s grey metal that looked out of place under the Victorian vaulting. There were ten stacks, and each one was labelled with the years of a decade. At the end of each there was a spoked wheel that you could turn to open the stacks up or close them together.

'So, 1888 will be here.' Henry took them to the second last stack, labelled '1880–1889'. 'What exactly are you looking for?'

'Not to worry, we'll take it from here, thank you.' Alice kept her brisk, professional friendliness and it actually brought a flush to the boy's cheeks. She was probably the hottest woman ever to show him some respect, James mused. And she knew it. For a moment – just a moment – he couldn't help contrasting her with Monica, a woman who essentially knew you were going to sleep with her eventually and acted on that basis in advance. Alice managed to be a decent human being, and treat you like one, and still get what she wanted. That was a class act.

'Uh, okay! So if you need help, don't hesitate to call for me, because I'm ready any time.' He waved at a phone on the wall. 'Just call 007. Just like James Bond! Hey, is there really a double-O department? Oh, yeah, and there's a copier at the front entrance next to the phone if you need it.'

'Thank you, you really can go now!' James said firmly. He walked slowly towards the boy to usher him out of the room. Henry actually stood his ground a moment longer, remembering his job.

'Well, actually, I just have to add that you have to be very careful with the files. Some are older than me. Well, that's no wonder, I mean, I'm nineteen, but you know …'

'Out!' James ordered. Henry pulled the door closed behind him a little more loudly than necessary. 'Thank God we got rid of him!' James said as he turned back to Alice.

'Well, he was just trying to help!' Alice defended the lad. 'I mean, MI5!'

James held his arms out.

'Hey, it might have been true for all I know. What was on that card you showed him? How did we even get in here?'

She rolled her eyes.

'Fellows of certain Oxbridge colleges are granted access to certain institutions for the purposes of research.'

'You're a fellow? And which colleges?

## CHAPTER 4

'Obviously not any you went to.' She took the spoked wheel at the end of the 1880s and tried to turn it. James stepped forward to help, wondered if that would just annoy her and hesitated. She threw him an irritated look.

'A hand?'

'Sorry, just trying not to be all macho and condescending.'

James gripped the wheel between her hands and they both put their strength into it. The stacks started to move with a loud squeak. They kept turning until the aisle between the stacks was wide enough for two people to walk next to each other. Rows of brown and grey and beige folders, floor to ceiling, stretched away on either side towards the brick wall at the end of the vault.

'So, after you,' James said. Alice walked slowly down the files, scanning the spines.

'Right, then. The murders began in August and Abberline filed his report at the end of the year, so we want anything from 08/1888 onwards. You take that side, I'll do this.'

They started their search.

It became fun, James thought, scanning a date at a glance, the flicker of hope as he saw that it came within the date range, the expectation as he pulled the file off its shelf and opened it up.

It became less fun as file after file yielded – nothing.

'Not a trace,' Alice muttered in disgust as she closed the last file at the end of her side of the stacks, half an hour later. James pushed his own file back into its place.

'The Met were certainly busy that year …'

There had been the expected quotient of other police matters. Non-Ripper murders, rapes, burglaries, riots, the works.

'… but you'd think Jack the Ripper never existed.'

There was no trace of the Yard's most notorious case anywhere.

They made their way slowly back down the stacks towards the entrance.

'It doesn't add up,' James insisted. 'You'd expect something. Absolutely nothing can only mean …'

'A clean-up,' Alice agreed. James was about to answer when his eye caught something – something they had both walked right past when they came in, because it wasn't labelled with the date. A big red folder, right at the start of the very first shelf.

'Oh, I don't believe it!' he groaned. The spine was stamped, in large letters: 'RELOCATED FILES.'

They looked at each other, neither quite wanting to blame the other for something they were equally at fault on. Then James opened the folder up.

In the table of contents, he quickly found what he was looking for. He turned to page 190.

'Yes! New Scotland Yard Main Safe Archive. And there's a proper reference number. No. 123_08/1888 JtR. Gee, JtR – what could that mean?'

'New Scotland Yard.' Alice pulled a face. 'I'm not sure even my college connections will get us in there.'

'One step at a time.' James hefted the folder in his hands. 'Didn't Commander Bond say there was a photocopier upstairs?'

## CHAPTER 4

*

Henry could never have looked happier than when the MI5 agents told him they wanted to use his copier.

'Absolutely! This way. Oh, this is the coolest thing ever.'

He led them into a cubbyhole mostly filled by machine. It looked surprisingly smooth and modern compared to everything else about the place. It even had an LCD display and a range of controls.

'Can I explain it to you?' Henry said eagerly. 'You lift this up …'

'Thanks. I think I can handle a photocopier,' James said. He lifted the lid and inserted the page they wanted. Alice punched the big green COPY button and the machine whirred into life.

'Yeah, but it's actually so much more than just a copier,' Henry said. 'It can collate and sort …'

'Uh-huh …'

James plucked the copy up as it slid out on to its tray, and held it up with a grin for Alice to see. She smiled back.

'And it automatically scans and digitises …'

Alice took the original out of the machine and replaced it in the file.

'Henry, could you be a dear and put this back in the stacks? The 1880s decade? Thank you so much.'

James was already halfway out of the building. She turned to hurry after him. Henry clutched the folder and slowly deflated, finally a little hurt that his visitors didn't share his enthusiasm.

'… and sends a digital record of everything to the central computer,' Henry muttered. 'But, you know, whatever.'

# CHAPTER 5

'Very nice,' Alice murmured as they stepped out of the lift into the restaurant. The cafe was on the National Gallery's fourth floor, a long room taking up the entire facade of the building, flooded with light from the large windows that overlooked Trafalgar Square and Whitehall.

'One of my favourite eating spots,' James said as he led her to a table.

'I guess it's your local.'

They sat at a table for two at one of the windows. When the waiter came, they each ordered a coffee and James also a cake.

'Cake,' Alice said wistfully. 'I wish I could allow myself that luxury.'

James grinned.

'I guess I'm still a teenager inside. I can just pack it in and not put anything on. In fact, I used to be so underweight my mother wanted to send me to fat school to plump me up a bit. I went into food writing so I could enjoy my hobby on expenses.'

'Totally the opposite for me,' Alice said sadly. 'One bite of chocolate and I just suck fat in from the air and end up looking like Pavarotti.'

'Well, Pavarotti was a very stylish dresser,' James teased. She narrowed her eyes as a very gentle warning he should back off.

'He'd never have got between those stacks. So, New Scotland Yard. How do we get in there?'

'Beats me,' James said with a sigh. He pulled out his phone and started to scroll through his contacts.

'I'm sorry, am I keeping you?' She sounded irritated.

'Eh?' He glanced up. 'Oh, no, sorry. I was just seeing if I know anyone, or anyone who knows anyone, who could be the slightest help. Even we part-time food writers meet the occasional people.'

A pause.

'And?' she asked as he kept scrolling.

'No one in the As. But there are twenty-five more letters to go. We could try just walking in again, like this morning?'

'Well, why not? Maybe Henry's idiot younger brother will be on duty and we could tell him we're from MI5?'

'Uh-huh ...' James grinned. The grin faded. He stopped scrolling. She noticed.

'Have you found someone?'

'Unfortunately. MI5 might be the answer ...'

He was interrupted by the arrival of their order. Alice's eyebrows had shot up, but they both waited until the woman serving them had moved a good distance away.

'MI5,' she said. 'Really?'

He paused.

'I have ... a friend.'

'And you think this friend would help?'

## CHAPTER 5

'No,' he said, more bluntly than he intended. It was strange. When he had bumped unexpectedly into Monica yesterday then sure, all the old feelings had come rushing back, right on cue – the hurt, the anger – but he had been able to control them. Now he was deliberately bringing her to mind he felt a lot less in control. 'I don't think she would piss on me if I was on fire, and it's mutual.'

A slow grin spread over Alice's face.

'Oh, an unhappy love affair! You have to tell me everything! After you've told me what good she's going to do us.'

James gave a slow, bashful smile in return. He was with a woman who already outstripped Monica in every class. That had to be some kind of victory.

So he told her, watching her eyes go rounder and rounder as she spoke.

# JACK

# CHAPTER 6

'Miller, MI5.'

Sean Miller held his ID out to the wide-eyed old geezer behind the desk. Behind the old guy was a young kid with long red hair who looked like he was about to faint.

'I have to verify this, sir,' the old guy said once he had got over his surprise. Sean nodded abruptly.

'Of course.' He stepped back as the old man picked up his phone with a shaking hand, and glanced around the ancient, dusty lobby where his two companions – a man and a woman – waited with expressions of stone.

Sean Miller was a sporty, well-built man with dark hair and blue eyes hidden behind dark sunglasses, which he reluctantly took off because the dim lobby made him almost blind while he was wearing them.

Sean had known what he wanted to be a long time ago. At school, he was always the best at sports. He was doing judo by the age of three, moving on to other martial arts as he grew older. He had been hired at the age of twenty-one, straight out of university, by the Security Service; MI5, as the public called it, or just Five, as it was known to those who actually worked there.

But he had no idea why his unit had been dispatched to a mouldering old archive in Old Scotland Yard. He knew the bare facts – that someone had photocopied something here less than an hour ago, and the digital scan that was automatically sent to various agencies had immediately recognised a certain number, and that triggered an alert. But why it had done that – no idea.

The kid behind the old guy plucked up the courage to speak.

'You guys are like buses!' It was a very feeble smile that he offered. 'You never see any and then two visits come along all at once.'

Sean looked quickly from one to the other.

'Two? Who else—'

'They weren't MI5, Henry,' the old man, Wallis, said tiredly. 'That was their joke. They were Oxbridge researchers. But these gentlemen' – he hung the phone up and passed Sean's ID back – 'Are the real deal.'

The boy looked as hurt as if he had just learnt Santa wasn't real.

'Tell me about these researchers,' Sean ordered. Wallis quickly gave him the basic facts. 'Chris, Monica …' Sean gestured at his team. 'You two go with young … Henry? … and check out the archives. Mr Wallis, I'll need to see your CCTV.'

The group split up. Henry led Monica and Chris through a door at the back, and Sean peered over Wallis's shoulder at the grainy moving pictures on his monitor.

They didn't look much. Two IC1s, nondescript male, female very easy on the eyes. Appearances meant nothing, of course. If every villain looked like a villain then there would be no need for Five. Still, they weren't on the obvious records. Even a place like this was part of

## CHAPTER 6

the security network: their faces would have been tagged automatically if they matched anyone in the system.

*Great*, he thought. *Two unknowns.*

'Excuse me,' he said, and took the old man's place in the chair. His fingers tapped on the keyboard as he shunted the images over to the main server for closer analysis.

Monica and Chris had returned.

'Well, they didn't take anything,' Monica said. 'Seems they were looking for something from 1888 – but if they consulted the removed records file, I guess they didn't get it.'

'1888? What happened in 1888 that deserves a security tag to alert us if anyone comes looking?' Sean thought out loud. 'Well, we're done here. I've grabbed the images. Thank you for your help, Mr Wilkins.'

The MI5 agents left the building and climbed into the black Land Rover with tinted windows that waited outside, in defiance of any traffic wardens willing to try their luck. Then they drove the short distance – barely a mile, but still a twenty-minute walk, and Sean detested wasting time – to Millbank's Thames House, an art deco office building originally occupied by ICI and now the headquarters of Five, on the banks of the Thames, just by Lambeth Bridge.

Once there, they split up into their different offices. An email was waiting on Sean's monitor: 'Require immediate report on case.' Sean's eyebrows went up, but an order was an order. He called up the images from Old Scotland Yard and ran off two large, manhunt photos of the man and the woman. With this material he marched off in the direction of the director's office.

'Ah, Sean. This our best man, the one I was telling you about,' the director said to his visitor.

The director had reached his position because of his razor-sharp mind, a fact that could be lost on anyone who saw him in the flesh. His grey suit looked made to measure, but it was unironed and large wrinkles were spread over his body. He blinked at people with grey eyes through slightly smeared round glasses.

Sean was more interested in the visitor. If the director hadn't addressed him, Sean might not have noticed he was there. He wore a sharp black suit, creaseless and immaculate, decorated with a red handkerchief and a grey, very fashionable, thin tie. He had lanky black hair down to his shoulders and dark, burning pits of eyes.

'William Johnson. What is your report, Mr Miller?' the man said coldly.

Sean had no intention of being ordered about by someone he didn't know.

'May I know your clearance, sir?' he asked. It was very unlikely that the director would want him to give information to inappropriate personnel, and Sean was already certain this case was a storm in a very small teacup, but it was still a perfectly proper question to ask.

He saw at once that it had been a long time since Johnson didn't get his immediate way. The man's face froze for a second, before he stamped a smile on to it.

'Fair enough.' He passed over an ID card. 'Does this satisfy you?'

## CHAPTER 6

Sean studied the card.

'I've ... not heard of this department, sir,' he said.

'It's a very small department,' Johnson agreed icily.

'And don't Protection Command handle royal security?'

'It's more of an advisory role. But you do recognise the clearance level?'

'Yes. Sir.'

William Johnson outranked the director of MI5. Shit!

'So.' Johnson smiled like someone had once described the process to him but he hadn't really understood it. 'Your report?'

Sean had no choice but to go with the facts.

'Two researchers from an Oxford college ...' His scrupulous mind reminded him that he did not know this to be entirely true. 'One researcher from an Oxford college, female, and an unidentified companion, male, entered the archive of the Old Scotland Yard building in Whitehall, and made a copy of a file number that triggered an alert in our system.' He handed the pictures to the director, who passed them on to Johnson. Johnson looked at the pictures long and hard.

'Names?'

'The old coot on duty at Old Scotland Yard was too awestruck to ask them to sign in. He remembered one of them was named after a bird. They were looking for records from 1888.'

Johnson looked abruptly up.

'1888, eh? Do you know what documents were stolen?'

'No documents were stolen. They're all still there,' Sean said. 'What they wanted is at New Scotland Yard. They took a copy of its file number, and for some reason our system decided this was worth alerting us.'

Johnson nodded slowly.

'We're done for now.' He held up the photos. 'I'll keep these. Mr Miller, you'll be reporting to me for the time being. I've already cleared this with ...' He waved a vague hand; he had obviously already forgotten the director's name.

Sean looked at his boss in surprise. The director just gave a small, weary nod.

'But I work for MI5,' Sean pointed out, 'not for royal security or whoever you are. I have several cases lined up relating to possible terrorism leads, and —'

'And you will be at New Scotland Yard tomorrow morning at 10 a.m.,' Johnson said harshly. 'We understand each other? Good.'

And with that, he left the room.

\*

Alice's smile had vanished. She studied James's face closely, appraisingly.

'You're serious,' she said – a statement, not a question.

'Yes. I know her domestic routine well enough. If I can get into Room 101, Sanderson Hotel, then I may be able to find something to help us.'

'However did you two meet?'

'At a party thrown by my late father, but that's not important.'

## CHAPTER 6

'True.' She continued to stare at him. He looked back, and had to agree with what she was no doubt thinking: *What the actual?* He was doing a favour for a bonkers old man. How did he suddenly come to be seriously thinking of breaking the law?

Because, he decided, it would be the most fun he had had in ages, and he would be doing it with the most gorgeous woman he had seen in the same length of time.

Something shifted behind her eyes – some decision had been reached. He braced himself for being told to take a hike. Well, it had been worth the try.

'Okay,' she decided. 'I'm in.'

# JACK

# CHAPTER 7

The Sanderson hotel was in Berners Street, a quiet side street not far from Regent's Park, away from the hustle and bustle of the big city. James had never been there before so he looked around curiously as he entered the hotel through the imposing main entrance, with a bouquet of roses and a bottle of champagne.

The lobby was very modern. Inviting sofas stood around with the seductive curves of the famous red Salvador Dalí lips. The magnificent ash wood flooring was warm and welcoming. All in all, the hotel made a friendly impression. *Well, Monica would never be staying in some Travelodge, would she?* James thought as he wandered over to the reception. This was a long green glass counter with a pretty, brown-haired woman behind it, talking on the phone. James waited and gave her a friendly smile. The woman's eyes lit up as she saw him.

'Yes, he may be here now ... Yes, certainly, Ms Leapman, that will be no problem. Thank you.'

The woman hung up and gave James another, professional smile.

'I think that call might have been about me,' James said. 'James Kent, for Monica Leapman, Room 101?' He hoisted the flowers and the bottle to show he meant business.

'Yes, Ms Leapman was just saying you would be here. She's told you she's been delayed? Well, you're to go straight up – unless you'd like to wait for her in the bar?'

'Well, I would, but ...' James waggled the flowers. 'Can I just say, we had plans?'

'Of course.' The woman gave him a roguish smile. 'I'll get you a key card ...'

Soon, James was in the lift going up to the first floor.

'Nice one, Alice!' he murmured.

Of course, they had called Room 101 to check Monica Leapman wasn't actually in. Then Alice had made the call James had just eavesdropped on, claiming to be Monica. She was held up, her boyfriend would be turning up any second, please render all assistance!

The glass doors slid open. James strolled quickly down the long, bright hallway, past the rows of doors until he reached 101. The corridor was L-shaped and 101 was right on the bend. He juggled the bouquet and bottle in one hand, and with the other stuck the card into the slot beneath the door handle. The door opened with a quiet click.

James entered and instinctively looked around. Here, too, the motto was: white is beautiful. The window was veiled with white, transparent linen curtains. The floor had the same texture as the one in the lobby, light wood, a sharp contrast with the black leather sofa in one corner and two matching leather armchairs. In the other corner was the large, white double bed.

## CHAPTER 7

He peered through the door into the bathroom. The washbasins, the shower and the large bathtub were all white marble.

James set his burden down and started his search.

Tucked away under the bed base he found Monica's service weapon, a black Walter P99. He grinned. Monica hadn't changed her habits since she had shown him this little trick. Neither of them had had any clothes on at the time and James had quickly forgotten it until now. The gun was loaded, but secured. James suspected leaving a weapon unattended was probably some kind of disciplinary offence, if anyone ever found out – one that even Monica couldn't sleep her way out of.

Well, not his problem. He put the gun back and looked around. He was here for a reason and he couldn't waste time.

His eyes settled on the reproduction satinwood bureau across the room, and he felt in his pocket for his Swiss army penknife. *The advantages of an expensive, private education*, he thought wryly …

James had shared a study with a boy at school with whom he had only one thing in common. It had led to a great friendship, because the one thing was that they were both desperately unhappy.

The other lad was the son of an East End barrow boy made good, who had shrewdly grown his business up from nothing until it was worth millions and he could send his son to the kind of school he would never have dreamed of in his own childhood. But the son was painfully aware of the gap in breeding between him and the other boys around him, James included.

James, for his part, loathed the world of entitlement that he had been born into. It wasn't real. For some reason the fact that you were descended from some lord who couldn't keep it in his pants made you important.

And so the two lads had swapped skills. James had taught his friend the social graces that went with his new position. And it had worked – at the last report, the young man had married the daughter of a duke and they were very happy together. In return, James's friend had taught him certain skills that would never feature on the school's curriculum. Such as, the skill he was about to use.

A few moments later he felt the bureau's lock click open under his knife's pick.

There was a laptop in there – he didn't even bother with that. It would be secured in several different ways that he didn't know how to crack, and it would probably alert all kinds of undesirables if he tried.

But there was paperwork here too. He shuffled through it, and a slow grin spread over his face as he found exactly what he was after.

# CHAPTER 8

The black Land Rover ground its way through London's evening traffic. Sean Miller kept his eyes firmly on the road, so that he wouldn't have to watch his partner's pout, and his hands clamped squarely on the wheel so he wouldn't fantasise about throttling her.

'I don't know how we're expected to be partners if you won't tell me what the boss,' Monica complained.

'And I don't know how you can work for Five and not grasp the concept of security clearance,' Sean snapped. 'So shut the fuck up.'

'Yes, but I have to work on this case too.'

'No, you don't.'

'What?' She stared at him as if he had slapped her. 'Why not?'

'I can't tell you that.'

Sean could feel her stare burning into the side of his face

'Hey, what are you doing? We swore we'd always be honest with each other.'

Sean rolled his eyes. The 'honest with each other' thing had been her idea; she had taken his silence as consent. *Jesus, why am I still with her?* he thought to himself.

*You know exactly why*, he answered, and he knew the reason did not paint him in a good professional light.

This was exactly why relationships with co-workers were forbidden.

'So, where exactly do you have to go before dinner? To the hotel?' he asked.

No answer. Monica had now decided to give him the silent treatment, but Sean decided to drive to the hotel anyway since she would squawk the moment he headed in the wrong direction.

Five minutes later, he pulled up in front of the Sanderson. Monica had not spoken a single word for the rest of the trip, which suited him fine. They entered the hotel together.

'Room 101, please,' Monica said to the receptionist.

'Oh, your friend has it. He's in your room right now,' the woman assured her with a smile. Then she registered that Monica had come back to the hotel with another man and the smile began to waver.

'I beg your pardon? You let a stranger into my room?' Monica exclaimed. 'Are you stupid?'

'But … But of course not! … You called me on the phone …'

'We'll deal with it,' Sean said curtly. He steered Monica towards the waiting elevator and pressed '1' for the first floor. He waited until the doors had closed before pulling his Walther from its kidney holster.

'Did you bring your service weapon?' he asked.

Monica's jaw dropped.

'It's in my room!'

'I'll pretend I didn't hear that.' Sean grimly worked the slide, feeding a round into the breech.

## CHAPTER 8

'You think that's needed?' Monica asked.

'A man uses deception to break into an MI5 operative's room? Let's just say I have grounds.'

The doors opened. The corridor was empty – this arm of the L-shape, at least. They advanced down it towards 101, Sean holding his gun in both hands, aimed at the floor, finger alongside but not on the trigger, ready to whip it out of sight if any civilians appeared.

The door to 101 opened and a man slid quickly out of it. Sean's eyes went wide with recognition, at the same time as he whipped the gun up, sighting down the barrel straight into the man's midsection.

'Security Service! On the floor! Now!'

For a brief moment, no one moved. Then Monica pealed with laughter.

'James! Really? I never thought you'd be so romantic!'

'Eh?' Sean forgot himself enough to glance at her, and when he looked back, the suspect had bolted down the other arm of the L-shaped corridor.

'That's the man from Old Scotland Yard, you daft bint!' Sean bellowed as he sprinted forward. He hurtled around the corner just in time to see a fire door swinging shut ahead. He shouldered it open again and barged through. Concrete flights of stairs led up and down. From below was the sound of running footsteps. He craned his neck over the stairwell and aimed down, his gun wavering as he tracked the movement. There was a shadow, flickering as it hurled itself around the bends below, but nothing he could get a clear shot at.

'Shit and fuck and bollocks!'

He flung himself down the stairs after the fleeing suspect. A few moments later he burst out into reception.

'Which way —'

The receptionist went pale when she saw the gun, but she pointed at the main doors. Sean pelted out to the pavement outside the hotel, barely remembering to holster his gun before anyone saw him waving it about in public.

He was just in time to see the rear door of a black taxi slam shut. The taxi pulled away, at speed, as he started to run towards it. Furious, Sean went back into the hotel.

'Should I call the police?' the receptionist asked, now clearly terrified.

'I'll let you know,' he snapped.

A couple of minutes later he strode into Room 101. Monica was giving the room a thorough going-over. At least she could be professional about that.

'What the hell was about?' he demanded.

Monica looked stunned.

'That was the suspect from this morning? But he's an ex-boyfriend! I bumped into him yesterday and told him where I was staying. I didn't think —'

Sean wasn't interested in excuses.

'Is anything gone?'

'Well, the gun's secure and nothing else is missing,' she reported. She flushed when he stared at with narrowed eyes.

'Are you absolutely certain?'

## CHAPTER 8

'Absolutely. Everything's where I left it. Apart from my weapon, the only Five material in here is my folder …'

Her voice trailed off as Sean cocked an eyebrow. She ran to the bureau and opened it.

'This was locked when I left it … but look, here's the folder …'

She shuffled through the documents, before looking up at him, bewildered.

'There is something missing. The letter from the director in which I was appointed to the team! Do you understand that?'

Sean shook his head. No, he really didn't understand that.

# JACK

# CHAPTER 9

That was a close one! Trembling, James sat in the taxi and took a few deep breaths to get himself back under control.

Okay, so MI5 aren't known for their sense of humour. But even so, he hadn't expected to be on the wrong end of a gun wielded by a man authorised to use it.

Then he grinned and pulled the folded sheet of paper out of his pocket. He unfolded it and gazed at the prize, scrawled at the bottom beneath a few lines of text. *All for a stupid signature!* he thought.

'I need to slow down or I'll get nicked,' the driver called from the front. James had promised him a very large tip if he got away from the hotel now.

'Fine, fine. Thanks.'

'Old friend was it, sir?'

James grinned again.

'Jealous husband.'

The driver chuckled as he slowed to the legal speed limit.

The taxi turned into Portland Place, which led directly to Regent's Park. James had given the address he had memorised to the driver but he hadn't really thought it through. He had pictured it as one of the great villas that lined the roads here, a legacy of John Nash's vision for an entire district with a direct connection to Westminster and the Court. Now they turned into the Outer Circle, with the Park on one side and elegant Georgian townhouses on the other. The taxi stopped in front of a small palace. James paid and got out.

*Wow!* he thought. *Not bad!*

The house was white plaster with a black slate roof, and a beautifully maintained lawn in front of it. Large windows let the light into the interior. Above the door was a balcony held up by Greek columns.

James worked the heavy door knocker, which had the shape of a lion. It thudded against the wood and immediately the door was opened by a maid in an honest-to-God black dress and white apron and cap.

'Yes, sir?' asked the girl.

'I'd like to see Ms Alice Gull. My name is James Kent,' James replied.

'Please come in! I'll tell Lady Gull you're here.'

She left him standing in a huge entrance hall. The floor was made of black and white marble slabs in a chessboard pattern. A marble staircase led to a first-floor gallery landing. Several suits of armour stood around the walls. But James was most impressed by the ceiling painting – a portrait of London from the nineteenth century, framed with white stucco, showing Parliament's clock tower and other famous London buildings against a red sunset.

The big grandfather clock was just striking seven when the maid came down the stairs.

'Lady Gull will see you in a moment. If you'll follow me to the salon, please.'

## CHAPTER 9

They went through the door on the right. The salon had green walls hung with many gold-framed pictures. The ceiling was also stucco. Two sofas and matching side tables stood on the large Persian carpet that had been rolled out on the black wooden floor. The room was laid out in the classic seating arrangement, with everything symmetrically furnished. The only modern item was a laptop sitting on the folded-down top of an elegant Chippendale escritoire, but the room was so tasteful that even that just blended in. Three Chinese vases stood on the mantelpiece of the marble fireplace. A family crest was carved above them – a coat of arms carried by two lions. After a closer look, James recognised the crown that showed a dukedom, which seemed to float above the crest.

'Can I get you anything while you wait, sir?' the maid asked.

'Yes, thank you. I'll have some tea.'

She left him and James looked out of the window at the huge rear garden. Everything looked as if it had been personally designed by God, entirely natural, but in reality James guessed it was carefully planned to the nearest millimetre.

'I'm sorry you had to wait!' Alice said behind him. James looked around. His immediate instinct was to ask why she hadn't told him she was a duchess.

But then, he wasn't completely blameless when it came to keeping family secrets. So instead of taking her up on it, he just grinned and produced the folded letter.

'One signature of the director of MI5, coming right up.'

'Excellent!' She plucked it from his hand and spread it out on a leather-topped desk. Her hair dangled down as she pored over the signature at the end, and he fought the temptation to brush it back on her behalf.

'I should mention that to get it, I had a gun pulled on me by an MI5 goon,' he added casually, looking closely to see her reaction. She smiled without looking up.

'That probably goes with the territory of breaking into an MI5 agent's room. You're here, so I guess you got away.'

No *'Oh my God!'* James noted. No *'Are you all right?'* Not even any questioning that he was actually serious.

'I guess I did,' was all he said.

Was she as bored with life as he was? James wondered. Was that why she just took mention of MI5 and guns in her stride? Why she had so casually agreed to blagging her way into Old Scotland Yard, with genuine credentials, and was now seriously considering an escalation to blagging her way into New Scotland Yard with forged ones?

God, she was amazing.

'Can you do something with it?' he asked.

'Forge a simple signature?' She still didn't look up. 'Promise not to tell *The Sun*, but yes.'

'Toff Girl in national security leak scandal!' James laughed. 'You can count on my discretion. They'd want to know your hair colour, age and statistics, of course.'

## CHAPTER 9

'The hair colour's natural so they just need to look; everything else, they can go whistle.' Her head moved from side to side slightly as she scrutinised the signature.

'You didn't learn this at school, I guess?' he asked, not mentioning that earlier that evening he had broken into a desk using skills that he oughtn't to have had either.

'Not officially. Just say that since my father wouldn't sign notes letting me off attending, I had to help myself.'

'You do realise this is slightly more important than forging your father's signature! And it's going to come under closer scrutiny.'

She finally looked up, and smiled.

'James, you're so pessimistic. Besides, I have all night to practice!' She made a circling gesture that was meant to take in the whole room. 'Feel free to call for refreshments, read any book, use the computer. It's all yours.'

So, that was what James did.

Five minutes later, with a beer and a beef sandwich at his side, he sat down next to the laptop. He shot a look at Alice's back. She was bent over the desk, radiating concentration, with the letter on a reading stand next to her and several blank sheets in front. James turned back to the laptop and his fingers hovered over the keyboard.

Then he tapped out a name.

Bit by bit, he pieced together the line of descent from Sir William Gull up until Alice.

He soon learned a very good reason why she hadn't told him she was a duchess. She wasn't one, and wouldn't be until her father, the Duke of Cardiff, died. Fair enough.

William Gull had been knighted for services to the Crown. That didn't make him a Duke. The dukedom had crept into the family line when Gull's daughter, Caroline Cameron Gull, married Theodore Dyke Acland. Acland was another doctor – they kept it in the family – but he was also heir to the Duke of Cardiff.

Alice's great-grandmother was born a year later. She had been an Alice too.

It was a fascinating way to while away a few hours, following leads of interest down endless trails of links to see where they led. James barely touched the sandwich.

Suddenly he became aware of Alice's shadow on the screen. He looked up and wondered why he felt a little guilty. But she was smiling, quite openly.

'Cyberstalking?'

He grinned back.

'Yeah, it's a hobby of mine. How did you do?'

'How did *you* do? Any unanswered questions?'

'No ...,' he began, then remembered. 'Yes, one.' He traced a line of links on the screen to illustrate. 'You're a direct descendant of Dr Acland, everyone born within wedlock – so why are you still called Gull? Not Acland?'

'Ah.' She nodded. 'That was a bit of family solidarity, apparently. After the rumours began that Sir William Gull had been the Ripper, we changed the surname back to Gull to show we weren't having any of it.'

## CHAPTER 9

'That's certainly a vote of confidence,' James agreed. 'They must have had pretty good grounds to believe it.'

Her eyes flashed.

'How about the fact that he had had a heart attack in 1885 from which he never properly recovered, and his arm had been paralysed ever since? At the time of the murders, between August and November 1888, he couldn't even move his hand properly. I, however, can move my hands very well and have produced a pretty good fake signature. Want to see it?'

James pushed his chair back and stretched to unkink his back.

'Hell, yes!'

# JACK

# CHAPTER 10

Sean Miller was boiling with rage as they entered the restaurant.

This was meant to be a romantic evening out with his girlfriend and the setting was perfect. At first sight, the Yauatcha looked like an aquarium. They were surrounded by underwater light. Blue glass walls shone like the Mediterranean in summer, with fish behind them making their slow, casual way around the room.

But it was a very tense end to the day. The case he had been working on during working hours had crept into what was meant to be his time off. Not only had he not managed to catch the intruder from Old Scotland Yard, but he had drawn his weapon, and that meant a report had to be filed.

And now Monica was insisting on learning everything, and he wasn't allowed to tell her, because of national security and the clearance levels that apparently came with working with William Bloody Johnson. Which made no sense, he told himself angrily, because she actually had inside information – that is, had slept with the suspect, on and off, for a two-year period – which might help the case.

At least he now knew the suspect's name, so he had put a low-level operative on watch at James Kent's flat and then tried to get on with his romantic evening.

'Look' – Sean put a cap on his rising temper and just about bottled it – 'I thought we wanted to spend a nice evening. Can we talk about something else?'

Monica paused, then gently stroked his right cheek, a feather-like touch that soothed him.

'Of course, Sean. This place is fantastic. Thank you!

Passers-by could be seen through the glass. At a long marble counter, a petite woman in a kimono sold poison-green French patisserie with mango pieces and ginger sprinkles. Steaming bamboo baskets of dim sum were served with Japanese teas and filled with Chilean sea bream and chilli or local lobster and black beans.

A petite woman showed them to a table for two. Orange fish from South Africa swam behind them. The guests at the next table were smartly Asian, while the couple opposite them with Rasta plaits could be rock stars from New York. That wouldn't be uncommon in the Yauatcha, where the celebrities met for dinner.

Sean ordered a large fish platter and a good Japanese rice wine for them both. The woman nodded with a nice smile and left them alone.

'I'm sorry I upset you,' Monica said. 'I'm a bad girl.' She leaned across the table. 'In fact, I'm *evil*.'

He leaned back towards her so that their lips were almost touching.

'Oh, it doesn't matter at all if you're an evil girl.' Their lips brushed, then came together more firmly, lingering with each touch. 'In some situations I even find it—'

A loud buzzing made the two flinch.

## CHAPTER 10

'Damn, why now!' Sean pulled his phone out of his jacket. 'Sean Miller!'

'Good evening, Mr Miller!' said a cold voice that Sean recognised immediately, though he didn't remember handing his personal number out.

'What can I do for you, Mr Johnson?' Sean asked as politely as he could.

'I heard you had a little meeting with our guest from Old Scotland Yard?'

Sean winced. Had that report reached him already?

'I saw him for a second,' Sean replied. 'I didn't have time to invite him over for coffee.'

'Very funny, Mr Miller. You screwed up. I don't think you fully understand the seriousness of the situation. It's clear you still regard this as a very low-level affair. In fact this is very important for the Crown and for national security.'

'The situation is in hand, sir. There's a watch on his flat and I'll be alerted if he returns. Ditto if he uses his credit card or mobile.'

'It was still an inexcusable lapse. His address, please.'

Sean frowned.

'Sir?'

'The address of Mr James Kent, please. Now.'

Sean bit back on a sharp 'Oh, for fu—' Johnson could find out Kent's address at the press of a button. He probably already had. Asking for it now was just an alpha male way of showing off his seniority.

And Sean had no choice but to go along with it. He recited the address of Kent's Trafalgar Square apartment.

'Thank you very much. Our appointment tomorrow morning at 10 a.m. at New Scotland Yard still stands.'

'I'll be there.'

'Of course. I wish you a nice evening. By the way, the dumplings in the Yauatcha are supposed to be really good.'

Mr Johnson hung up. Sean looked spiritlessly at Monica's uncomprehending face, all thoughts of romance and sex turned to ashes. Who exactly was this Johnson?

Sean knew MI5 had considerable power. He had always felt comfortable using it because he also knew the legal framework that governed it. He had faith in the rules.

Rules that Johnson just seemed to ignore, like he was never going to be held to account, like they only applied to other people. And he was quite possibly right. And that ... that could be frightening.

# CHAPTER 11

The desk was covered with discarded signatures, with Alice's latest and final effort in the middle beneath the lamp.

James's eyes went back and forth between that and the original, several times. For good measure he also scanned the discarded efforts.

'Perfect!' he decided, eventually, 'although I don't see much difference from the others.'

She shot him a surprised look.

'And you an art student, James! Look closely, the hook here is quite different from here, isn't it?' Alice held out two papers in front of him.

'Just write the damn letter,' James muttered.

With the signature perfected, it didn't take long to write the words above it.

*I hereby permit the handing over of the documents with the number 08/1888 JtR to Alice Gull for transfer to MI5 headquarters. Signed_____*

'You look beat,' Alice said. 'Do you want to stay over?'

James glanced at her thoughtfully, and guessed that probably meant …

'In the spare room,' she added for clarification. 'Well, one of them.'

He grinned.

'Thanks, but I'll get a cab.'

'Oh, we can do better than that …'

Five minutes later, James and Alice were at the front door and James was admiring the dark green 2002 Bentley Arnage R with tinted windows that was waiting for him. A man stood in front of the open passenger door, which gave a glimpse of cream-coloured seats inside.

'Just give Charles your address,' Alice said, smiling at his obvious car-lust. 'See you tomorrow? Say, nine?'

They said good night, and James sank gratefully into the plush seats while the Bentley pulled silently away under Charles's expert hand. There was no vibration. Had James not known they were driving, he would never have guessed. He closed his eyes and leaned back. It had been a long day and he still wasn't over the adrenaline rush-and-drain of what had happened at the hotel, which felt like it had added several hours to the normal twenty-four. He was so exhausted that he would have liked to fall asleep immediately.

'We're here, sir,' Charles said suddenly. James really had dozed off and hadn't noticed that they had arrived.

'Thank you, Charles.'

James watched the rear lights of the second beautiful car he had ridden in within twenty-four hours pull away. Then he pulled his key out and went into his building.

He hung his coat on the hook inside his front door, and dropped his key and phone into the bowl on the side table. Then he strolled to the living room, turned on the light – and froze.

A man was sitting in one of his chairs. He could have stepped out of the movie *Men in Black*. He wore a black

## CHAPTER 11

suit, a white shirt and a grey tie. Unlike the Men in Black, he had long, black hair hanging either side of his slender face. And he had a gun pointed at James, with a silencer screwed into the end.

'A wonderful evening, Mr Kent! Now let's finally get to know each other.'

His voice was clear and cold, without any excitement, as though it was the most normal thing in the world to wait with a gun, at night, in other people's apartments.

James's mind spun. If this man wanted him dead, he would be dead already. He could have been gunned down and never known it. Therefore the man wanted something; therefore the man probably wasn't actually going to kill him.

Though – and James was no expert here, but still – he was pretty sure a man with a gun could inflict a lot of non-lethal pain. But *why?*

James had faced down bullies at school who were twice his height and half his intellect. He knew how to keep his face straight and his voice level.

'May I know what you're looking for in my apartment? And how did you actually get in? Who are you?'

'My name doesn't matter, and *I* will ask *you* a few questions. If I don't like the answers' – he waggled the gun – 'I have ways of showing it. Do we understand each other?'

'I think we do,' James said carefully.

'Now. Why are you looking into Jack the Ripper?'

The question was so unexpected that James's resolve to take the man seriously couldn't stand up to his sense of absurdity.

'Well, I like to solve puzzles! I can do the *Times* crossword in fifteen minutes!'

The gun was aimed a little more firmly at him, but the man waved towards a side table. With his mind taken up by the intruder, James hadn't noticed Anderson's file spread out there. He had left the papers neatly stacked. His visitor had gone through them thoroughly.

'These records originally belonged to Sir Robert Anderson. Who gave them to you?'

*George Anderson, what the hell have you got me into?* James thought. But he wasn't going to give his employer's name. The one thing worse than this nutter with a gun being here was the thought of him threatening a helpless old man with it. Minus the gun, James and this guy would be equally matched, he reckoned – if he could just work out how to get past it.

'No one,' James said promptly. 'I'm acting on my own behalf.'

The man stood up and aimed the gun directly at James, sighting down a straight arm and over the barrel. The movement looked professional – he had been trained to do this. James could see a gold signet ring on his right hand. He tried to memorize the design so that he could Google it later – if he got out of this in one piece.

'You don't get hurt if you tell me what I want to know,' the man promised, and James realized he was

CHAPTER 11

not supposed to be leaving this room alive, one way or another.

He clicked his tongue, as though he was admitting defeat.

'The folder arrived this morning. I've no idea who sent it. You know I'm a journalist? We get sent all kinds of crap anonymously.' He went on, warming to his theme. 'I guess you've at least looked me up already? I write for *Time Out*. Why would I want a pile of crap about Jack the Ripper?'

The man's eyes narrowed.

'That is at least plausible. Next question. Who was the blonde woman at Old Scotland Yard?'

Now James was frightened. So he knew of Alice's existence. If he learnt her name then she too would be in danger.

'Her? She was a tourist. I showed her the way there …'

The man fired the gun. It gave a small cough and a small crater appeared in the floor just in front of James's left foot. Every muscle of James's body froze.

'Every lie from now on, Mr Kent, and I aim one inch higher than the shot before. I know you were together in the archives looking for the year 1888. So, who is she?'

'Okay.' James's heart pounded, but he made himself sound cool and collected, and nowhere near as terrified as he felt. 'I'll tell you two things that are true.' He paused, then held up one finger. 'One, I'm not going to tell you.' He held up another finger, with his other hand, bringing his hands within inches of each other in front of him. 'And two, if you kill me, you'll never know who she is.'

The man smiled faintly.

'I really don't think you appreciate how much pain can overcome the strongest man's resolve, Mr Kent, but you clearly need to learn, so –'

'Okay!' James said quickly. He was still holding his hands up. Careful not to make any sudden movements to provoke a shot before he was ready for it, he stood with palms out, the classic gesture of appeasement.

'Okay,' he said again. 'You've got me. Where should I start?'

The man relaxed, just a fraction.

'Start at –'

James clapped his hands together, and the apartment went dark.

The gun coughed again, several times, but James could find his way around this apartment blindfold and was already hurtling through it. He threw himself at the door to the roof terrace and yanked it open. On the way through he fumbled for the latch beneath the handle and heard it go click. When he pulled the door shut after him, the door would stay locked. Working out how to unlock it would cost the man valuable seconds.

Of course, he did have a gun and the window was only glass …

The lights blazed on in the apartment again. The man had worked out the clapping trick for himself. James could clearly see him inside. He grinned to himself as he swerved around the two deckchairs and the hammock,

## CHAPTER 11

and the first faint drops of rain pattered against his face. By turning the lights on again, the man had just turned the windows into black mirrors. If he wanted to see out into the dark, the best he could do would be turn the lights off again ...

Sure enough, the lights went abruptly out.

*Fuck.*

James vaulted over the balustrade and came to an immediate dead end – a sharp drop thirty metres down to the road, and a very small ledge leading towards the next building. He had often wondered if he could actually do this. He had never been bored or scared enough to try.

*Crack.*

A quick glance back showed his apartment was still in darkness, but a massive star had appeared in the plate glass window. James didn't know how strong it was when it came to gunfire, and he didn't know how powerful a handgun was compared to a more powerful hunting rifle. He had gambled it would take more than one shot to get through it – but probably not many more after that.

*Crack.* The star was twice the size and he could hear the glass creaking. No, not many more shots at all.

No time to think about it. He faced the wall and inched his way along the ledge, barely fifteen centimetres wide. Just in time, before he lost his balance completely, he reached the drain pipe and slid down to safety.

# JACK

# CHAPTER 12

From the terrace six floors up, William Johnson watched through the drizzle as James Kent fled around the corner into the Strand. There was no point trying to shoot at this distance. Too many witnesses, and no handgun was that accurate.

Besides, he could guess the fugitive's next destination, fifty metres down the road in the direction James was running.

*He'll want to get to the girlfriend to warn her. He can't phone her because I saw him put his phone down here. Unless she lives very close, that will be too far on foot. He won't take a taxi, because it would just require one police alert to make every driver take a long, hard look at any single male passengers. So –*

'Next stop, Charing Cross,' he said out loud.

\*

James had been hopping up and down with nervous impatience on the platform, waiting for the train to appear. He had done his best to lurk behind something – anything! – but the cylindrical platforms of the Bakerloo line offered very little cover.

He had realised halfway down the drain pipe that he no longer had his phone. Thank God he had his wallet, with its Oyster card, in his trouser pocket.

He was aware of other passengers looking sideways at him. Not really dressed for the time of day, no coat and a grimy white polo shirt, smeared with dirt from the pipe and torn. Well, let them look, he thought. There was only one person whose gaze he did not want to attract, and he wasn't here.

James felt the first breeze on his face as the oncoming train pistoned air down the tunnel ahead of it, and he wanted to cry with relief. He threw himself into a seat the moment the doors opened and he didn't relax until they beeped to announce their closure and the train began to pull away, all without the man from the flat and his ugly, merciless face.

*That was the second time today someone pulled a gun on me!* he thought as the train plunged into the tunnel, cutting off sight of the platform for good. *What the hell is going on?*

As the train rattled its way towards Piccadilly Circus, he could think a little more analytically.

*Okay, first time I had just conned my way into MI5 territory. Maybe that does kind of arouse suspicion …*

But then he remembered:

*'The man from Old Scotland Yard'?* That's what the guy at the hotel had shouted. *What did I do this morning that deserves this kind of attention?*

While he could just – *just* – imagine some bizarre way in which his and Alice's researches at Old Scotland Yard had maybe broken some kind of obscure rule, he couldn't see any reason at all that a gunman would break into his apartment with the intention of torturing him for information and then killing him. No way!

## CHAPTER 12

*I saw that coat of arms on his ring. I can't look it up on my phone but maybe Alice can do something with it …*

A tinny voice announced that the train was now arriving at Baker Street station. James leapt to his feet, ready to exit the moment the doors opened.

Outside, at street level, it was no longer drizzling – now it was raining cats and dogs. He set off at a fast trot towards the Outer Circle of Regent's Park.

\*

From the outside, it was a small, inconspicuous office building with a sign over the door announcing 'Transport for London' in blue.

Inside, floors and ceilings fell away into a three-storey space lined with monitors. When the mayor of London had introduced the Congestion Charge in 2003, hitting anyone who wanted to enter the centre of London with a £10 fee, cameras had been installed all over town. Various authorities had taken the opportunity to install a few more of their own, and all the feeds came here. Anyone who had second thoughts about it had been persuaded by the speed with which the police had caught the associates of the 2005 bombers.

William Johnson waited impatiently for a sufficiently senior manager to come and attend to him. He had overawed the subordinates with his security clearance; for this, he needed to go to the top.

The shift manager finally showed up, obviously nervous at getting such a senior visitor.

'How can I help …?' the man began.

'All footage from Charing Cross Underground, starting half an hour ago until now.'

'You'd better come into my office.'

The small room next to the main hall was also stuffed with computers and monitors. The official showed William to a seat and took his own place at the keyboard. His fingers flew over the keys very briefly. Twenty-four separate monitors switched to different views of Charing Cross.

'As of thirty minutes ago,' the man reported. 'We can filter for biometrics if you have some kind of description?'

William thought.

'Late thirties. Brown hair. Slender build. White top …'

More key tapping, and even before William had finished speaking he could see different angles of James Kent running into the lobby of Charing Cross Underground.

'Perfect.' He flashed a grin that was just bare teeth. 'Where did he …?'

The manager was growing in confidence as he got to show off his toys. The screen changed to an image of James jumping on to a train. They kept watching until the doors closed, to confirm he hadn't jumped off again.

More keyboard tapping.

'No show at Piccadilly Circus …' the manager murmured. 'Oxford Circus … Regent's Park …'

The screen showed a train pulling in at a fresh station, and James leaping out. They followed him by a series of cameras up to the street level, up Baker Street, left into Outer Circle and …

## CHAPTER 12

'Where's he gone?' William snapped. The manager shrugged.

'He's off TfL's system now. You might have to contact the Met? Lots of cameras around that route. All those nobs, very security conscious.'

William scowled; the man looked innocently back. William grunted something that might have been an acknowledgement, but certainly wasn't 'thank you', and left.

*

No one was answering the ringing. James resorted to using the heavy door knocker, shaped like a lion's head. He could hear the echoes in the entrance hall. When there was still no answer, James reached out to use it a second time, just as the door slowly opened.

Charles, James's chauffeur earlier that evening, looked disdainfully out at him. He wore a bathrobe over woollen pyjamas.

'Yes, sir?' he asked, managing to make 'sir' sound like a rude name.

'I have to speak to Ms Gull immediately!' James said. 'I mean, Lady Gull. Lady Alice. Her. You know who I mean!'

'Sir, it's two o'clock in the morning and Her Ladyship will be asleep,' Charles pointed out.

'Yes, I understand you, but I wouldn't bother if it weren't important.'

Charles didn't blink. James stared at him. What was wrong with him? Well, apart from the obvious fact that he must make a pathetic sight. He was soaked to the skin and his shirt was torn and filthy.

'Charles, it's me! Remember? You drove me home. It's a matter of life and death!' James blurted out. He probably wasn't exaggerating, he thought. The stranger had been prepared to kill him, and had wanted to know who Alice was, so put those two facts together …

'I remember driving you, sir. Perhaps if you made your own way back there, and returned here in, say, eight hours' time?'

'Who is it, Charles?' Alice's voice asked. Charles twisted his head to look back and James peered around him. Alice was on an upper landing. She wore silk pyjamas and her hair, so neat and elegant when James had seen her during the day, was a bewitching mess.

'It's Mr Kent, ma'am, but I have already told him that you will not be able to speak to him until tomorrow.'

'Oh, Charles!' Alice's expression ran through the bad temper of a woman woken up at two in the morning, through irritation and then concern. She at least seemed to guess James was a well-brought-up man who knew that you didn't come casually visiting at such a late hour. 'Let him in.'

'But, my lady, it's two o'clock—'

'Take him to the library and give him something dry to wear. I'll be with you in a few minutes, James!' Alice took the stairs back up to the top floor and Charles turned to James with an even grumpier expression.

## CHAPTER 12

'Follow me, please.' He still managed to make it clear he would have preferred to simply slam the door in James's face.

Charles led James up the stairs and along a long, high corridor. At the end, they turned left into one of the most beautiful rooms James had ever seen, every wall lined floor to ceiling with old wooden shelves, stuffed and overstuffed with books. The sheer smell of old books was everywhere.

'I'll find some dry things, sir,' Charles said and disappeared. James had a little time to take a closer look about him. The books spread from the shelves and on to tables around the room, and they were all old. On one side, the wall of books was interrupted by a large stone fireplace – not burning, at this time of day. The Gull coat of arms was emblazoned above it. James kept on looking around. He liked the smell of old leather books, and there was a very old one in a showcase that he wanted to have a closer look at. The butler came back with a pile of new clothes just as James was taking it out of the cabinet. Charles shuddered and winced.

'That, sir, is a very rare volume of the *Encyclopaedia Britannica* and is worth thousands of pounds! Please return it to the display case immediately!'

James hastily put the book back down.

'I brought you a selection of the Duke's clothes, sir. You are about the same size and he is not in residence at the moment. Will you mind changing here, sir?'

James guessed that Charles was obeying his instructions to the letter: having been taken to the library,

James was not going to be allowed into any other room of the house if the butler had his way.'

'Of course! That's really very kind of you. I won't win any more beauty awards with these', James joked, pointing down at himself. The butler acknowledged the weak joke with a tired smile.

'Is there anything else I can do for you, sir?'

'No, thank you.'

James changed quickly after the butler had closed the door. The gear didn't look very modern but it did its purpose. Linen trousers and a new white shirt, and he pulled a green sweater over the top. The combination didn't really go together but it was warm and dry. He was looking at himself in the mirror opposite the fireplace when Alice came in. She had tamed her hair and was wearing a plain blue jogging suit.

'Dad!' she exclaimed. 'When did you get here?'

James pulled a face as she broke into laughter.

'Thank you. I feel as old as him.'

She gestured him to one of the many leather armchairs.

'So, James, joking apart, what's happened? Were you mugged?'

James began to talk. He told her about the stranger who had ambushed him in his apartment. He described exactly the coat of arms he had seen on the ring, and how he had got away, and how he was here.

Alice's face had gone very solemn, but he could see she was taking him seriously.

'One obvious question, James. Why didn't you go to the police?'

## CHAPTER 12

It was a question James had asked himself.

'Because I think if the police even get a hint this is tied up with the Ripper, they'll just treat it as a joke. I mean, I would too, if I hadn't had two, count 'em, two guns aimed at me today. And the first guy was official, MI5, so how do I know the second wasn't too? This is something we have to sort out ourselves.'

At that point, he suddenly realised, she could just say 'what do you mean "we", white man?' and leave him to work it out for himself. But she just nodded, and he felt a stab of – what? Admiration? Amazement? He had turned up at two in the morning to drag her into some kind of extra-legal adventure, and she didn't lift a finger in protest. She just considered herself part of it. What other woman in the world would be like that?

'Okay,' she said firmly. 'Describe this coat of arms again.'

'It looked like a ruler bent at ninety degrees, with the two ends pointing up, and a pair of compasses like you use to draw circles, pointing down. And there were heraldic animals but I couldn't make it all out.'

Alice looked impressed.

'Pretty good. I doubt I could have remembered my own name in the circumstances.'

'I thought we could Google the description, see what comes up?'

'No need, I think.' James watched in surprise as she got up from her armchair and went to one of the bookshelves.

'Do you know what it means already?' James said hopefully.

'Yes and no.' Her face fell. 'Unfortunately. I hope to God I'm wrong, because otherwise we are dealing with a very powerful organization.'

She walked up and down a few times until she found what she was looking for and pulled out an old book bound in leather. It wasn't very thick but it was secured with a lock, which Alice opened with a small key from one of the cupboards. She leafed through it and then went back to James, laying the open book on his lap.

'So, there we go,' she said.

James whistled. The picture in the book was a thing of beauty, hand inked in bright colours. It didn't completely match the coat of arms he had seen, but it was close enough. The right-angled set square and the compasses were identical.

Then he read the caption under the picture: 'Common insignia of the Freemasons.'

It hit him like a slap in the face. He had heard of the Freemasons. Granted he hadn't heard anything bad, but nothing good either.

Alice was talking.

'The Freemasons go a long way back and a long way in every direction. There's no exact list of all the celebrities who belong to them, but four of the founding fathers of the United States of America are said to have been Freemasons. That is why the omniscient eye is supposed to have been printed on the one dollar bill. It's another of their symbols. And they are very closely linked to the

## CHAPTER 12

Crown. The King used to be their Grand Master – George VI, and George V and Edward VII before him. Prince Philip had to become one so he could marry our future Queen, though they say he never practised and he never made Charles join. When Charles becomes king he'll be the first non-Mason king since goodness knows when. And I know for a fact my great-great-great-grandfather himself was a Mason.'

'What, Sir William?' James asked. 'How do you know that, if it's such a secret?'

'From his memoirs. You have to understand that the Masons we're talking about have nothing to do with today's variety. Today, anyone can go to a Masonic lodge and register, as long as they're male, but back then, only true gentlemen were accepted. You couldn't register or volunteer – you had to be nominated by an existing member. Everyone had to take an oath to protect the secrets of the Order, and they kept quiet in public so that no one knew who was a member and who wasn't, unless you looked for the clues.'

'Okay, so they've got a bit more open than that!' James laughed. Alice didn't smile.

'And that is the problem. Over time, they loosened up to the point where they began to think about sharing their ideas and ideals with the public. Not everyone was thrilled – so-called gentlemen would have to share their knowledge with the lower class rabble! And I mean *all* the knowledge – all the dirty little secrets and tricks, going back for centuries with the Crown right at the centre of it all. So a few of the more loyal royalists founded their own secret society, an even more secret society, to make the really important and incriminating knowledge disappear. Of course, that's all just rumour. Like I said, it's secret.'

James was fascinated.

'You think that's who these people are? This even more secret society?'

'It would explain a lot, wouldn't it? That coat of arms you described. Part Mason and part …'

Alice closed the book. The cover was stamped in gold with probably the most famous coat of arms in the country. And now James knew why it had looked so familiar.

On the left was a lion wearing a royal crown, and on the right a unicorn. A knight's helmet hovering over it all, with a large crown, which in turn had a small lion with a crown on top. It was the royal coat of arms of the United Kingdom.

They were combined on the ring the stranger with the gun had worn.

He whistled.

'I dunno,' he said eventually. 'I just can't see the Queen sending out her own private hitmen.'

'She's not what this is about,' Alice said. 'It's not about her, it's about the whole idea of monarchy. They probably take the whole thing even more seriously than she does herself. To them it's all about reputation and honour, and they are so embedded in the establishment, going back so far and in so deep – well, there's no knowing exactly what they can and can't do. They predate most of our

## CHAPTER 12

existing laws, so most of our existing laws were written to accommodate them.'

James could feel goosebumps prickle his skin. He looked out of his window. It was still raining cats and dogs. You could hear the raindrops hitting the window.

*

James wasn't the only to hear the raindrops.

In front of the house, an old blue Rover was parked. William Johnson sat in the driver's seat, with headphones over his ears, plugged into a very sensitive, very accurate laser-based microphone. A beam shone on to a window and registered the vibrations of the glass, turning them into voices and other sounds. Software filtered out everything like the raindrops that obviously wasn't a human voice, and made its best guess as to the rest.

Once he had seen James Kent running on foot into the Outer Circle, it had been a matter of moments to call up the names of all the private residences there. Under the circumstances, the name Gull had stuck out like a sore thumb. He had followed his instincts, and here he was now.

'Lady Gull,' he murmured, as he heard the secrets of the club casually being spilled out to a complete stranger. 'For shame.'

It showed what was wrong with the world, that a daughter of the aristocracy could be mixing herself up in this. Such a beautiful woman, too.

Unfortunately, it also complicated things. He could have killed James Kent and made it look like a burglary gone wrong. This would be harder. For a start, it went against every instinct he had to hurt the aristocracy. He was meant to be protecting the hierarchy, not killing off its members. People would pay more attention to the death of the daughter of the Duke of Cardiff, and anyway, a house like this would be secured with multiple security systems that even he couldn't just override.

He would have to back off … for now. He had their names and their faces. They wouldn't be going anywhere without him knowing. It might take a bit longer, but soon they would both be taken care of.

# CHAPTER 13

A few clouds still hung over the metropolis, pierced with increasing confidence by rays from the new day's sun. The streets of London smelled fresh after the night's rain and everything was covered by a thin film of water. One beam came straight through the window and hit James full in his tired face as he sat in the dining room of the mansion of the Gull family.

'You look terrible!' his hostess greeted him. James looked up from his fried bacon with scrambled eggs. Yes, 'terrible' was probably the word.

After they had finished talking, Alice had led him to his guest room. There he had lain awake all night and thought. He couldn't believe the Royal Family wanted him dead. He was not an avowed monarchist, but he respected them and the work they did for the country. He saw the Queen as a symbol of Great Britain, with all its principles and values and rule of law. And that rule of law included not sending killers with guns after you.

He remembered what Alice had said: these people took the Royal Family more seriously than the Royal Family themselves. It was possible for any group of fanatics to love something too much, like terrorists so infatuated with their god of love that they had no problem slaughtering people in his name.

But, how do you go about fighting people so embedded in the establishment that they *are* the establishment?

On the other hand, he had thought before he finally dropped into a vague sort of doze, the fact they put a killer on to him was a great compliment. They felt threatened by him.

'So, what do you think for our visit to New Scotland Yard?' Alice asked, proudly spreading out her arms. 'I put on something extra exciting.'

She turned around once. She wore an elegant white pantsuit, with matching white high heels with white leather straps. The suit was just tight enough to show the curve of her breasts to perfection. Under the jacket she wore a white vest with a generous neckline. She had her hair down, as James had always known it.

James had another stab of that feeling he had had last night. She knew the danger now, and she still wasn't even questioning that this was what they were going to do! She was still determined to press on with the plan they had come up with yesterday, before the man with the gun had turned up: get into New Scotland Yard, get that file.

'You don't look like an MI5 agent, more like a model!'

'Thank you for the compliment! I want to provide as much distraction as possible from the letter, so that they don't look too closely at the signature.'

'I think you'll succeed!' James said with a smile, and then his face fell.

'Problem?'

## CHAPTER 13

'Just thinking. I don't know if I was followed last night ... How do we know they won't get us the moment we step outdoors?'

'I've thought of that. How about a secret passage?'

'You're kidding!' he exclaimed.

She was kidding, he thought five minutes later. It wasn't really a secret passage. It was a narrow alleyway, sunk so that their heads were just below the pavement. It ran all along the back of the row of mansions where Alice lived, so that once upon a time the servants and tradesmen could come and go without offending the sensibilities of sensitive Victorians.

And when James and Alice emerged up to street level, they were a quarter of a mile from the Duke of Cardiff's London residence. Alice wore a wide-brimmed hat with dark glasses; James wore one of His Grace's flat caps. They didn't look like a couple trying to disguise themselves but neither did they look like the James Kent and Alice Gull that anyone who knew them would be expecting.

They flagged a taxi to take them to New Scotland Yard, and there was still no hue and cry as they got in and the cab pulled away.

We might actually make it, James thought to himself. It all depends on what Alice finds when we get there ...

# JACK

# CHAPTER 14

The video surveillance room of New Scotland Yard was lined with at least fifty screens. Sean Miller was there already when William Johnson entered at ten o'clock prompt. Sean felt a small stab of satisfaction at being first to arrive.

He still had mixed feelings about the man who described himself as the Queen's Security Counsel. Although Mr Johnson could smile, sometimes, his eyes were always cold, like a killer's.

Johnson, of course, didn't even acknowledge the fact that Sean was already there.

'Report?' he said.

Sean was standing over one of the Yard's surveillance operators, who was busy flipping through possible hits on screen. Johnson had already – far too early in the day for Sean's liking – fired off an email full of instructions, followed immediately by a phone call to check they were received and understood. Essentially they were the details of the man and woman from Old Scotland Yard, with orders to locate them. The man, Sean already knew about from Monica. The woman had a description but so far no name – or at least no name that Johnson was letting him know, though Sean suspected he knew. Johnson was just one of those people who like to withhold information to make themselves feel important, and then bollock their juniors for not having guessed what they deliberately weren't told.

'Both profiles fed into the system,' Sean told him. 'Searching now. Neither of them have yet registered, certainly not in the vicinity of the Outer Circle.'

And that was another thing, Sean thought. Johnson almost certainly knew which address in the Outer Circle was the one to look for, but he wasn't letting on. They could have put a drone up above it, or just pointed a camera at the front door – but no, Johnson had to play it this way. Was he protecting someone?

'Assuming either of them are out and about, how long will it take for the system to find them?' Johnson asked. Sean looked to the operator for an answer.

'If they don't move about and stand in sight of a camera, about twenty minutes.'

Johnson snorted.

'Last night I was able to track Kent from Charing Cross station immediately! Why twenty minutes?'

'I'd guess you already knew where to start looking.' The operator didn't peer up from his screen because he had no idea who Johnson was and didn't have much time for spooks either. 'We don't have that information so we're already running through thousands of hits from all over the capital.'

His tone obviously irritated Johnson, which in turn made Sean hide a smile, but he was clearly a professional doing his job and Johnson couldn't reasonably complain.

## CHAPTER 14

'All right, I'll give you fifteen!' Johnson barked, because he had to show he was in charge somehow. 'Miller, you're with me.'

\*

The current version of New Scotland Yard was in its third home since the organisation began. It had moved into what was once the Curtis Green Building, just off the Embankment, in 2013. The words 'Scotland Yard' were engraved in the middle of the white floor of the entrance hall, in large letters. As Alice entered the lobby she registered at least two surveillance cameras. After a short pause in which she took two deep breaths, she crossed with a sure step to the young man at the counter.

With Wallis yesterday, she had deliberately been brisk and professional. Here in the headquarters of the Met, she assumed she would be surrounded by people who were brisk and professional, so she would hardly stand out. And so she decided to go for the fine balance line between brisk, professional and sexy. She generally despised women who depended on being good looking to make their way in life – but frankly, as she often told herself, wasn't that the man's problem, not hers?

'Hello, handsome man! Maybe you can help me?' She leaned on the counter, giving the seated man a direct view of her well-formed neckline.

'Of course ... madam!' said the young man.

'I have this letter of authorisation here, and I need what it says to be done as soon as possible,' Alice said with a big smile. She handed the letter over with simple assurance and not a scrap of doubt that what she wanted would be achieved. He scanned it quickly with his eyes and reached for the phone next to him.

'Mr Smith, could you please come to reception as soon as possible? Thank you.' To Alice, he said, 'Mr Smith manages the main archive as well as the security archive.'

'You're a treasure! How can I ever make it up to you?' Alice beamed. The young man grinned bashfully.

'Well, are you busy tonight?'

Alice realised she may have been too successful with the distraction.

'Hmm, a little cheeky!'

'Well, I had to ask!'

'Now, there you may be right. I'll get back to you.'

'I'll be here. I'm not going anywhere!'

To Alice's relief, Mr Smith came into the reception hall. He was a stocky man in his fifties, with a grey, receding hairline and an old, washed-out suit of brown corduroy. He seemed a little neglected and shabby and Alice's first thought was that he was perfectly suited to be working in a basement.

'Hello, madam! John Smith, the most important one here. Man, that is.' He laughed loudly, as if he had made the joke of the century, and quickly stopped laughing when he noticed no one else was. *Brisk and professional*, Alice told herself. 'Well, you can laugh later. How can I help?'

Alice handed over the forged permit. He read it quickly and nodded.

## CHAPTER 14

'Hmm. File number 08/1888 JtR ...' He squinted thoughtfully at the permit, but then nodded. 'If you'll come with me?'

Alice followed him towards a large glass door. He quickly typed a four-digit code on the wall-mounted keypad and the door opened with a quiet buzz.

'08/1888 JtR ...' Smith murmured again as they walked down a white corridor.

'Is there a problem?' Alice asked innocently.

'Well, I think, if I remember correctly, it was picked up this morning by a man I didn't know at all and moved to another archive. But I might be wrong!' he added quickly, when he saw the dismay that Alice tried unsuccessfully to hide. 'It could have been another year, or something else from the same one. I've got it logged downstairs.'

They had reached a pair of steel elevator doors, which opened promptly when Smith swiped a slot next to them with his security pass.

Alice's heart was beating even faster as she stepped into the elevator with him – not just with the audacity of forging her way this far, but the thought that somebody had beaten them to it. Then what would they do?

The elevator slid smoothly downwards for a couple of floors and opened again on to a drab, grey-painted corridor. They had to walk some distance until they stopped in front of a large round door, which looked like it should be guarding gold bars in a bank vault. This time Smith typed a ten-digit code. A small box slid out of the wall and he pressed his thumb on it. Then he scanned his eyes. That made five separate security checks since they had left the reception area, Alice counted. This place was secure.

Mechanical noises sounded behind the metal and the one-metre-thick door swung open.

'After you!'

Alice entered the room and was speechless.

She had been expecting a larger and more modern version of the brick vault under Old Scotland Yard. Instead she was standing on a gallery halfway up the side of a vast underground space. There were more galleries below and above her, and the walls were lined with shelves that had to be holding thousands of books and folders. A cluster of showcases stood in the middle of the room, holding even more documents.

'Yes, I know what you're thinking,' Smith said pleasantly. He headed along to where a computer workstation sat on an ordinary-looking work desk covered with more files and bits of paper. 'Beautiful, isn't it? I felt the same way the first time. As far as I know, there are over a million documents here, going back even before Scotland Yard was founded.'

He tapped at his keyboard and checked the screen.

'Oh, yeah, here we go. The documents you're after were picked up earlier today at 9:45. Hmm, not long ago! You must have just missed them.' He looked up thoughtfully at Alice. 'Just one file, but a thick one.' He held his hands apart to show the distance. 'A very obscure file, and suddenly two people are interested in it the same day?'

## CHAPTER 14

Over her pounding heart, Alice remembered that Smith might not be a policeman himself, but he did spend his days surrounded by them. Maybe their thought processes rubbed off. Considering all the security measures they had gone through to get down here, he could very well keep her contained if he thought anything at all was suspicious while he called for backup.

'It sounds like crossed wires,' she said calmly. 'My research supervisor could well have got here first. Is there a name for whoever took the file?'

Mr Smith looked back at the screen, and his eyebrows went up.

'No,' he said, sounding surprised. 'Which itself is unusual. Not forbidden, though. But I can describe him. Slim. Very expensive-looking suit. Black hair. Not very communicative.'

Alice hid a shudder. Based on James's description, it did sound very much like the unknown gunman.

'How so?' she asked.

'Well, I asked the usual questions. You have to lift the mood a little, right? Things like where he works, what he was planning to do with the file and where the documents were going?' He sniffed. 'Just told me to mind my own business. Though he did graciously unbend enough to tell me it was going to, quote, one of the safest places in England and it was good enough for the Crown, unquote.'

'That does sound like my supervisor,' Alice said, with her warmest, friendliest smile to soothe Mr Smith's ruffled feathers. 'He can be very brusque, I am sorry. He takes his work very seriously.'

She was a better actress than she had realised. Nothing gave away the turmoil in her thoughts. If last night's gunman was on the case, and had got this far … She had to get out of here, she thought. He might still be around. She could not let herself be trapped with him.

'Not a problem, dear lady. Well, after all that, I suppose I'd better escort you back to the surface. Wouldn't want you wandering around here all day, ha ha!'

On their way back to the elevator he pulled a half-finished muesli bar from his pocket and offered her a bite. He just shrugged when she politely declined. The elevator started to move up.

\*

'Sir! I have the female suspect!'

Sean and Johnson came hurrying over.

'Where is she?'

'Uh … right here in the building!'

The screen showed Alice Gull walking across the reception area towards the main doors. Johnson was actually so surprised that stared at the screen for half a second before moving.

'That's impossible! Miller, with me!'

Johnson was already running towards the door with Sean close behind. The operative at the screen looked after them, then back at the image. The suspect was almost out of the building. She would be away in another moment.

## CHAPTER 14

He grinned to himself. This was what every operative wanted to do but hardly ever got the chance.

He flipped up a cover in the desk next to him and pressed his thumb down on the red switch beneath it.

*

Alice was almost of the doors when the alarm sounded – an ear-splitting screech that clearly announced trouble.

At the same time a calm, pre-recorded voice spoke over the PA system.

'This building is in lockdown. Remain where you are. This building is in lockdown. Remain where you are …'

And the doors began to slide shut.

Alice pelted forward. The nice young man who had hoped for a date blocked her way.

'You can't leave, madam …'

She shouldered him aside, sending him staggering, and threw herself through the doors. They just nipped her heel as they closed and she stumbled slightly, waving her arms to keep her balance, but then she was out and running towards the Embankment and the road where she had left James and the taxi.

'What the …?' James gasped as she fell into the back of the car.

'Drive!' she gasped.

The driver twisted round to stare at her.

'Lady, I'm going nowhere if it gets me in trouble with the cops …'

Alice pulled her sunglasses case from her bag and shoved it into the back of the driver's seat, keeping it out of his sight.

'There's a gun in your back!' she said. 'Now, drive!'

Uniformed, armed cops were running towards the taxi. The driver gunned the gas and the cab powered away.

James stared at her. He didn't say anything about the fact that she was holding up a taxi with her sunglasses, but his eyes begged a question.

'Your friend from last night got there first,' she murmured in answer.

He mouthed 'Shit' but kept quiet. At least now he understood why they had to get away, at all costs. Even being arrested by legitimate cops would not protect them, if half her theories about the guy were true.

\*

It took valuable seconds to reverse the lockdown and get the doors open again. By the time William Johnson burst from the front of the building, the taxi was already fifty metres away, heading south with the river on its left, down towards Westminster Bridge.

He was boiling with rage. That stupid idiot sounding the lockdown! If he hadn't pressed the alarm and made her run, they could have trapped the woman in the building – maybe the man too.

Two black-clad armed policemen were running towards the main entrance, Heckler & Koch MP5 automatic rifles at the ready. They went tense when they

## CHAPTER 14

saw Johnson reaching into his inside pocket, but it was only to get his ID to show them.

'Do you recognise my authority?' he snapped.

'Yes, sir ...'

Johnson wheeled around and pointed at the dwindling taxi.

'Then on my authority, open fire on that vehicle!'

*

The first shots shattered the rear window. Two more shots hit a side window in the passenger compartment and the taxi driver screamed as one just winged his shoulder, leaving a nasty welt on the skin.

'Holy shit, that hurts!' The taxi swerved dangerously to the left as he clutched at his shoulder, scraping the curb and the cars parked there until it shuddered to a halt.

James and Alice stared at each other, pale white. They had been shot at! They had actually been shot at!

Then they looked back. If someone could open fire on them without any warning at all, in public, then they had no intention of surrendering. They could step out of the cab with their hands held high and still end up riddled with bullets.

Alice dug her glasses case harder in the driver's back.

'Get moving!'

'Fuck you!' the man screamed.

James swore and threw himself out of the taxi's back door, bracing himself for the impact of bullets as he pulled the driver's door open.

'Move over!' he shouted. 'I'll drive!'

The man stared at him.

'You need a license for that!'

'Shut up and move!'

The driver clambered clumsily across into the left-hand seat and James swung himself in. He jumped on the accelerator and the taxi shot off. The driver slid down into the footwell and crouched there, curled into a ball and making himself the smallest target he possibly could.

Westminster Bridge loomed on their left, with the northern end of Parliament and the base of the clock tower directly ahead. James's first thought was to get across the river, away from the crowded centre of London, until he heard sirens and saw blue flashing lights appear at the far end.

'Can you see if they're still behind us?' he shouted. Carefully Alice straightened up and looked out of the broken window.

'Two police cars,' she reported.

James swore and did the only thing he could. He hauled on the wheel and the taxi swerved right, into Parliament Square.

'Where the hell are you going?' Alice shouted.

'I have no idea! I just know we can't stop!'

'Just stop already! Why can't you just stop?' the driver begged.

'Because there's people back there with guns,' James said through his teeth. He couldn't be bothered to navigate the one-way flow of Parliament Square. They shot illegally across the top of it, against the oncoming

## CHAPTER 14

stream – the same route he had walked home after meeting Steve, what felt like years ago. James swerved the taxi around the traffic light island and continued down Birdcage Walk, racing towards Buckingham Palace with St James's Park on their right.

'Just surrender to them!' the driver wailed.

'In case you hadn't noticed, they just shot at us without warning. Sorry, mate, but we're all in this together.'

The driver groaned but kept quiet. Alice and James glanced at each other in the rear-view mirror. He saw resolve and agreement in her eyes. Neither of them liked what they were doing but it beat being shot dead by the Met.

The Palace loomed ahead and across the park, James could see the gold and marble glory of the Queen Victoria Memorial. He swung with screeching tyres into the Spur Road one-way system, then around the monument. The taxi skidded abruptly to a halt, facing down the broad, tree-lined avenue of the Mall towards Trafalgar Square.

'What's going on?' Alice demanded. The sirens were getting louder and closer behind them. 'Why are we stopping?'

'The road's closed,' James said dryly. The Mall was blocked by police cars. Alice twisted around. The road in the other direction, Constitution Hill, leading to Hyde Park, was blocked the same way. Armed cops in black helmets and body armour had their guns levelled at them. The tourists that had been busy photographing Buckingham Palace stood as if rooted and watched the spectacle. The police hadn't had time to clear them away. Most of them had their phones up to record the event.

And in the forecourt of the Palace, the sentries, in their bright red comic opera jackets and towering bearskin hats, were running towards the entrance with their utterly modern loaded weapons. James remembered that those guys might look like something out of Gilbert and Sullivan but they were real soldiers and they really were there to guard the Queen. They would not take kindly to a gunfight outside her residence.

Behind the taxi, the two cop cars that had chased them Scotland Yard pulled up. A pair of men in civilian suits got out, both of them recognised by James, plus a couple more police officers armed with automatic rifles.

An amplified voice crackled from a loudspeaker.

'Throw your keys out of the window and come out of the car with your hands up.'

'So, what do we do now?' Alice asked anxiously. 'Just give up?'

'Yes, please just give up!' the driver sobbed.

James pointed behind them.

'For information,' he said, 'the guy built like a rugby player is the man from the hotel and the one in the dark suit is the guy from my apartment last night.' Alice turned around to stare.

'So,' she said, 'our chances of surviving if we surrender have just gone from minimal to zero.'

'Oh, God!' the driver wept.

Suddenly James grinned down at him.

'Hey, if you want out so badly …!'

## CHAPTER 14

*

Johnson kept his eyes fixed on the taxi. What were those two up to? They couldn't seriously believe they could get out of this!

Unfortunately the Met seemed to have taken over. It was a regular police officer who was giving the fugitives orders over the loudspeaker. Well, let them. Once they were in custody, then Johnson would make his move. It would mean exposing himself to more public notice than he enjoyed, but he could manage that. If that was what it took to eliminate them, it would be worth the extra trouble.

Suddenly the taxi door opened and a man crawled out on to the road. The air was full of the sound of guns being cocked and every weapon there was levelled at him. The man shuffled forward on his knees, both arms stuck straight up in the air.

Johnson frowned.

'We don't want him! He just looks like a taxi driver!'

'Nice start,' said the voice on the loudspeaker, 'but you have not yet obeyed our instructions. Throw the keys out of the car window ...'

As soon as the man was between the taxi and the armed men in the Mall, the engine roared and the taxi swerved around. Johnson stared in disbelief. It was aiming for the public stairs that led down into St James's Park.

'Open fire!' he ordered the man behind him. 'Now!'

The man raised his weapon to his shoulder.

# JACK

\*

Inside the taxi they heard the shooting start up like a fresh war had broken out. A few more bullets hit the vehicle and another window shattered. But then the taxi was racing along the wide pathway beside the lake, with trees between them and the Mall, and there was no clear shot for anyone to take at them.

Still, the shooting continued: from the sound of it, there were a lot more bullets flying around, and not all were at the taxi. James frowned as he tried to piece the noises together at the back of his mind. Were the Palace sentries shooting back? Shit, that would get someone in trouble!

James kept his hands on the wheel while Alice waved out of the window to clear the way of tourists. Most of them used their own initiative and jumped away in terror. James could already see the route ahead in his mind – he had done this many times before on foot. He just hoped there were no bollards or other obstacles in the way that he had never had to notice before.

The staircase loomed ahead. James had to throttle right down so as not to wreck the car, but it lurched bump by bump up the steps and back into the Mall. They had bypassed the roadblock. James floored the pedal again and swerved past Horseguards Road, towards Admiralty Arch and the Mall.

## CHAPTER 14

*

'Cease fire!' William Johnson bellowed into his radio. 'All units *cease fire* for Christ's sake!'

The popping of rifle fire gradually died down. The order had got through to the police, and someone on the Palace side – in a different chain of command, he had to remind himself; I need to do something about that – had given the same order to their men.

Johnson and Miller slowly straightened up from behind their car. Johnson stared in horror at the starred window on the facade of Buckingham Palace. Jesus Christ, someone had actually hit the Palace!

Then he took in the crowds lining the Mall. Many of them had had the sense to lie down when the shooting started. Others were still standing, lined up like cattle with their cameras out, recording everything. God, why couldn't a stray bullet or three have taken them down?

He raised his radio again.

'HM Security Counsel. We need total suppression on all social media channels.'

Sean stared at him.

'You can't just shut down social media!' he exclaimed. 'Even Five can't do that.'

Johnson smirked back.

'Maybe you can't, but believe me, I can.' His face fell. 'Oh God, I can't believe those fools hit the Palace!'

'Perhaps you should do something about it,' Sean said cheerfully. 'You know, being the Queen's Security Counsel, like it says on your card.'

Johnson whipped around to face him.

'You have been about as much use as a third tit so far. Get out of my sight and find something helpful to do.'

He stormed off, Sean hoped to make nice to whoever was in charge of the Met officers and the sentries.

'Fine,' Sean said out loud to himself, already making plans. 'I will.'

\*

When James had been a kid, he and his dad had gone for a holiday in New York. One day, from their hotel they had seen the kind of car chase he had thought you only got in movies. Twenty or so police cruisers howling and whooping their way in convoy down FDR Drive. It had been the most exciting thing he had ever seen.

Twenty-five years later, he finally knew how the guy they had been chasing felt. The taxi shot out of Admiralty Arch towards Trafalgar Square and the National Gallery beyond it, with what felt like half the Met giving chase.

Rather than skirt around the small, low roundabout between the Mall and the Square, with its statue of Charles I astride a horse – the official centre of London from which all distances were measured – he shot straight across it while passers-by jumped screaming out of the way. They hit the road again on the other side and shot into the Strand.

'You do know, at some point we have to get out?' Alice called from the back seat.

'I know. We just need a few seconds to lose ourselves – but we have to have those few seconds! For all I know,

## CHAPTER 14

those guys have orders to shoot the moment they get a clear shot.'

'I find that hard to believe.'

'So did I,' he muttered grimly, 'until last night that guy tried to shoot me.'

'Fair point …'

The taxi weaved across all the lanes, in and out of the city traffic, shooting through the gap between two open-topped double-decker buses giving tourists the city tour. The block of patrol cars behind them was slowed down but did not give up the pursuit.

'Do you have a plan for getting us those few seconds?' Alice asked.

'Actually I do.'

The Strand became the Strand Underpass, then the Strand again as they hurtled past the Royal Courts of Justice. Both of them wondered for a moment if they would ever end up in there. At the same time, they became aware of a muffled *thud, thud, thud* in the air. Alice peered up out of the window at the police helicopter that was dogging their moves.

The road now became Fleet Street, once the seat of the English press. Then they were on to Ludgate Hill and passing St Paul's, the great cathedral of the City of London. The police phalanx was still in pursuit.

'This is the last stretch,' James called over his shoulder.

'Oh, good, the plan! Let's hear it?'

'We're going to cross the river, ditch the car and split up. We can't do this together.'

Alice gaped in dismay.

## JACK

'No, I can't leave you alone!'

'Alice, they'll be looking for a man and a woman together. Once we're on our own we've each got twice as much chance of making it. So, I'm going to go over Tower Bridge, then I'm going to jump out and you keep going. I can lose myself in Shad Thames – I know it like the back of my hand. They'll stop to get me while you head off. You'll get your couple of minutes to lose the car, then double back and we meet at a safe place.'

Alice groaned but couldn't get around the logic of what he was saying.

'Okay, but where? They'll have both our homes nailed down under surveillance.'

'I've thought of that. Jack Straw's Castle. It's a pub on the Heath in Hampstead that belongs to a good old friend from university. There's no way even MI5 could draw that connection.'

'I'll find it,' she promised.

'Ask for Jack, he owns the place. No relation to Jack Straw. I'm sure he'll help us.'

'Jack,' she said dryly. 'Easy name to remember, under the circumstances. Okay.'

Now they just had to get over the river ...

The taxi hurtled around the green space of Tower Hill and on to Tower Bridge Road. The Gothic towers of the bridge loomed ahead as James pressed the pedal further down. On the south bank beyond it, on the right was the space-age glass construction that was City Hall, office of the Mayor of London, and beyond it H.M.S. *Belfast*, the old World War II warship that had now found its calling

## CHAPTER 14

as a museum. And on the left was Shad Thames, once a warehouse complex serving the Port of London and now a maze of renovated apartment blocks and shops and cafes and restaurants. If the cops knew their way around it better than James then he would eat his hat.

Warning lights flashed ahead and the barrier began to swing down in front of the first tower. The bridge was closing to traffic, prior to opening for a ship. Or maybe there was no ship – maybe the police had just phoned ahead and ordered it to happen.

If they stopped now, they would be trapped this side of the river, in a dead end.

James bared his teeth and pressed the pedal to the metal. The taxi accelerated, hitting the barrier at fifty miles per hour. The barrier flew away in pieces, though James was sure it had taken a chunk out of the taxi's grille as well.

The road in front of them began to rise as the two halves of the bridge swung upwards. James kept going, with only a slight lurch as the taxi hit the rising slope. Ahead, the view was cut off – they couldn't see the other side. James just went with his innate Londoner's knowledge of how quickly the bridge opened – it was something he had watched too many times to count from one of the many restaurants in Shad Thames that overlooked the river.

The gap was still only a couple of metres when the taxi reached it. The cab shot across and hit the road on the other side with a thump and a grind that tore off the front and rear bumpers. James braked hard as it slid down the southern ramp of the bridge and pulled up in a big half-circle drift at the entrance to Shad Thames, just past the arch that acted as a gateway on the south bank to the rest of the bridge.

James and Alice each started to leap out of the vehicle even before it had come to a full halt. James left the driver's door open so that Alice could clamber in.

'See you later,' she said tenderly. James acknowledged the statement with a smile, and was running even before she had powered the accelerator and the taxi was lurching off again, with a screech of tortured metal.

He ran down the stairs from the road to the river walk, swung around towards Shad Thames and —

A voice snapped behind him, cold as steel.

'Security Service. Hold it right there! And turn around slowly!'

James froze. It wasn't the voice of the man from his apartment. Had he heard it before?

He had no choice. He turned around.

Yes, he realised, he had seen this man before. It was the rugby player, the other guy who had chased them from New Scotland Yard, and before that James had seen him at Sanderson's. Monica's boyfriend. The first man to pull a gun on him.

'I never caught your name last night,' James said.

'Sean Miller, not that it matters.' The man sighted grimly down the barrel of his gun and James slowly held his hands out to show he was unarmed.

## CHAPTER 14

'Lucky I followed you on the south bank, so I didn't have to cross the bridge, right?' Miller said in satisfaction. 'Though what the *hell* you thought you were doing —'

'Trying to get away from a small but legal group who believe they can get away with murder and who therefore won't have any qualms about plugging me,' James said. 'The fact that you actually gave me a warning suggests you're not one of them.'

He was aware of tourists lining the parapet above them, looking on, partly in horror, partly curious about what was happening.

The man's lip curled.

'Paranoid bullshit.'

'One of them was at my apartment last night.'

'That is —'

'I take it you know my address?'

Miller paused, frowned.

'Of course.'

'Well then, send someone you can trust round to have a look at it. The main window has been shot out, from the inside.'

Miller shook his head.

'I don't know what you're trying, Kent —'

'To stay alive. Which won't happen if I go with you quietly, whatever you think.'

In the distance they could hear police sirens. From the south side of the river, getting closer.

'I'll be handing you over to the Met,' Miller said, 'but if you're so worried about your safety I'll take personal care of you.'

He glanced sideways at movement in his peripheral vision. A group of Asian tourists was slowly approaching, eyes fixed on their guides or their screens and none of them yet noticing that an arrest was taking place here. A small woman was in charge, armed with a furled umbrella and explaining the sights on the other side of the river.

'Come on now!' Sean ordered. But James didn't move, and in a moment the group was between them – a herd of about thirty tourists, blocking any chances of a clean shot from Miller.

James ducked and ran, along the promenade and away from Tower Bridge. Behind him he could hear Miller cursing and ordering the uncomprehending tourists to get out of the way.

*Damn it, I should have gone the other way!*

Ahead was only an unbroken stretch of riverside walk with nowhere to hide. It wouldn't take Miller long to fight free of the Japanese and then it would be a straight race, except that the guy behind had a gun and sooner or later might get around to using it.

H.M.S. *Belfast* lay at rest fifty metres away, her guns neatly aligned fore and aft, grey and gleaming in its World War II colours, as powerful and as shipshape as when she had hunted down the *Scharnhorst*. A gangway at the stern linked the venerable battlecruiser to the shore.

James swerved and ran on to the gangway, barging his way through the tourists buying tickets at the desk.

'Stop! Do you have a ticket?' the ticket seller bellowed.

## CHAPTER 14

'Season ticket holder!' James shouted over his shoulder, not breaking step as his feet pounded on the gangway with metallic echoes. A moment later he had disappeared into the ship.

The ticket seller stared after him, open-mouthed, while the tourists he was meant to be serving milled about uncertainly. They all turned when they heard more running footsteps approach.

The seller braced up to the newcomer.

'Look, I don't know what's going on but—'

The man silently flashed some kind of identification in his face. The seller abruptly stepped out of the way and pointed towards the ship.

'He went that way.'

'Don't let anyone off,' Sean ordered, 'and call the police!'

He had seen James enter the ship. He ran along the gangway and stepped cautiously through the same hatch, gun held in both hands before him.

His eyes first had to get used to the gloom of the warship's interior. He had a choice of directions. Sean pulled up memories of long-ago school visits to the old ship. One route led down, towards the machine shops and engines and weapon rooms. The other led up to the crew quarters and the bridge. Which way would Kent go?

The guts of the ship, he remembered, were a labyrinth of machinery and bulkheads and dark corners. So that was the direction he went.

JACK

Poised like a panther, ready to leap at any moment, Sean made his way down the metal steps. They were gratings so he could look through them at the floor below. Kent wasn't hiding there.

Arriving at the bottom, he bent his head to duck through the hatch leading to the cavern of the engine room. Here in the belly of the ship, he was below the waterline and the room was full of shadows and dark corners and nooks and crannies. It smelled of oil and metal. Before Sean were the mighty blocks of the engines. Above his head were the pipes that fed steam from the boiler room to the turbines. Slowly he crept forward along the gangway between the engines.

He had circumnavigated the first of the three blocks of machinery. He crept on.

Something moved to his left and he whipped the gun around.

Nothing. It was a shadow. He started to lower the gun …

No, it was *two* shadows, which meant the other guy was —

Sean started to turn, too late. A heavy blow struck him on the side of his head. The shock ran through his body as he dropped to his knees. His gun slipped free of his numb hands; his finger pulled the trigger as it fell to the metal grating. The boom of a gunshot echoed around the metal cave and the bullet whanged off into the distance, ricocheting off a hundred different metal surfaces.

## CHAPTER 14

James Kent was standing over him, an iron bar in his hand. He had scooped up the pistol before Sean could gather his wits to grab it.

Sean squinted up at the dark hole – the barrel of his own Walther P99. He couldn't help noticing it wavered a little. His head was throbbing but he slowly pulled himself into a more comfortable sitting position, resting on his butt, his legs bent in front of him as he hugged his knees.

'Do you even know how to use that?' Sean asked.

'I know that as long as this end is pointing at you, you're going to keep still.'

Sean shrugged.

'You know they'll get you, don't you? And that they'll throw away the key?'

'That's not my worry,' James said bluntly. 'I've already tried to tell you once. There are people who want me *dead*. Now, try to see my problem. You're either one of them anyway, in which case you'll slot me as soon as my back is turned, or you're straight, but in that case I can see why you just plain won't believe me, and you'll blithely turn me in and deliver me straight into their hands. So, you see, there's not a thing I can do to make this easier for myself except get them before they get me. What would you do in my place?'

Sean shifted on his backside, like sitting on the metal floor was uncomfortable, which it was.

And then his legs shot out, to wrap his feet around James's ankles. He pulled hard, James flew over backwards and the gun dropped into the depths of

H.M.S. *Belfast*. Sean was moving even before James had hit the floor, landing on top of him, pinning him down, pounding with his fists so that all James could do was wrap his arms around his head and take it.

But Sean had taken a blow to the head, which no one just walks away from, and the barrage faltered as the exertion brought a wave of dizziness sweeping over him. It was only for a moment, just long enough for James to grab his fists. Arms straining but not moving, the men glared at each other through the gloom of the engine room.

'You're ... going ... nowhere ...' Sean grated. James was underneath him but Sean's knees were on either side of James's leg.

James brought his leg up, hard and fast, mashing Sean's testicles so that Sean screamed and toppled off him. James made himself be merciless, because if he had stopped to think about it then the violence would have made him sick. With both hands, he scooped up the pipe he had dropped earlier and brought it down hard on the back of Sean's neck.

The MI5 agent slumped to the floor and didn't move.

James stared down at his motionless body.

'Oh ... *shit* ...'

In the great scheme of things, it had been Sean or him. Life or death, as simple as that. Every word he had said had been true: if he went into custody, he was dead.

But James felt he had been brought down to the level of the people he was fighting.

## CHAPTER 14

There was one thing he could do. He crouched down and touched his first two fingers to the side of Sean's neck, then breathed a sigh of relief as a pulse beat strongly against the tendon there. James snatched his hand away as Sean groaned and started to pick himself up – and slumped again.

James guessed he had about five minutes of grace before Sean was in any position to call anyone. He started to run.

He paused at the foot of the stairs. Maybe the MI5 agent had called for backup? Maybe the hatchway was already covered, up on deck? He didn't know, but he couldn't take the risk.

So instead he ran further inside the ship, along the passageways towards the bow. At the very end a small ladder led up to a hatch. James quickly climbed up and out on to the foredeck, standing below the triple six-inch guns of *Belfast*'s A-turret, saluting the sky at a 45-degree angle.

There was obviously some kind of commotion going on at the stern, which was taking up the attention of the other tourists on the foredeck so that none of them had seen the man covered with sweat coming out of the hatch. James peered past them. He could see uniformed police swarming over the stern area.

He tapped a rubbernecking tourist on the shoulder.

'What happened?'

The man didn't look round.

'Well, there were two guys who ran into the ship, and a few minutes later we heard a gunshot, sounded like? And then the cops came. They said to wait here.' He started to look around. 'Are you …'

'Hey, look, cameras!' James said, pointing at the bank. A TV news van had pulled up beside the police blockade.

'Oh, right!' the man said happily. He pulled out his phone and started to take pictures of the scene on the bank.

James moved swiftly back to the bow and peered over the railing. He was just above the anchor chain that led down into the dark brown water of the Thames. He quickly hopped over and wrapped his feet around the links, then let himself down to the level of the river, carefully so that no one would hear a loud splash.

Finally he slid into the water's cold embrace, feeling it first fill his shoes, then soak into his clothes. He swam the few metres to the shore and climbed the stairs to the river path, dripping wet.

He didn't stand still. The distraction at the stern still had everyone's attention and as long as no one looked at him directly he was just some other guy.

He quickly ran along the path with soggy, squelching footsteps until he came to the Hays Galleria, another legacy of the gentrification of the South Bank – formerly a warehouse and wharf, now a traffic-free street lined with tall buildings full of restaurants and shops and apartments and offices, shielded from the weather by an ornate glass and steel ceiling. Carefully not catching anyone's eye, like all this was perfectly normal, he padded down its length until he reached Tooley Street.

## CHAPTER 14

For a moment he stood still, looking left and right. Left, out of the question: that's where the police were. So, all he could do was escape to the right.

But he had no desire to do it on foot. His wet trousers chafed and clung to his legs, and his shoes were full of water.

But there was a row of scooters there, and a careless fellow citizen had left their key in one. James swung his leg over the saddle and started the engine.

#  JACK

# CHAPTER 15

*Where was he?*

Again and again, Alice looked out of the window on to the busy road. She hadn't expected James to be exactly quick – but it had been more than seven hours since she dropped him off at Tower Bridge.

Alice herself had driven on for barely more than a minute, weaving her way into tight little side streets before abandoning the old taxi, walking a few metres around the corner and waving down a new one.

It had taken her over the bridge into the City of London, and from there she had got a bus to Hampstead. She got off at Heath Street and walked the short distance to Jack Straw's Castle.

As she walked up to it, she had remembered where she had heard the name before. It seemed grimly appropriate. Jack Straw had been one of Wat Tyler's lieutenants in the Peasants' Revolt of 1381, said to have built a camp here from which he had wanted to march on London. But before the march could take place, he had been captured by the king's men and hanged.

Charles Dickens had helped make the pub famous, but the building he would have known no longer stood. The modern, castle-like building only dated from 1962.

Alice had scanned the road up and down for police cars as she approached, but could see none. And so she had gone in. Her eyes had to get used to the dim interior before she could see a few tables and chairs and a long bar on the other side of the room. The place was empty so she had rung the bell on the counter, which summoned an overweight little man with thinning hair who scurried out of a door behind the bar. He wore a coloured sweater that was much too short over a yellow shirt that was way too long. He was the most mismatched person Alice had ever seen but she had more important things to worry about.

'Hello,' she had said in her friendliest voice. 'Are you Jack?'

He had been less friendly.

'And who's asking?'

'I'm a friend of James Kent.'

And with that he became her new best friend.

'You're a friend of James! Fantastic. You're very welcome. Will James be joining us?'

'I hope so. We should be meeting if he isn't … detained.' It only took a brief quarrel with her conscience to make her keep quiet about exactly what might detain him. A warm smile appeared on his thin lips.

'Well, yes, I'm Jack and I own this lovely place. Sorry it's so quiet. People don't come by as much as they did. They usually go straight to Parliament Hill. It's only a few minutes from here, for the best view of London.'

'Quiet is absolutely fine,' Alice assured him.

'Well, anyway. Will you be staying? Can I give you a room while you wait for James?'

## CHAPTER 15

Alice was surprised, but realised that yes, she really did need to take a rest, now that the adrenaline of the chase was finally draining away.

'Yes, that's very kind of you, if it doesn't cause you too much trouble.'

'Hey,' he laughed, 'I own an empty pub! No trouble at all. Come this way.'

Alice followed Jack out of the room. On the right was the kitchen and straight ahead was a shaky old wooden staircase. Jack stomped up it and Alice climbed carefully after him. With every step it creaked loudly and the whole wooden frame shook.

'I can understand if James has been held up,' Jack said over his shoulder. 'Sounds like the whole city centre's on lockdown. Apparently someone took a pot at Buck House, can you believe it? What is the world coming to?'

Alice made polite noises of agreement. If there was nothing on the news about a man being captured then that was all to the good.

Jack took a left at the top and stopped right in front of a brown wooden door, with a brass number 1 attached.

'So here we are. Room number one, for my number one guest!' Jack said and pushed the door open. Alice entered the small room.

'Oh, my!' she exclaimed in delight. And then she thought, *oh, my* ... as she put two and two together and realised Jack thought she and James were a couple. More than half of the room was taken up by a large four-poster against the left wall. A narrow door on the right led into the separate bathroom.

159

## JACK

'Everything all right? I'll get you some tea and biscuits and then I'll leave you alone.'

'Thank you very much! Can you please let me know as soon as James arrives?' Alice asked politely.

'But of course. See you soon!' Jack closed the door behind him and trotted down the stairs again.

Well, whatever the status of her relationship with James, Alice wasn't going to miss this opportunity. First, she took a bath. Then she put on the clothes that Jack's wife Sara brought her, and sat down with the tea and biscuits in an armchair in front of the large panoramic window. From her comfortable little nest, she could see the park across the road, and all of the street in front of the house.

And there she stayed, for hours, and still he just didn't come.

She thought of calling him, and got as far as getting her phone out before remembering that she didn't know his number ... and now she thought about it, he had said his own phone was back at his apartment. She also noticed her own battery level getting dangerously low. A quick enquiry downstairs told her that no, Jack didn't have a charger she could borrow for that kind of phone. She went back to the chair and stared back out at the road.

Her eyes were getting heavier ...

Alice had a bad dream. Again and again she had the impression that a dark stranger with long black hair and a knife in his right hand was following her. Driven by fear she kept running into a dark alley without a street light, the pursuer always after her. Suddenly the road

## CHAPTER 15

stopped! She was standing in front of an old brick wall. With a big grin, the man with the knife stepped forward her and pressed the point of the knife into her skin. Her skin broke and the blade slid into her—

'Have you been waiting long?' a voice said. Alice jerked awake and saw James grinning down at her.

'You made it!' She leapt to her feet and pulled him into a hug, which turned into a kiss. A little self-conscious, they both stepped back from each other.

'I was so worried!' she said. 'Where have you been?'

She looked him up and down. The clothes borrowed from her father had turned into trackie trousers and a hoody and trainers that were trying hard to be Converse but were obviously cheap knock-offs. He looked down at himself and grinned.

'Uh – yeah. I had to get changed and this was all I could get with the cash I had on me. My card's PIN chip wouldn't work after it got dunked. Thank God for plastic banknotes! I'm afraid your dad's things ended up in a bin.'

That detail wasn't what interested Alice.

'Dunked?'

And so they sat down in leather chairs on either side of the window, and in short sentences James told her everything that had happened since they parted ways at Tower Bridge.

'So this guy on the *Belfast* – he was the one in the hotel?' Alice asked.

'Yes. With Monica. They have the same employer.'

'How can you tell?'

JACK

James ticked the points off on his fingers.

'One, the same kind of gun, and two – well, he said so! Security Service, which is MI5's official name. Plus ...' He winced at the memory. 'He was in really great shape.'

'I expect that's standard for an intelligence agent. Do you think the stranger from your apartment also works for British Intelligence?'

James pulled a face as he thought.

'Again, the gun was the same. But the guy on the ship ... you know, I almost felt I might be getting through to him? Just for a moment. What I was telling him – it came as news to him. So, Apartment Guy – if he's also in intelligence then it's a different department.'

Alice sighed.

'And now? Shouldn't we go to the police? Or seek help?'

'No.' James shook his head emphatically. 'These people are probably in control of the police. There are all kinds of warnings police are meant to give before they open fire, but they just did it, remember? If that was the guy from my apartment telling them to do it then he seems to have a lot of influence. You remember your split-off ultra-secret Masons? My guess is he's one of them.'

'So who knows how deep his power goes?' Alice grimaced. Then, slowly, her face settled down to a more deliberately neutral look. James shifted in his chair, sensing that she was having an idea that she only wanted to let out very carefully.

'Or,' she said. James leaned forwards, hands on his knees, silently encouraging her to go on.

## CHAPTER 15

'Or,' she said again. 'We find the highest-profile person we can think of. We go to them and tell them everything. Then they accompany us to Scotland Yard in a blaze of publicity, cameras everywhere, uploads to every social media feed you can think of. We make a public statement on the steps and then we turn ourselves in. Meanwhile this person raises the highest stink they can in Parliament. Try and see Apartment Guy disappear us after that.'

James smiled with one corner of his mouth.

'You say Parliament – you were thinking of the House of Lords, weren't you?'

'I was.'

'And the highest-profile person you can think of … is your father, the Duke of Cardiff.'

'Correct. What do you think?'

'I think it could work,' James said after a moment's thought. It had already occurred to him but he had turned it down because he didn't want to be the one who suggested, '*Say, let's submit your father and loved ones to terrible danger!*' 'I also think … is your mother still with us?'

'She is,' Alice said, puzzled.

'Any brothers or sisters?'

'No, just a couple of cats and dogs. Why?'

'Doesn't matter. Just your mother's enough. I don't think Apartment Guy would hesitate to strike against her, if he thought it would silence your father.

Alice's face fell. Then she rolled her eyes.

'You're right. We still can't drag anyone else into this. Not if there's the slightest chance we can do it ourselves.' She clapped her hands together, like a teacher, dismissing the idea. She was abruptly firm and businesslike. 'Okay, what now? London is the most filmed city in the world. All those CCTV cameras he has access to – they'll have to find us sooner or later.'

'So, let's make it later,' James said grimly. 'The moment we start moving tomorrow, it'll be a race against time – so we just have to keep one step ahead.'

'Okay.' Alice smiled and James felt another of those thrills stab inside him. He had pretty well said they were going to be outlaws in their own home city, and she just accepted it! God, she was amazing. Right now, he could just … Well, never mind.

Alice was checking her watch.

'And on another subject, aren't you hungry at all? It's already late!'

James grinned.

'I asked Jack to take care of that on my way up here. Let's see what he's done for us!'

To Alice's surprise, James didn't lead them back downstairs. He turned in the other direction. They went up some more stairs and he held the door open for her at the top. She gasped. They were on a roof terrace, paved beautifully with large, natural stone slabs. Here and there were large flower pots with exotic plants, including banana, lemon and orange trees. In one corner stood a wooden pergola covered with ivy. Under the ivy's

## CHAPTER 15

natural roof was a table with a white tablecloth, set with porcelain tableware and silver cutlery.

'This place is amazing!' she said. He nodded.

'The best view in London.'

He led her around the table and now they could both enjoy the magnificent view. From here they could see the City of London, the heart of the financial world, its many skyscrapers glowing with light against the evening sky. The view also took in the Heath across the street, but at this time of the evening there was only darkness and the barest hint of its many old trees.

'Well, you can say what you want, but London is just a beautiful city. Everywhere you find such quiet romantic places! Even on the roof of this somewhat run-down pub,' Alice said with a smile.

'I can't imagine a nicer city,' James agreed. 'Now, please, have a seat!'

James pulled a chair back so Alice could sit down as Jack came hurrying across the terrace.

'May I offer you a good house wine? I recommend the white. This one comes from Kent and my personal wine cellar!'

'Then it must be good!' James assured Alice. 'Jack is the best cook in the world and his cellar has more than two hundred wines.'

'Well, I guess it might not be that much – but there's more than a couple down there,' Jack confessed. 'I've been collecting for a long time. My oldest wine is over fifty years old and I also have schnapps that are even older.'

'Jack's been in trouble before. He had to choose between wine or woman,' James joked.

'And what did you chose?' Alice asked seriously.

'What a question!' Jack acted outraged. 'Of course, the wine. My wife understood.'

'How'd you guys meet?' Alice wanted to know.

'Well, James and I both studied art history at Oxford a few years ago, at the same time, although I am a few years older than him. We just hit it off. Then I chucked in my studies to buy the old pub up here and expand it. I was a bad example to James, because a short while later he also dropped out! He started writing for *Time Out* so he would get free meals here.'

'Rumpled!' James said. 'And I thought I hid it so well.'

'In your dreams, mate.'

Alice looked interested. This was something about James's past that she hadn't known. Though, come to think of it, there was a lot of James's past – in fact, most of it – that she didn't know.

'Well, there were other reasons,' James went on quickly. 'Oxford was too like school. In both places I was surrounded by people like me – rich kids with everything handed to them on a plate – and I didn't like who I was. It's hard to put into words, but I knew I'd never need to really try in life, and I *wanted* to try. So I chucked everything in and came to London to live off odd jobs.' He smiled bitterly, without humour. 'Which was the final nail in the coffin as far as my father was concerned, because – I now realise – he had given me so much and it was like me throwing it all back in his face.'

## CHAPTER 15

Alice tried to reconcile the image of James deliberately dropping out with the young man who lived in a very nice Whitehall apartment. He must have guessed what she was going to say.

'I struggled along for a few years,' he said, 'and then my father died and I got everything in his will. The only heir. So now, guess what, I still don't need to try. See? I couldn't even drop out properly.'

Alice wasn't sure how to react. Family heritage was important to her and she could never understand people who were as indifferent to their heritage as James seemed to be.

She also knew she had scraped away a layer of self-protection and seen something inside him that probably didn't come out very often. She felt privileged.

'Everything you've done today,' she said, 'I'd say you did all that pretty properly.' He smiled awkwardly, and to change the subject she asked, 'What's for dinner?'

'This is a surprise, but you won't regret it!' With that, Jack disappeared towards the ground floor.

'I can only agree with Jack,' James said with a smile. He obviously didn't realise how what he had just said had affected Alice. 'No one ever regrets his cooking.'

'I'm sure my spoiled palate will enjoy it.'

'You will love it!' James agreed. Silently they sat together on the roof and enjoyed the tranquillity of the city.

'Where do you want us to go next with our investigations?' Alice interrupted the silence.

James pulled a face.

'Yeah, we do need to get that straight. Fact is, I don't know! What did the man say again in New Scotland Yard?'

'He said ...' Alice thought back. 'The stranger who removed the files only said that they would be taken to one of the safest places in England and it was good enough for the Crown. What could that be?'

'The safest place in England? Where valuable things are kept? It must be the Bank of England!'

'Maybe ... Is that owned by the Crown?'

'Well, it was founded by the king. William III, I think. To finance the war against France.'

'Yeah, but the Crown doesn't own it, does it? There must be some other place ...'

'So, here comes the starter!' Jack had reappeared with a plate in each hand. 'Green salad with fried salmon strips, in a lemon sauce.'

'It looks delicious!' Alice praised. James just nodded his head approvingly.

'Thank you. It's my signature dish. Do you want to know where I ate the worst salad ever?' Jack asked.

'At McDonald's?' James asked.

'No! Worse than that. I was at the Tower of London with my wife, a long time ago. I just wanted to show her what jewellery she'd never get from me. Near the Tower there is a small tourist restaurant and it served a salad with just three limp leaves and a terrible vinaigrette. And that's when I said to myself, 'I can do better than that!' So, every salad I make now, I try to make it the exact opposite of that terrible one!'

## CHAPTER 15

Jack disappeared again, leaving Alice and James staring at each other like fools.

'The Tower of London. Duh!' James spoke both their thoughts out loud.

'They keep the Crown Jewels there. It's probably safe enough for a few documents,' Alice said.

Neither of them wanted to ask the most obvious next question: how do you break into the Tower of London? They ate their salad and waited for the main course, which followed quickly: lamb in peppermint sauce. This, too, was of the highest quality.

They ate in companionable silence.

Twenty-four hours ago, James thought, it had been pissing cats and dogs and he had turned up at Alice's place, soaked and dirty. Like a true English summer, the weather couldn't decide what it wanted to be. Tonight it was dry, maybe a little humid, but just warm enough to enjoy sitting out on a roof terrace eating a fantastic meal with a fantastic woman.

Eventually the meal was well and truly finished, the last specks of sauce mopped up.

'So, how do we proceed?' Alice asked as they sat back, their stomachs comfortably full.

'I say we go to the Tower tomorrow and take a look around. Maybe we'll see a door that says "Secret archives!"' James joked.

'Yeah, sure! But, you know, the idea of going to the Tower isn't bad? At least then we may get an idea of what we're doing.'

'Sure. We won't be able to hang around but we can certainly do a reconnaissance. Okay, that's tomorrow sorted!' James checked his watch. 'Nine thirty – still early. What do to do next?

Alice read his mind.

'How about a little walk now? We have one of the most beautiful natural parks in London just around the corner, and I need to do some walking off.'

'What about the dessert?'

'I'm just too full for that now! I hope Jack will forgive me,' Alice said.

'What can I forgive you for?' asked Jack, who had appeared with a large cheese platter.

'That I can't eat anything more right now!'

'Oh!' Jack looked at the cheese platter with a long face. 'All right, I'll put it in the fridge. Maybe you'd like something later.'

Jack trampled sadly down the stairs, followed by James and Alice.

They left the house through the back door to stand in the dusk. A large lattice gate led off the pebble-covered courtyard into the street. The two of them crossed the road, which barely had anyone about, and enter the large park that was Hampstead Heath, eight hundred acres of natural heathland stretching between the elevated districts of Hampstead and Highgate. It had been created by merging different plots of common land and was striking for its diversity. Woods alternated with meadows and hills. Ponds and lakes invited you to fish, even swim in the summer. Unlike the parks of central London, there

## CHAPTER 15

were no buildings and statues here, apart from the magnificent eighteenth-century pile that was Kenwood House at the very northernmost point. This was as close to the original natural landscape of London as anyone could ever come.

James and Alice walked together, and at some point bumped into each other in the dark so that their hands brushed together. Their fingers entwined and after that they didn't come apart again as they strolled towards Parliament Hill. From this romantic point, one had an overwhelming view of the British capital. It was properly night time by now and the city was ablaze with light

'Let's sit down for a while?' James suggested. Alice accepted the offer gratefully, as her legs were aching from the long walk.

They sat side by side on a bank. She leaned into him and it seemed the most natural thing in the world to slide his arm around her waist.

'This is something extraordinary,' she said after a while. 'I've never been here at night. By day it all blurs together and you don't realise how much you can see. Look, you can even see the dome of St Paul's!' She pointed in that direction.

'And there's Big Ben and the London Eye,' James added. 'But the most beautiful thing about this city is sitting next to me right now.'

Alice turned to James and looked into his brown eyes.
'That is so corny.'
'Did it work?'

# JACK

She slowly bent her head forward. James followed her example and their lips met, first brushing together, then more firmly. Alice had never known a man could kiss so sensually. James's arms slid around her. She felt him stroking against her blouse, caressing her, taking nothing for granted until he knew exactly what she wanted. And so she let his hands slide inside her blouse and slowly begin to stroke her soft skin.

He was still wearing the hoody and a T-shirt under it. It was easy to slide her own hand in, feeling and caressing the smooth strength of the muscles of his ribs and back, feeling the heat of his skin.

Then, very quickly, she lifted her hands and pulled his clothes over his head. He stared at her in the moonlight.

'Here? On the Heath?'

'Why not?'

Slowly he grinned, and then leaned forward to kiss her again, at the same time as he gently opened her blouse and she felt his hands move around her, feeling for the clasp on her bra. Alice spread his discarded hoody on the ground and lay down on it, pulling James's naked upper body on top of her. She slid his trousers down his legs and he kicked them off, and felt him opening her own trousers up and sliding them down. They paused only a moment to admire each other's naked bodies. Then he lay on top of her again and their kisses grew more urgent. It was still warm enough that they didn't feel cold as they lay together, kisses and caresses working each other up to a near frenzy, the night air playing gently on their bare skin. James kissed Alice on her breast, then gently touched

## CHAPTER 15

the tip of his tongue to her nipple before bringing his open mouth down on top of it, teasing and tickling with his tongue and lips, at the same time as he shifted his hips to lie on top of hers. She reached down to guide him with her hand as he carefully penetrated her. Alice moaned quietly as she felt him move inside her, slowly, gently, then more and more urgent, peaking, and then slowing but still keeping on until eventually he heard her gasp herself and felt her shudder with pleasure beneath him. And then they lay together and let the night breeze gently dry the sweat from their skin.

# JACK

# CHAPTER 16

Most of the lights in the Palace had been turned off. Its most famous occupant had always had one eye on household expenses and was also determined to set a good example for energy conservation.

But there was still light in a small room, where an old woman was meeting a forty-year-old man and his assistant. The woman sat in an armchair and looked at the two gentlemen. Her grey hair was no longer perfectly styled after a long working day.

'I am sorry that we have to disturb you at such a late hour, ma'am, but this is a matter of the utmost urgency.' As the older man spoke, the younger drew a picture and a report from the inside of his black suit. He put them on the woman's side table. She took the report and scrutinised it intensively.

'Well, gentlemen, as you know this man works for me and I have always trusted him. But I will certainly not tolerate actions like we saw today.'

'Thank you, ma'am,' said the older man. 'But we must act quickly. This man is like an out-of-control machine.'

'Then why do you not dismiss him?'

The two men looked at each other.

'We … can't, ma'am. This man's appointment is entirely in your gift. Officially he works only for you.'

'What do you expect me to do?' The old lady looked at the older man. She generally appreciated his advice.

'Act now, ma'am! Release him from his duties and dismiss him. That will render him powerless. If you don't, there could be serious consequences for you.'

The room went silent and he cursed himself silently. He was aware that what he had just said sounded almost like a threat – and she did not respond well to threats. Appeals to duty were the way to get through to her.

Thoughtfully, the old lady looked at the photo. She chose her words slowly, as if it were hard for her to say what she thought.

'Thank you for your advice and rest assured that I will think about it. But this gentleman has given me nothing but the most loyal and dedicated service, until today, and he deserves better than to be cast out without notice. I will find a place for him where he can do no more harm. Now, if you'll excuse me.'

She stood up and held out her hand to the older man. Whenever she did this, the meeting was over and there was no going back. He bowed and kissed her hand, then walked out of the room with his young assistant.

'I don't understand!' He began to complain after a few steps down the hallway, just far enough to be out of the hearing of a woman in her nineties. 'Why does she never take my advice until too late? It was like this in '97. She just prevented a catastrophe by finally coming up to London, but it was damned close and it didn't have to come to that. And here we are again.'

## CHAPTER 16

They walked up a narrow staircase, because the conversation had taken place in the basement of the Palace. No one should know about this, which was why the meeting had taken place so late, after the close of official business.

'What are we supposed to do now, sir?' the younger man asked.

'I have no idea!' admitted the interviewee. 'Since she won't just fire him, it would be best if the problem solved itself.'

The younger man studied his fingernails.

'I may be able to initiate a few things that will help the problem do that, sir.'

They had reached a large black wooden door, which was opened by a servant. A black armoured Jaguar waited in the courtyard outside. A bodyguard opened the back door and the two men got in. After the guard had taken a seat next to the driver in front, the Jaguar started moving.

'This conversation never happened, understood?' the older man said. 'But I agree with your last suggestion. Get it all started, but never forget, you won't get support from Number 10.'

The younger man just nodded his head slightly.

After a short drive they reached a small, closed-off road just off Whitehall. In front of house number 10, they stopped.

# JACK

\*

William Johnson was more than just angry. Everything that could go wrong yesterday had gone wrong.

He strode down a long corridor. The walls here were shabby and not as grand as in the other rooms of the Palace. The morning sun was already shining through the windows. The boss got up early, so Johnson had to as well

*This can't be happening! If the guy could just die, I wouldn't be having this problem*, Johnson thought to himself.

He liked his profession and he admired his employer. It had been a long and rocky road to become what he was now: Security Counsel to the Queen of Great Britain. Counsel, rather than advisor. It had a better ring to it. That at least was his title now, because it sounded more modern and less dangerous. What harm could a counsel do, after all?

In fact, Johnson had inherited a very old job that had been known by a number of titles and had once carried a great deal of power and autonomy. He had looked it up when he got the job to see if those powers were still on the statute books. They were. Someone, somewhere had thought they might be needed again someday. And that day was now.

Johnson had enjoyed a rigorous training in a Scottish regiment as an enlisted man, before going to Sandhurst, the smithy that forged the career of army officers. Here he had shone with very good marks, very much ambition and diligence. After five years in the army he had decided

## CHAPTER 16

it was too constraining and had taken his skills out into the commercial world. He had moved into the lucrative profession of personal protection. His first celebrity to protect was the Duke of Marlborough, a relative of the famous war premier Sir Winston Churchill. The Duke's family was deeply rooted in the politics of the land, so the Duke had recommended Johnson to the British Prime Minister and he became security adviser to the head of government.

He was well regarded at 10 Downing Street, seen as a man who took his work seriously and did not let anyone dissuade him from his course. He had also met his current employer there. Johnson had been captivated by her personality from the very first moment. He had asked the Prime Minister for permission to change jobs. After a few days of reflection, the PM had consented and so William Johnson now worked directly for the head of the Royal Family at Buckingham Palace.

In the years he had worked for the Queen, he had never had a problem with her. On the contrary. The Queen respected and liked her security counsel.

But now William was in unknown territory. He didn't know how she would react to the current situation, as it had never happened before.

Johnson reached a tapestry that appeared to cover the wall at the end of the corridor. But he knew exactly where to touch, to open the hidden door. Behind it was a narrow spiral staircase leading up. After stepping through another door at the top, also camouflaged on the outside with a picture, he was now in the hallway of the Queen's chambers. On the left were the bedrooms and dressing rooms of the Duke of Edinburgh and of the Queen herself. On the right were the office, the tea room and the audience room of the Queen. A liveried servant opened the last door for him and Johnson stepped inside.

The room had high walls decorated with stucco. It was lit brightly by the rising sun that shone through the large windows overlooking the private park where the garden parties were held every summer. In the middle of the room stood a large table, bearing several ornamental bowls. Behind the table sat an old woman with grey hair. She wore a green knitted sweater and a matching green skirt, and she held a folded newspaper that Johnson recognised as *The Times*. She read it every morning and she would have already solved the crossword long ago.

She set the newspaper aside, and gazed steadily at him through her glasses.

'Well?' she said.

He didn't need to ask. Every headline, at home and abroad, had been about shots being fired near Buckingham Palace.

'There were two very dangerous people in the vicinity of this building, ma'am. The officer on the ground —'

'You.'

'I believed that lives were at risk. It was a calculated decision – which sadly proved to be the wrong one.'

'What I fail to understand,' she said, 'is, if these two are the dangerous terrorists you make out – why is there no hue and cry? Bulletins at all the ports, stations, airports, rental agencies, hotels, bed and breakfasts? I remember

## CHAPTER 16

9/11. I remember 7/5. It took just hours for the first clues as to the identities of the bombers to emerge, and after that there was no hiding place. Homes were raided up and down the land. Why are my security services so silent now?'

'Because I have told them to be, ma'am.'

She frowned.

'Why on earth …?'

He kept his face like stone and did not utter any of the words that bubbled inside him.

*'Because, ma'am, in the case of all those other terrorists you've mentioned, they had friends and families who knew they had been radicalised, who knew exactly what they were. If we make Kent and Gull's names public, in no time at all a few hundred people will be coming forward – friends, family, some of them very senior and respected – to say that* no way *are these two terrorists. They might be arrested and whisked out of my reach; they might make their story known before I'm able to silence them. No, they must not be identified until I can get to them first. And that is why any reports come to me and to no one else.'*

But he couldn't say any of that to her.

'You've always trusted me before, ma'am; please do so now. Just believe me that any hue and cry at this stage would only be counterproductive. A secret, silent investigation will have much less chance of being compromised than anything louder and more public.'

She looked sceptical.

'I have had representations from within the Civil Service asking that you be dismissed. They say you went too far – and I have to say, I agree with them.'

'And I have to confess that they are right, ma'am.' God, that hurt, but there was only one way to deal with this: to confront it directly. Representations, eh? He could guess exactly who she meant. So, they were coming for him. The knives were out. Well, he had seen off better enemies than them. 'I let things escalate out of control. I can only give my word that it will not happen again. Transferring this operation to another command will create a moment of weakness, a window of opportunity that could let them slip away.'

She held his gaze for a long time. He returned it openly, innocently, without blinking.

'And how long will it take you to get these people arrested?'

'With respect, ma'am, the longer I have to spend in this meeting, the longer it will take.'

'Then I had better let you go. But be in doubt about my displeasure at yesterday's events, William. If I am not to dismiss you, as I have been asked, then I make one condition.'

'Ma'am?'

'They will be taken alive. They will be brought before a court and they will receive their just punishment there. I will not tolerate vigilante justice!'

'I can't promise, but I'll try my best, ma'am.'

'Just see to it, William.'

## CHAPTER 16

She nodded, and that was the sign that he was allowed to leave. He bowed to her and went to the door.

'Oh, and William?' she said as he reached out for the handle. 'If you have anything else to tell me, this would be the right time.'

He smiled back.

'No, ma'am, there's nothing else. Nothing at all.'

# JACK

# CHAPTER 17

Much of the Tower's nine-hundred-year history was associated with fear and terror. Those who had incurred the wrath of the monarch often languished for years in the gloomy fortress. Many met a violent end on nearby Tower Hill. Today, Tower Hill was a bustling subway station where nothing remained of the dark past, with many thousands of tourists passing through wanting to visit the Tower at the foot of the slope by the river.

James Kent and Alice Gull were two of them, leaving the station hand in hand.

As long as they kept moving, they felt safe. They had heard people could be tracked by their phones – well, that was fine because Alice had switched hers off, as it was almost flat, and left it with Jack. Neither of them looked anything like the pair of fugitives who had fled New Scotland Yard the day before. James had his hood up and hadn't shaved – though that had been forced on him by all his shaving gear being back at his apartment. Alice had borrowed clothes from Jack's wife and she was wearing her hair up, pinned untidily (but, James thought, beautifully) by a pair of multicoloured scrunchies. Their shapes and their gait were subtly different to anything that would be on record. If they simply stood still then sooner or later the algorithms of the intelligence services might pick up their facial features, but as long as they kept moving then they were always presenting something new to the ever-vigilant computers.

And they had one more thing in their favour. The algorithms might be looking for a single man and a single woman, maybe together or separately. They were not looking for a couple whose body language fairly screamed that they were falling for each other. They had already made love twice more since their time on the Heath – once before going to sleep in the double bed so presciently provided by Jack and once more on waking; once urgent, desperate to recreate the amazing thing that had happened a couple of hours earlier, and once more leisurely as they slowly woke up together, taking their time as if they had all day to do this and nothing else on their minds.

They crossed under the street that was still busy with the back end of the morning rush hour, then walked down the cobbled slope towards the Thames and the West Gate. The closer they came to the main entrance of the castle, the denser the mass of visitors became.

Finally they stood in line in front of the forbidding stone arch between the twin turrets of the West Gate, where two bobbies efficiently checked all the bags with a metal detector. Alice looked nervously at James. He knew immediately what she was thinking. How much had the stranger done? Had he already distributed their picture to cops across the country? There had been nothing on the news – but then, in a manhunt, the media were often denied details so that the fugitives never knew exactly

## CHAPTER 17

how far ahead they had got. It didn't mean their details hadn't been sent out secretly.

And so – both as camouflage, and because he wanted to, and if they were about to be arrested then he would never get another chance – he kissed her.

The smirking policemen let them pass without further ado.

'Now what do we do?' Alice asked as they made their way up Water Lane, the high-walled cobbled alleyway between the inner and outer walls, on their way to the inner ward. She looked around as if she hoped to see a sign to the secret archive.

'I suppose the best thing is to join a guided tour by one of the beefeaters and hypothetically ask if there is a royal archive here,' James said.

They headed for a group gathered around an older man in a long frock coat, black with red piping, and a matching black and red hat. 'E$_{II}$R', the insignia of Elizabeth II, was proudly emblazoned on his chest, with a royal crown hovering above it.

James had heard that the beefeaters – the Yeoman Warders, to give them their proper name – were all retired soldiers and no one should be taken in by the fancy clothes. They were as much a proper uniform as the battle fatigues worn by a soldier out in Afghanistan. And this one looked the part. He held himself ramrod straight and had a good-humoured, authoritative way of speaking that immediately commanded respect and made you want to pay attention. James would have bet good money that he had once been a sergeant in the army.

Now he was a tour leader at the Tower of London. His group gathered in front of the Traitors Gate, once a direct entrance to the Tower through which prisoners had entered by water. Most of them did not leave the Tower alive, though one obvious exception had been the future Queen Elizabeth I. She had fared a lot better than her mother, Anne Boleyn.

The beefeater was telling raven-black stories with a lot of British humour, and most of the time he laughed at the jokes the loudest. Once he had gathered enough tourists, he led them off towards the inner ward, giving them a rapid patter of history and anecdotes that on any other day James would have found fascinating.

As the group moved on, James managed to work his way close enough to ask.

'Excuse me, I've heard that the Royal Family are keeping all the documents that have ever been written, and that this is supposed to be the place where they are kept?'

The man chuckled.

'Well, not quite. It's true that everything is kept, and of course some of them are top secret so they have to be looked after properly. But not here.'

'No?' James and Alice made long faces. The man recognised that it had not been the answer they were after. For James at least, it wasn't so much disappointment, or even that they could have saved on the extortionate entrance fee – just that they had wasted their time.

## CHAPTER 17

'Well, you know, the Tower still officially belongs to the Queen, but it hasn't been used by her for a long time. As you can see, it's just a museum these days. So, to keep the archives close by in case she needs to brush up on something, they're held in Windsor. In the Round Tower, I believe, but the best thing would be to ask someone there. Not that they let just anyone in – no offence, of course – but you do need a good reason. Valid research, or something like that. Does that answer your question, sir?'

James and Alice thanked him. They let themselves fall back, and when the group turned one way, they turned the other. They left the Tower the same way they had come in.

'So, let's go to Windsor!' Alice said.

*

Sean Miller's head was still buzzing with the clout he had got off James Kent.

He had made his own way off H.M.S. *Belfast*, on wobbly legs. Unfortunately the paramedics had taken one look at him and whisked him off to hospital, where the doctors had confined him for his own good, even though he insisted he was perfectly okay. Just for observation, they had said. One night.

He had woken up, still with a sore head, and recognised Monica Leapman by his side, staring at him with tears in her eyes.

'I thought you were dead!' were her first words.

'Come off it. You know us double-O agents don't die that easily,' Sean joked. He tried to sit up, and winced as his head gave an extra hard throb.

'That's licence to kill, not be half-killed. I want you to lie still, Sean, so you can get well quickly.'

'First, there's no doctor around and second, I'm fine. I'm fully functional again! Okay, the head hurts. But that's okay again,' he added quickly when he saw Monica drawing in a breath to contradict him. 'So, situation report. Please tell me we have Kent and Gull in custody?'

She silently shook her head.

'They've vanished. Out of sight of the cameras, anyway.'

Sean snorted.

'Technology is only as good as the people using it. Okay, we're using good old fashioned intelligence. Get a list of all their known associates. Go as far back as university – school, even. The older they are, the less likely they are to be on our system.'

'You could get that from Facebook,' she pointed out. Sean's eyes flashed.

'Or, I could get them from you!'

'You're awake. Good.' A sadly familiar voice was heard behind the curtain that separated the bed from the rest of the ward. William Johnson pushed it aside and stepped in.

'I don't have much time. I'm about to brief Her Majesty. Mr Miller, your help is no longer required. That is not just my decision – your director has also said you need a few days' rest before you can report back to duty.'

## CHAPTER 17

'You can't do that! I'm on top form!' Sean said indignantly.

'Top form?' There was an unpleasant glint in Johnson's eyes. 'You've been knocked down by an inexperienced civilian, a failed art student with not one scrap of combat training. Thank heavens you weren't feeling below par or you'd be dead. Ms Leapman, you're now on the case. I'll see you in your office at ten o'clock.'

Johnson disappeared as fast as he had come, leaving Sean slack-jawed, but not so much that he didn't notice the delight on Monica's face.

'You traitor!' he exclaimed. 'How did you do that?'

'I'm surprised too! It was so sudden,' Monica defended herself.

'Oh, don't give me that!' Sean was boiling with rage, and Johnson's criticism – that he had been brought down by James Kent, of all people – stung because it was true.

'Maybe it's for the best, anyway,' Monica said. 'You've always held me slightly back. Never quite given me the responsibility I felt I could handle.'

'Responsibility?' Sean couldn't believe his ears. 'From an agent who leaves her service weapon unsecured in a hotel suite? Whose idea of intelligence gathering is to go to a suspect's friends list on Facebook?'

'Say what you like, Sean.' Her voice was cold as ice, no longer the teary 'I thought you were dead' that he had woken up to. Sean recognised the signs. He had exhausted his usefulness to her – and he had been a fool to think what they had meant anything more than this. Apparently it took two colossal bangs on the head and a kick in the balls to make him see straight. Given that he had been thinking with his balls and not his head, it served him right.

She went on.

'You're the one invalided in bed, and I'm the one who just received a field promotion. Well, lover, I guess this is it. I'll see myself out.'

She paused on her way through the curtain and looked back with a coquettish smile.

'And don't be sad. You're not the first.'

Two minutes after she had gone, Sean was discharging himself from hospital. His phone rang while he was halfway across the lobby.

Which was why, at lunchtime, Sean was walking south across Westminster Bridge. He descended the few steps at the end to the waterfront in front of County Hall. Still absorbed in thought, he walked past the queue snaking its way into the London Eye for the half-hour ride up and around and down again in a dangling greenhouse.

As instructed in the call, Sean walked to Jubilee Gardens. The so-called gardens, laid down in honour of the twenty-fifth anniversary on the throne of Elizabeth II, was effectively a large lawn, surrounded by trees, directly on the Thames. Sean amused himself by watching the queue for the Eye. The wheel was 135 metres tall, which made it about as high as the queue was long. Okay, on a good day you could see up to forty kilometres from the top of the wheel, but he found it funny that so many people would willingly stew in the sun just to ride it once.

A man came to sit with him on the bench.

## CHAPTER 17

'Wouldn't it be nice to have such a carefree life, like these people?' he asked, indicating the queue with a nod of his head.

'Personally, I'm not averse to a little risk in life,' Sean said. He scrutinized the newcomer. The man wore a white shirt and a spotted tie under a black pinstriped suit. He could be anyone at any level from Westminster, just across the river. It was perfect camouflage for this part of the world.

'I'll keep this short, Mr Miller, since I need to be back in the office very soon.' The man slid an envelope over to him, which Sean opened. He found himself holding a photo of a man he knew only too well.

'This gentleman is one of the most hard-working and loyal servants to Her Majesty that you will ever find.' The man paused a beat before adding: 'So much so that he has become a liability, not just to Her Majesty, not just to the intelligence community but, frankly, to the entire country. He is a fanatic. Each man kills the thing he loves, as Oscar Wilde so rightly observed. If this man goes on as he is then he will destroy everything.'

Sean thought back to yesterday's fiasco in the escape from New Scotland Yard.

'I can see where you might get that from.'

'Legally, he is untouchable, unless Her Majesty herself decides to do something about it – which she has so far been unwilling to do.'

'And this is my problem why?'

'Because we need to neutralise him, preferably by legal means, and that means compiling an absolutely waterproof, ironclad case against him. He is very good at hiding his tracks, either by being subtle or simply ordering people to forget him and delete the evidence – which he can do. We want a dossier off you, Mr Miller – a dossier that will convince the most sceptical doubter in the land that Johnson must be dismissed and arrested.'

'He fired me, just this morning.'

'Perfect – he won't suspect that you are after him. In fact, such is his arrogance, you are probably not even on his radar – he will regard you as a problem dealt with. Mr Miller, he has brought this on himself. We can't control him anymore because his methods are just too dangerous for us. We want a clean finish. Can you do that?'

'You never really answered my question. Why me?'

'You have all the authority and power of the Security Service behind you, and no active case to distract you. You're perfect for the job and you come highly recommended. Well, I have to go. We'll be in touch, Mr Miller.'

Sean looked again at the picture.

'Just how high up does this go? Who else's toes will I be stepping on?'

He looked up, but the man had already disappeared into the crowds like a shadow.

Sean stood up and headed to the nearest bar, which was in the hotel of County Hall. He ordered himself a large Martini.

'Well, cheers!' he said to himself as he drank up. 'Looks like I really am a double-O.'

# CHAPTER 18

Windsor Castle shone in the sun that streamed in beams through the cloud cover. Alice and James could see it enthroned above the town, even from the small station where they disembarked from the train from Victoria along with a hundred other tourists. The artificial earth mound put up by William the Conqueror in 1080 had grown into five hectares that included a mighty fortress, a royal palace, a magnificent chapel and accommodation for a large number of people, and it was the architectural epitome of the nation's history.

James was old enough to remember seeing the devastating fire of 1992 on the news. The castle had been rebuilt and restored out of the Royal Family's private funds and the scars were undetectable.

They strolled up the hill, along the lower walls of the castle, until finally they reached the queue that wound back and forth in front of the gatehouse. In front of the gate there were several benches where tired visitors had already settled.

'Well, we could join that and wait,' Alice said, 'or get some lunch and come back when it's gone down? We could get some sandwiches and sit down in the park.'

'I've always wanted to have a picnic in Windsor Great Park, but we can do better than sandwiches!' James said mysteriously.

They strolled into the little town of Windsor. The shops were specifically geared towards the tourist trade and the tastes of international customers. James could see several fast-food chains, as well as gift and tourist shops, but that wasn't what he had in mind. Before long, they had reached a small delicatessen. He grinned triumphantly.

'I always wanted to come here! Never quite got round to it.'

She looked at him sideways, then realised.

'Let me guess – you were at Eton?'

'Seven years at Slough Comprehensive, as we like to call it,' he confirmed.

The most famous and expensive boarding school in the country lay halfway between the castle to the south and the much larger town of Slough to the north. An education there cost the discerning parent a significant five-figure sum each year.

They went in, and Alice saw that the shop even offered fully equipped picnic baskets. James was reaching for one when he saw the price.

'Eighty flipping quid?' he gasped. 'Shit, so that's why I never came here!'

'Including the basket, it says!' Alice said cheerfully. 'And I have my card.'

They left the shop with a medium-sized basket and followed the signs to the gate into the Great Park at the end of Park Street. Immediately they were on the Long Walk, the long gravel road that led straight away from the castle for a kilometre. To the right and left there was a meadow like a large green lawn, the monotony of grass

## CHAPTER 18

broken up by trees planted at regular intervals. Like Alice's garden back in the city, it was carefully designed to look natural.

James and Alice walked along, slightly uphill and away from the castle, for a good fifteen minutes. When they looked back, they were awestruck. They could now see the enormous scale of the site – the walls, the towers big and small, the gables, and the Round Tower above it all, the ancient heart of the castle, built by Edward II on top of William the Conqueror's mound. And that, according to the beefeater that morning, was where they would find the Royal State Archives.

The Union Jack flew above the tower, which meant the Queen was not in residence. If she had been there then it would have been the royal standard. In her absence, the state chambers would be open to the public.

'You see, that's where we have to go!' James pointed in the direction of the Round Tower.

'So, we've set ourselves a goal. Now let's eat something while we figure out how to do this.'

They sat down under a shady big oak tree, where they had a great view of the castle. James opened the basket. Two glasses, two plates, knives and forks, along with pâté, eggs, bread, cake, sausage and even a good English wine. Okay, James thought, probably worth eighty quid.

After the full meal they leaned against the tree and enjoyed the beautiful weather. For just a little while, they could forget they were wanted fugitives. Alice put her head on James's shoulder and closed her eyes. James kept his eyes open and just enjoyed watching the people.

Mothers and fathers with their children, joggers, Japanese tourists and many more. All reminders of normality and how things could be again. You never really valued what you had always had, he mused, until there was a danger it would be taken away.

After about half an hour, Alice stirred and took a breath.

'So, enough sleep. Let's go up and see if that queue's got any smaller.'

\*

Monica Leapman could hardly believe her luck.

First, the sudden promotion to poor old Sean's job. Her former boss and lover had looked so sore! Well, he was no longer her problem.

And then, almost at once, as if she could take personal credit for it – people always tended to remember who brought them good news, she had learned – she could let her new boss know that the two suspects had been detected. Alice Gull had used her card to make a purchase in Windsor.

Then came the surprise. She assumed the order would go to the Berkshire constabulary to pick them up. Instead, Johnson leapt into his battered old blue Rover, barely giving her time to climb in at the passenger's side, and they were off down the M4, driving as if speed limits were just things that happened to other people. As, Monica suspected, in this case, they were.

'You haven't asked one very obvious question, Ms Leapman,' Johnson said as he undertook a car in the

## CHAPTER 18

inside line at over ninety. She was glad that, insanely fast though his driving was, he kept his hands on the wheel and his eyes on the road, driving calmly like a professional. Monica wondered how he got away with it. Did he just pull rank on anyone who tried to stop him? Or was his number programmed into the computers that monitored the speed cameras so that he could just be ignored?

His tone was neutral. It could have been a fact, it could have been a criticism. Coming right on top of her self-congratulatory thoughts, it felt like a warning shot to her ego. *Don't take this for granted. You can still screw it up.*

And speaking of screwing, she already had the feeling William Johnson would be a lot harder to control that way than Sean Miller had been. So far he had barely looked at her twice.

'What's that, Mr Johnson?'

'You must be wondering why it is so important that Gull and Kent might have seen certain documents? Mr Miller would certainly have asked.'

She still wasn't sure if it was a criticism.

'I assumed it's on a need-to-know basis, Mr Johnson,' she said truthfully, though she certainly had been wondering just that. 'I like to think I have more discretion than Mr Miller, and also more trust in the judgement of my superiors.'

He pursed his lips into a thin smile, not taking his eyes off the road.

## JACK

'That's a commendable attitude, Ms Leapman, if just a little fawning. But, yes, the fewer who know what they might find, the better for the security of the nation.'

They drove in silence for a few minutes, until Johnson spoke again.

'This case is important in more ways than one, Ms Leapman. It is already adversely affecting my standing with Her Majesty. Apparently, they've been thinking about giving me an ultimatum. If I don't get this right, I'll be deposed.'

'Oh, that's terrible!' Monica said, though at the same time thinking, *shit!* Just when she thought she was sitting pretty, maybe she was tying herself to a millstone.

Well, maybe she was – in which case she would cut herself loose. If Johnson was already history, maybe she could be the one to fill his vacant position. Get a nice, well-paid job at court. After every battle, she usually got a better job. That was how it had been with Sean Miller, pointing out to Johnson that she was far better placed to take on the case than the man in the hospital bed.

'Of course, I'll survive. I've worked too long and too hard for this.' Johnson broke into her thoughts. 'No one will destroy my dream, not even traitors to their class like Kent and Gull. You must know, Ms Leapman, that I have sworn to protect the Crown from all its enemies, and I will destroy any threat.'

Johnson's face was turning red, his eyes murderous.

Monica chose her next words carefully.

'I understand perfectly, Mr Johnson.'

## CHAPTER 18

She didn't, but whatever he said, showing approval would help her work her way even further into his good books. And it did seem to defuse him.

'I thought you might,' he said dryly. 'Tell me about Kent, Ms Leapman. How far would he go to reach his own goals? I had thought him a dropout from the files, but he seems annoyingly persistent.'

'He's obstinate about getting what he wants.' She paused: he seemed to expect her to continue, so she began at the beginning. 'James was an only child. His mother died giving birth to him, which can still happen. He grew up with his father. Lord John Kent didn't have that much time to take care of his son so James grew up pretty much alone on the family estate in Cornwall.'

'What did you say the father's name was?' Johnson interrupted abruptly.

'Lord John Kent.'

'Oh! Well, well. You don't know what he did for a living?'

'Not exactly. He wasn't idle rich, he had a job: some kind of law work, I think. He worked for various clients. The one thing I would say he and James have in common is a strong sense of justice. Did you know Lord Kent?'

'Only fleetingly. We met once. Please continue.'

'Well, James went to Eton because that's where all the Kent boys go. He was a very good student, one of those who barely needs to try to get straight As in all his A levels. But even then he never used his title, even when he turned eighteen. He just wasn't interested in the aristocracy. His father assumed he would be doing a typical thing like go into the army, or follow him into the law firm. Instead he went up to Oxford to study art history, because that was what he wanted to do. I know it led to a rift with the old man that never quite got healed, especially after he quit. Then his father died in a car accident, but even though James is now Lord Kent in his own right, he still doesn't use the title. He sold the family estate and lives off the interest.'

'And you were a couple?'

'Yeah, for a couple of years. Unfortunately it went to pieces.'

'And why was that? Whose fault do you think it was?'

'I would say … his,' Monica said carefully. She could tell she had all his attention, though he kept his eyes front. She was telling the truth, as far as it went. 'He just didn't like career women.'

Which was not quite what James had said when they split. James did not like women who just used men to further their careers. Well, Monica thought, whatever. Once it had become clear that James was not going to pick up his aristocratic heritage again – become Lord Kent, with her as Lady Kent at his side, with all the openings into high society that went with it – then the relationship had been doomed.

Johnson nodded slowly.

'You probably never had cause to find this out during your time together, but would Kent be willing to kill to defend himself?'

## CHAPTER 18

'I honestly can't say. In our time, he was a very peaceful man. He basically stayed out of trouble. He preferred using words to using muscles.'

'But as we saw in the case of Mr Miller, he's not afraid of using muscles when he has to. Well, I guess everyone acts the same in an emergency,' Johnson said soberly. 'Obviously, I would rather not have to gun him down without warning. If he can be provoked into acting to defend himself, then of course opening fire in return will just be self-defence on our part ... You did bring your weapon, Ms Leapman?'

Monica had been listening with growing disbelief, but running through everything she had just heard, there was no doubt that Johnson didn't just want to arrest James and Alice. He wanted them dead, and he was going to make it happen. They were driving to an execution. This realization made Monica shiver.

'Are you cold, Ms Leapman?' asked Johnson. 'The air conditioning can be a bit too chill. Should I turn up the heat?'

'No, no, you don't have to. And yes, I have my gun.'

She sat back and gazed forward, though she barely saw the motorway rushing towards them. She was just picturing James Kent, dead. That body she knew so well, riddled with bullet holes, empty and lifeless.

And, very slowly, she smiled.

*You should have stuck with the title, James.*

The grey outline of Windsor Castle loomed massive on a hill ahead of them.

# JACK

\*

The sun stood high above the castle and warmed the air. Only a lukewarm wind blew across the castle wards and the temperature rose ever higher, with hardly any shade to shelter in.

The interior of St George's Chapel was cool and pleasant. The magnificent tombs and monuments of ten monarchs were to be found here, and James's artist's eye found much to admire.

'It's one of the most beautiful examples of the Gothic perpendicular style in Britain,' he said enthusiastically. 'By the end of the fifteenth century, this place was pretty well complete.'

'And it's the spiritual home of the Order of the Garter,' Alice added. She pointed up at the eight-pointed star above the small side entrance to the chapel: the star of Britain's oldest chivalric order. 'I always loved that story about how the Order was founded.'

'Someone had lost a garter, or something?'

'Catherine Grandison, Countess of Salisbury and the lover of King Edward III! They were at a ball and her blue garter fell off, which was social death back then. So to spare her embarrassment, the king picked it up and put it on his own leg. And he said …'

She pointed at the motto around the star, and they said together:

*'Honi soit qui mal y pense.'*

'"Shame on him who thinks evil of it", roughly translated,' said Alice. 'And every member since then has

## CHAPTER 18

sworn to protect the realm and their monarch. Maybe we should ask for advice.'

James's eyes went wide as they rested on another familiar sign.

'Hey, I've seen that before!'

They looked up at the carving of the two compasses and the set square.

'Yes,' Alice said sadly, 'that was in my book too. A lot of members of the Order were or are Masons too.'

'Maybe we won't ask them, then …'

Eventually they strolled out again into the lower ward and gazed up at the Round Tower, which housed the royal archives.

'So, there it is! What now?' Alice asked.

James bit his lip. He had to admit that all their wandering around had accomplished nothing. They had been pretending to plan, as a displacement activity for having to face the harsh fact that they didn't know what to do.

'I have no idea. We would need someone who knows their way around and can tell us the quickest way to find the documents we need—'

'*Charles!*' she exclaimed suddenly. She was looking across the ward. James followed her gaze.

'The Prince of Wales? Where?'

'Not that one! Charles Brown! He studied with me at King's College in Cambridge!' She waved frantically above her head. 'Hey, Charles!'

A tall, lanky man in a grey tailor-made suit paused and looked around, and a huge grin appeared on his face.

'Hello, beautiful!' He hurried towards them. 'I haven't see you in ages. How are you, Alice?'

Alice didn't give a straight answer to that question.

'Charles, this is my friend James.'

The smiling man held out his hand. 'Any friend of Alice's! Charles Brown.'

'James Kent, pleased to meet you,' James said pleasantly, hoping the small stab of envy didn't show in his voice, though to judge from the chatty tone these two had never been more than friends. 'And how about you? Are you here on holiday?'

'No, I don't think I've been on holiday in months. I work here, in the archives!'

For a moment no one said anything: Alice and James were simply too stunned. Charles's smile began to fade. 'Something I said?'

'No, no!' James recovered quickly. 'We'd just been talking about that earlier, that's all. You know. What it must be like to work for the old lady.'

Charles smiled easily.

'Well, you don't do it to get rich! A lot of work for a little money, but huge amounts of job satisfaction.'

'How did you get into this?' Alice asked.

'Well, you remember when we were at Cambridge, I volunteered at the university library? The librarian told me there was a vacancy in the archives at the Houses of Parliament – someone had retired – so I applied there. I worked there for some years, and then a few months

## CHAPTER 18

ago my boss asked me if I would like a promotion to Windsor Castle. Sure, what a question! I immediately said yes. Now I'm here! Like I said, not much pay, but the perks are great: I get free rations and an apartment in Windsor Castle. Over there, in fact.

Charles stretched out a long arm and pointed to a row of narrow terraced houses located against the wall, to the left of the main gate.

'And you work in the Round Tower now?' James asked. 'That's where the guide said the archives are located.'

'Yeah, that's the place. But look, it's hot and I'm on a break. Can I get you tea? I know a lovely place in town. We can chat more easily!'

Gratefully, James and Alice accepted. Maybe they had found a solution for their problem. Now they just had to make it work.

Charles held up his briefcase.

'Just let me drop this off at home and we can all go out. Come with me.'

They followed Charles through the crowd towards the row of small houses. Charles opened a black wooden door and they entered a small hallway. It was not decorated with much furniture. In the corridor there was only a narrow wooden staircase and a long bench. Two doors led into adjacent rooms. Behind one was a tiny kitchen and behind the other a living-dining room. It looked cosy and comfortable – a bachelor's quarters. In the corner was an old wooden table with two chairs. The small sofa table was covered with pictures framed in silver. Charles was in almost all of them, with one member or another of the Royal Family.

Charles dropped an ID card with his picture, a magnetic stripe and a chip into a wooden bowl next to the door. James tried not to fix his eyes on it. That was what they needed!

'Anyone need the loo? No? Well, I'll just pay a quick visit,' he said, and stomped up the wooden stairs. They groaned with every step he took, and they could also hear the floorboards creaking as he moved about upstairs.

James and Alice were left looking at the bowl and the card. Then they looked at each other.

'He'd notice if we just took it,' Alice said, reading his thoughts. James nodded.

'We'll find a way. We have to.'

The cracking of the old wooden planks on the stairs announced Charles's return.

'Well, I've got to say, you've got a nice apartment!' Alice said.

'Yes, I think so too. Everything I need is there. It's not too big to clean, and if I get bored then I can just take the train and be in London in half an hour. Great!'

Charles didn't take the card from its bowl, but he held the front door open for them to go first and there was no way James could just pocket the card on the way out.

'So, how long have you been together?' Charles asked as they strolled towards the gate. They glanced sideways at each other and suddenly felt very shy. Charles was the first person to identify them – accurately – as a couple. It felt weird. And right.

## CHAPTER 18

'We've only known each other for a few days,' Alice said. 'Come on, Charles. Just because you're single …'

'Hey, I just had a girlfriend! Her name was Anna and she worked as a cleaning lady in the castle. I met her at the Christmas dance. Unfortunately, she was transferred to Scotland. Now I'm alone again. So, how did you meet?'

'We met at the Jack the Ripper launch in London,' James said, more curtly than he meant. He did not want to be talking about himself. He wanted Charles to talk about his work.

But it was Charles who got there first.

'And what do you do?'

'My work isn't as interesting as yours! I work for *Time Out* from time to time. But what about you – what exactly do you do in the archives?'

'Well …' Charles had to slow down to concentrate as they worked their way through the knot of people around the gate. 'Well, I …'

'Oh, no,' James groaned, stopping dead in his tracks. They both looked at him in alarm.

'Problem, old boy?' Charles asked. James gripped his stomach.

'It's a problem I have. Just say I really should have taken you up on your offer of the toilet. Is it too late to go back?'

Charles smiled in sympathy.

'Oh, bad luck. Yes, of course.' He chucked James the key; James snatched it with one hand. 'You have to pull the door toward you when you unlock it. It's a little stuck.'

## JACK

'I will!' James promised, and hurried off.

Back at the house, he followed the occupant's advice and pulled the door towards him with all his might. Once inside, he pushed the door shut. He didn't take the card from its bowl immediately, just in case Charles decided to follow and check he was all right. For the sake of appearances he ran upstairs to the bathroom and timed two minutes on his watch. Then and only then did he run back downstairs. No sign of Charles.

James pocketed the ID card and hurried out of the door again, pulling it to behind him and wiggling it to make sure it was locked. He went quickly over to where Alice and Charles were waiting by the gate. Charles was chatting to one of the guards about something: his face lit up when he saw James coming.

'And here he is. See you later, John. Are you feeling better, James?'

'Much, thanks.' James returned the key, and as Charles turned away, he caught Alice's eye and patted his pocket.

Now they just had to work out how he was going to use it.

'You were saying about your job, Charles?' he asked as they headed into town.

'Well, sure. You must understand that for over three hundred years everything that the castle or the Royal Family has written has been collected. This includes letters, diaries, invitations, and a lot of secret documents too. The so-called catalogue of where everything is, on which shelf or in which filing cabinet, actually comprises

## CHAPTER 18

over thirty books itself, though obviously it's also all online now. So I can tell you, it's a lot of work!'

'And it's all in the Round Tower? These secret documents too? Is that safe?' James asked.

'Safe as anything, mate. The windows are made of thick bulletproof glass. The walls are over three metres thick. You can only get through the entrance door with a proper card and there's a soldier on guard around the clock by a soldier. Oh, yeah, I forgot the cameras. So that'll be all. No unauthorized person can get in,' Charles concluded happily. He glanced at them sideways. 'But why do you ask? It almost sounds like you're casing the joint!'

James laughed.

'No, we know when we're beaten!'

Charles had to laugh too.

They quickly left the tourist town behind and reached the river. They crossed the Thames over a long pedestrian bridge made of grey, old stone. Behind them, the medieval castle sat grandly on a huge rock and in front stretched the picturesque high street of the village of Eton, famous around the world for the school of the same name.

You wouldn't have thought, to look at it, that there was no much money in the area. Without the thronging tourists it would have looked like the high street of any home counties market town – narrow and cramped, not wide enough for two streams of traffic, and modest Georgian shopfronts not more than three floors high. James began to fret as Charles showed no sign of getting wherever they were going quickly and they went further and further along the high street. Somehow he had to find an excuse to double back to the castle with his stolen ID. The further they went now, the harder it would be to get back to the castle without Charles noticing.

At the end of Eton High Street on the right was the school itself – a Georgian-style building of plain red brick, the kind of simplicity that only comes from having so much money that you know it's vulgar to flaunt it. Charles led them down a winding street in front of the school until they stopped in front of a stone house. The gate was open and showed a beautiful little inner courtyard, greened with many small trees and shrubs. All around were round wooden tables where four people could sit at a time, but only a few were occupied.

'This is an insider tip. A lot of colleagues from the castle eat here – it's safely off the tourist trail.'

They took a seat at one of the tables. Immediately a tanned woman with long black hair came to them.

'Do you know what you want, or should I get you the menu?'

'A large plate of bruschetta and three glasses of wine, the good red one, please,' Charles said promptly. 'We'll use the menu of the day as the main course.'

'Will do!' The woman left the three alone.

'And what did you just order?' Alice asked.

'As a starter, there's bread with various spreads. Tomatoes are the classic, but recently the cook has started using olives. The main is usually the chef's idea, something really typically Italian like pasta dishes or

## CHAPTER 18

meat. I got an excellent fish dish the last time. Actually, I don't even like fish, but it was really very good. The wine comes from a vineyard on Lake Garda that the owner has known for a long time.'

James shifted a little on in his seat. Charles was being so friendly – and the promise of the food and wine was so good – that he felt a real heel for just using the man's basic niceness. But, he reminded himself what would happen if he didn't.

Charles himself noticed the movement, and unwittingly gave James his cue as the waitress reappeared with glasses, the wine and a carafe of water. She placed the glasses on the table and began to fill them.

'Is something wrong, James?'

James patted his pockets and let a look of dismay come over him.

'I think I've lost my phone!'

'Oh, bad luck!' Charles looked genuinely sorry. 'What a pain. Do you know when you last had it?'

'I can remember exactly. I was just checking it as we came over the bridge. Then I noticed my lace was coming undone and so I put the phone down to tie it again. And now I can't remember picking it up again. So, I bet that's where it is.'

'On the bridge?' Charles pulled a face. 'You'll be lucky if you see it again, old chap.' His concern turned to surprise and dismay as James pushed his chair back.

'Yes, but I have to try,' James said. 'Look, you two catch up. I'll be … well, not long!'

He left quickly, before Charles could muster any more arguments.

James made his way quickly through the small alleys of the village back to the high street. The shops he was after – the ones he remembered from his school days – were still there and he had enough plastic banknotes, just, to quickly buy the things he needed for his forthcoming operation. And then he ran back to the castle. He was almost out of breath as he reached the main gate, after running some distance up a hill, lugging a large shopping bag – and that was probably why the guard took more than one look at Charles's ID that James flashed on his way in.

'Just a moment, sir …' The man deftly tweaked the card from his fingers, eyes flickering from the photo to James's face and back. 'This isn't the entrance pass … and you're not Mr Brown.'

James felt like a trapdoor in the world had just opened beneath him, and sensed the sudden alert interest of the other guards on duty. He could have kicked himself as the biggest flaw of his plan suddenly became blindingly evident.

Of course this wasn't the ID you needed to enter the castle, or Charles wouldn't have left it behind. There must be two separate IDs. One to get in, and one – this one – to get around with. *Crap!*

'Oh, you're kidding!' he groaned. 'He must have given me the wrong one.'

'Given you,' the man said, without expression.

## CHAPTER 18

'I'm fetching something for him. From his apartment. Look, I can show I know him. He lives in the third apartment from the left in the row of houses over there.' James pointed.

'So you're fetching something for him – and why can't Mr Brown come himself?'

'He's a busy man, working in the archives. Right now he's entertaining an important contact at the Italian restaurant down the road from the school …'

He could see he wasn't getting through. The man just nodded and reached for his phone.

And then salvation came. James saw a familiar face in the background – one of the other guards. Charles had been talking to him.

'Look! Ask him! He saw me leave earlier with Mr Brown. It's … John, right? Don't you remember, John? I was with Mr Brown … and an absolutely stunning blonde.'

It might have been that last point that made John the guard remember. He grinned, and nodded, and James was waved through.

He hurried out into the lower courtyard. It was past the time where they let fresh tourists in and the crowd was thinning. There were still people working in the castle, he knew, but the total number of people out in the open was going down, which suited him just fine. It meant fewer witnesses.

Trying to look like he belonged there on business, James headed across the lawn of the lower courtyard towards the Round Tower. Despite the casual look, inside he was tense and nervous. This was his one chance: if he blew it then not only would the Ripper's trail be lost but so would any chance of fighting back against whoever was so determined to see him dead. What would happen to him if he was caught, he didn't even want to know.

He wondered how Alice and Charles were getting on.

\*

'What in God's name ...' William Johnson gasped.

As his car pulled up to the gate into the castle – the George IV gate, used by private visitors and the Queen herself, not the one frequented by paying tourists – a huge column of red smoke was billowing up into the sky from somewhere in the castle grounds.

A guard held out his hand and tried to stop him.

'I'm sorry, sir, the situation is—'

He went quiet as Johnson simply flashed ID at him, not breaking step as he ran past. Monica hurried after.

Groups of people everywhere were either hurrying around like ants in a disturbed nest, or standing and staring – maybe awaiting the official assessment of whether or not this was a terrorist attack, so then they would know whether they had to clear out or not. Monica stared at the column. It seemed to be pouring out of the ground from somewhere behind the Round Tower, a pillar of red flame ...

Monica frowned. No, not flame. The smoke itself was red. Surely any fire would burn grey or black?

Johnson was talking to some soldiers and boiling with rage.

## CHAPTER 18

'What do you mean, you can't put it out? Report, man!'

One soldier answered him with the polite contempt that the military use for civilians when they know perfectly well they belong to a different chain of command and the civilians can do nothing to harm them.

'It's some kind of smoke bomb, sir. You know, the kind of thing they use at football matches, only bigger. I heard it go off like an almighty firecracker, but I know what high explosive sounds like and that wasn't it. We tried to put it out, with extinguishers and with water, but whoever put it there is too imaginative.'

The man was barely suppressing a smirk. He had obviously made his own assessment that this presented no threat – in fact, he seemed to be amused. The military sense of humour. It was entirely the wrong attitude to take with the man responsible for the Queen's security.

Johnson had turned red. He didn't find it funny at all.

'Imaginative? What the hell do you mean?'

'He sprinkled it with some chemical substance that means it won't go out, sir. It just reignites. We've called the fire brigade, but frankly I think it will just go out if we leave it long enough, once the chemical is used up.'

'Unacceptable!' Johnson snapped. He pulled a two-way radio from an inside pocket. 'Control room, HM Security Counsel. I want a camera feed … What the hell do you mean, one of them's blank? Which one?'

A pause, during which his face turned puce and his eyes boggled.

'The entrance?' he almost screamed. 'The entrance to the royal archives is totally unguarded … No, I am not interested in excuses! Why wasn't it dealt with immediately it went on the blink? I don't care that it's not a Code 1 area!'

Another pause.

'No, I do not intend to wait for the anti-terrorist squad to turn up. I'm going in. No, this is on my own authority. Johnson out.'

He shoved the radio into his pocket and turned to face Monica. She braced to face his anger and rage, but to her surprise it was fading away. Instead, his face went almost bland and his eyes … She shuddered. His eyes had gone as dead and dispassionate as a shark's closing in for the kill. Monica remembered her realisation in the car: James Kent and Alice Gull were not meant to get out of this alive.

'I do believe your ex-boyfriend might be here, Ms Leapman,' he said mildly. 'Stay here and hold the fort. Use my authority if you need it.'

This was her chance. The right word, maybe the right two or three words, could still save James's life. She owed her ex nothing – but could she really condemn him to death?

Monica drew a breath.

'Very well, Mr Johnson.'

But Johnson was already heading up the little hill towards the tower.

## CHAPTER 18

*

There was no guard outside the door into the Tower. He must have run to check on the so-called fire. Johnson reluctantly had to admit to himself that he was impressed by James Kent's approach. However, Kent was by no means out of the castle yet.

He stood just inside the door, out of sight of any passing members of the public. Only then did he draw his gun from its kidney holster and work the slide, feeding a round into the breech.

'I should have known you'd be trouble ...' he murmured.

Now he thought about it, he remembered the younger Kent. The grieving young man at the funeral. Yet, James had actually made life easier for him.

Lord Kent had come too close to learning things that even a Lord shouldn't know. Johnson had solved the matter by doing what had to be done: the first time he had used his powers in that way. But Johnson had been young, new to his job, and he had overlooked just how well respected and well liked Lord Kent was. There had been wild speculations about the car accident: too many questions had remained unanswered. But luckily for Johnson, and unexpectedly, it was James himself who solved things. James had insisted after the investigation that this was a normal car accident and that it was now time to leave the deceased alone.

And then the press had found something else to worry about – some footballer cheating on his wife, probably – and the storm had passed.

Now Kent was back in his life.

*I should have dealt with you, too*, Johnson thought. *I didn't realise.*

With his left hand he felt for a light switch. The neon tubes flickered on with soft plinking sounds. He was in the anteroom to the archive, a bare stone room. On the opposite side was another door where Johnson had to swipe his ID. *So, how did Kent get in here?* he wondered. *Oh, he's resourceful all right …* The door clicked open.

This room lit up automatically as the door opened. As the tubes flickered, a large five-story room that filled the entire Round Tower appeared out of the darkness. The archives were kept on a star-shaped framework of shelves that lined the walls and protruded into the room. Johnson walked quietly and carefully along the shelves with his gun drawn and held before him in both hands.

'I know you're here, Mr Kent! You don't have a chance to escape. There are over a dozen armed policemen outside, just waiting to storm the room!'

Johnson walked further into the quiet room, glancing into every nook and cranny. A computer stood on a table in the middle of the floor. The screen was off but the PC itself was still humming. He pressed the monitor's power switch and it came back to life: 'Search result no. 123_08/1888 JtR = shelf 4, tray 10, box 12.'

'Well, I knew you were after this case! I just don't understand why you're so interested in it!'

## CHAPTER 18

Johnson circled the room slowly, looking down each of the corridors between the shelves.

'Your father took an interest too – did you know that? And you saw what became of him. So be a good boy and show yourself!'

A voice rang out.

'Stop talking about my father like that!'

Johnson allowed himself a tight smile. He had known James would respond sooner or later, if he found a spot that was sufficiently sore to prod. But the echo still didn't let him know exactly where James was.

'Why?' he called back. 'He was a snoop, verging on being a traitor! He had his nose stuck into things that were none of his business! If what he learned came out, the press would have eaten us alive. I did what I did to serve my Queen and my country!'

'What are you talking about? Stop it!'

Aha! Was James on one of the upper floors? Johnson prowled down one of the corridors. At the end was a narrow iron staircase.

'Ah, I understand. You don't even know how your father really died! Well, I'll give you a little tutoring. Did you know he entered the Queen's summer residence and knocked down a guard?'

'Never! My father wasn't a criminal!'

'Yes, he was!' Johnson climbed the stairs carefully, keeping his eyes peeled for any movement above him. 'He was in Balmoral without clearance. That is a crime. While everyone was looking for him like crazy, I went to his car. The idiot had just left it right in front of the gate.'

Johnson now walked along the small corridor along the bookshelves on the first floor.

'I mounted a small explosive device inside the front offside wheel well, next to the brake hoses. I followed him when he finally drove off. When we came to the river, I detonated the explosive remotely. The car swerved off and of course he had no brakes, so into the water he went. Yes, lad, that's how your father died. What a shame! But you shouldn't mess with the Crown!'

'I don't believe a word of it! The Queen would never approve of that!'

'You're right about that!' Johnson laughed. 'She's surrounded by advisors who are as old as she is. The old sacks have no idea.'

'And, of course, you're doing it right!'

Johnson pressed his lips together. This was where Kent was meant to be goaded into giving himself away, getting angrier and angrier, losing self-control.

But that last remark had sounded mocking. One thing Johnson would not tolerate was to be mocked for his devotion.

'Indeed I am!' Johnson started to get angry as he crept forward. 'I will do anything to protect this great institution and you won't change that!'

'We'll just have to see.' Suddenly there was a violent pressure in Johnson's back. He froze. 'Now, very slowly, give me your gun!'

The words were amplified by another jab. Johnson's mind was spinning. He had been the one to be distracted! Getting riled with James had meant he hadn't looked

## CHAPTER 18

closely enough into each of the side corridors. Now Johnson stood there as if rooted and thought feverishly about how he could become master of the situation again.

'You're just bluffing, boy. It's impossible to smuggle a weapon into the castle.'

In response, he heard a metallic *click*.

'You'd probably think that about getting a smoke bomb in too, wouldn't you?' James said coolly. 'Now, without turning round, hand me your gun behind you.'

Johnson stretched his gun hand back over his shoulder and felt James take the weapon.

'Now turn around.'

Carefully, Johnson turned to James. James was standing a safe distance back, with Johnson's own gun in one hand, aimed at him. In the other hand, he held an old brown folder. A pen dangled from a ribbon attached to it. So, that had been the weapon, and the 'click' had come from the lock of the folder. Johnson realised with dismay that he had fallen for the cheapest of tricks.

'So, what do we do now?' he asked cheerfully. 'I see you've found what you're looking for, but you're certainly not going home with it!'

James grinned.

'Yeah. You keep saying things can't happen. Then, guess what, turns out they can.'

'So, are you going to march me at gunpoint through the main gate? Maybe hope nobody notices? Or just shoot me now?'

# JACK

One thing Johnson felt quite sure of: James would not kill him. If he was going to do that, he would have by now.

And then he realised he had underestimated James Kent again. James glanced at him sideways, thoughtfully.

'Normally I don't hit defenceless people, but for you I'll make an exception.'

James lashed out with the butt of the pistol. Johnson only just moved in time but still it hit hard against his temple. He cried out as an explosion went off in his head, but had just enough control to throw himself forward and grapple with James. His whole weight fell on James just as James was pivoting to turn away. James tripped and fell to his knees. The gun dropped from his hand and skittered across the iron grating before falling to the ground below. It fired a single harmless shot as it hit the floor, but James and Johnson were too busy wrestling with each other to notice.

Johnson was determined and trained in combat, but he was less bulky than James and James was fuelled by hate based on what he had just learned. He clenched a fist and drove it as hard as he could into Johnson's kidney. Johnson cried out and his grip weakened. James delivered one, two, three more blows into the same spot until Johnson let go. He lay there, face clenched in agony, groaning and clutching his side.

*Screw this!* James thought. He had made his point. He quickly scooped up the file and ran to the staircase.

Incredibly, he could hear Johnson stumbling after him. *Should have knocked him out*, he thought – but somehow,

## CHAPTER 18

despite everything, he just couldn't find it in himself to do that. *I guess that makes me better than him.*

He hurled himself around and around the spiral staircase to the ground. Behind him he could hear Johnson stumbling after him.

James hit the ground level running. Where was the dropped gun? Never mind, no time. He crossed the floor of the round room and breathlessly reached the door leading to the anteroom.

Just as he reached the door there was a shot behind him, and every muscle in his body clenched as a bullet hit the door frame. He glanced back. Johnson had made it down the iron stairs, surprisingly quickly, and he had found the gun. It was waving all over the place as he clutched on to the shelves for support. No wonder he hadn't hit James.

James ran on into the anteroom, still looking behind him, then starting to look around and flinching as his peripheral vision saw someone standing there. He and the other person both instinctively raised their arms to protect themselves from the collision, and ended up entwined, him holding the other person's wrists.

He and Monica Leapman found themselves staring at each other.

'*You!* What the hell are you doing here?'

'I heard a shot ...'

For the first time, James realised she was holding a gun in her hand.

And the one thing he knew he couldn't do was hit her like he had hit the other guy.

With a grunt, he hurled her with all his strength back through the door. He heard another shot fire as he pelted towards the exit into the daylight.

*

'You stupid cow! You stupid, stupid cow!' Johnson snarled at the body.

He had fired his last shot at the door, more in hope than anything else, just she came flying in through it. It had hit her in the side of the head.

Monica Leapman lay in a crumpled heap at his feet, blood leaking from the hole in her head, eyes already glazed and clouding over. Quite dead.

He leaned against the wall, breathing heavily, and winced at a sharp pain in his side from where James had hammered him.

Then he reached gingerly into his jacket for his radio.

'All stations, HM Security Counsel. Code red, I repeat code red. Agent down. Lock the site down.'

# CHAPTER 19

James hurried down the small hill of the Round Tower. Several fire trucks of the Royal Berkshire Fire and Rescue Service had arrived in the lower courtyard of the castle and James could slip past the guards unnoticed, hidden by the metal bulk of the vehicles.

*Monica!* What the hell had she been doing there?

Well, he had known who she worked for, of course – maybe the chances of her being there weren't that surprising. Plus, she had always been very ambitious and had always made her way towards the top. But he could really have done without that meeting just now.

There must have been a guard just the other side of the nearest fire truck, because James heard a radio crackle and a hate-filled voice that he recognised. He missed the first bit but caught the end of it clear as day.

'… lock the site down.'

James swore to himself. The guy back there had been right. He certainly was not just going to walk out of the gate.

All the tourists had gone home: the only people here now were the emergency services milling around the Upper Ward, and bona fide castle employees still in their offices. That actually made it easier for James to get along without being noticed. Just keep moving, he told himself. Keep moving, don't give them a chance to catch up – because going unseen couldn't last forever.

He passed the portal of the state apartments, where he had been standing in the tourist line with Alice a few hours ago. The doors were locked, but there was a card reader next to them. He sent up a silent prayer and swiped Charles's ID. The doors clicked open and he was through.

Windsor Castle had one big weakness, he had realised. It was designed to stop people getting in, not out.

Very soon he reached the East Terrace lawn at the north-east end of the castle. In relation to the entire complex it was a small garden that could not be visited by the public, since the Queen and members of the Royal Family used it for private purposes – but it was still a good hundred metres of open space to get across. James ran.

He reached the wall at the end and looked down into the Great Park. It was only a few metres below. James glanced back, just in time to see uniformed figures emerging from the private apartments on to the East Terrace. And so he swung his legs over the top of the wall and dropped.

James had misjudged the height. He thudded harder than he intended into the ground, and swore as pain stabbed into his left ankle. He limped his way into the bushes of the park, still clutching the thick file on Jack the Ripper.

Just in time. A few seconds later he heard voices behind and above him, and orders crackling through

## CHAPTER 19

on the radio: something about 'authorised to use lethal force …' Monica had once told him that the whole idea of shooting to wound was a polite Hollywood fiction. In real life, if you opened fire with live ammunition then you intended to kill.

So, he kept stumbling through the park, doing his best to put distance between him and the East Terrace. Normally James would have found the park's many trees and bushes quite beautiful, and he was grateful for the cover, but the wilderness also slowed him down. He ran as best he could through several bushes and shrubs until he finally reached a large green area. James slowed down to catch some air, but still held close to the bushes so as not to be seen.

In his right hand he was still holding the heavy file on Jack the Ripper. If it hadn't been what this was all about, he would have dropped it long ago to help him get away more quickly. He hoped very much that this file would be worth all the effort he had taken.

It had to be, he told himself. He still couldn't think how, but it had almost got him killed at least twice. The guy back there in the Round Tower had thought it was important enough to commit legalised murder. Whatever he and Alice were on to, it mattered to someone.

After a quarter of an hour he reached a small lattice fence that separated the private from the public park. James climbed over and marched down the Long Walk towards the exit, away from the castle. It was the same way he had walked with Alice this afternoon. The gate to the Great Park was not locked yet so he could walk straight through, then circle around the castle, through the town and back to the small stone bridge across the Thames and to Eton.

James hurried through the dwindling crowds, always looking around, tense for the first hint of sirens and alarm. He expected a policeman to come and arrest him at any moment. He could hear sirens but they were behind him, across the river: fire brigade and police called in as reinforcements at the castle. This side of the river there was no hue and cry, but just in case he avoided the high street and went by the back alleyways back to the Italian.

And now what? He thought. He had been gone for over an hour, he was sweaty and rumpled from his escape, and he was carrying a file he hadn't had with him when he left. Plus, if the guy in the Tower traced his break-in back to Charles's ID then Charles, who was completely innocent in this, could be in big trouble.

No, James's mind was made up. Charles had to be told. He might not believe a word of it, but they had to be honest.

Charles and Alice were still at their table with the remains of a meal in front of them. James headed straight for his seat as though it was the most natural thing in the world.

'So here I am again!' said James and sat down. Charles looked at him with amazement.

'What on earth happened to you?'

'We were getting worried …' Alice began. James acknowledged her concern with a nod as he slapped the file on to the table.

## CHAPTER 19

'And where did that come from?' Charles asked in surprise. He leaned forward to study it more closely, and then his eyes went wider and his face clouded with anger as he recognised the label. 'Hey, that looks like—'

'We owe you an explanation, Charles,' James said bluntly. Alice looked at him in alarm. To her he added, 'Let's just say it didn't go smoothly, and also the guy from my apartment – well, he was there with the same open-minded, friendly attitude as before.'

It didn't help the alarm.

'James,' she whispered, 'we decided not even to tell my father, so …'

James knew what she meant: they had kept her father out of this precisely so as not to bring the killer down on the rest of the family. Wouldn't they be doing the same to Charles?

Charles looked from one to the other.

'You decided not to tell your father what?'

'Knowledge that could get him killed,' said James, just as blunt as before. 'People who stumble into this – the one thing that lets them get out again is not knowing what it's about. So we're not going to tell you that. But I will tell you enough.'

'Oh. Oh, nice.' A predatory gleam came into Charles's eye. He rested back with his hands behind his head. 'I can't wait!'

Alice put her hand on his.

'Before he says anything, please remember one thing, Charles.'

'And what's that?'

'That we're friends, and I would never lie to you.'
Charles frowned.

'Okay. But let's hear it anyway.'

And so James told him, starting with his commission from Lord George Anderson, his meeting Alice ... The one thing he didn't mention was the man at the root of all this: Jack the Ripper. That seemed to be the bit of information that got people killed. He wasn't going to put Charles in that danger.

Charles kept quiet, though he obviously had to bite his tongue on a couple of occasions, until James got to the man in his apartment. Charles almost said something, but bit his tongue. For the Scotland Yard episode, he just grunted, 'Uh-huh'. When he got to the man's third appearance in the story – in the Round Tower, just now – Charles slapped the table angrily with both hands.

'That's impossible! He wouldn't do a thing like that! Okay, he's unpredictable and very ambitious, but not that!' Charles exclaimed.

'Who's the man? Do you know him?' Alice asked with interest.

'As James has described him, it sounds like the Queen's Security Counsel. His name is William Johnson. But like I said, I can't imagine him capable of this! Hold on.'

Charles took his phone out and searched quickly, fingers tapping on the screen. Then he held it out to Alice and James, one eyebrow raised in enquiry.

James took one look. The man was lurking in the background behind a picture of the Queen at some event

## CHAPTER 19

– he was only in the picture by accident – but there was no question about it.

'That's him,' James confirmed.

Charles seemed to subside slowly in shock.

'But I can't believe he's capable of killing someone!'

'Believe it,' James said bluntly. 'If not me – well, he told me himself he killed my father.'

Alice looked at him in horror.

'Really, James? Oh, I'm so sorry!'

Charles stared.

'And who was your father?'

'Lord John Kent. Johnson said he got too close to finding out stuff he shouldn't, so he faked a car accident. He blew the brake hoses. That's what he told me!'

Charles frowned, remembering.

'John Kent. That was just a few years ago, wasn't it? Didn't he fall from a bridge into a lake in Scotland? Wow, and that was your dad? I'm really terribly sorry about that and you have my deepest condolences. But,' he went on stubbornly, 'let's be realistic. No one could tell then whether it was murder or an accident. There was no proof it was a murder and so that's what I believe, as long as no one can prove anything else to me.' We folded his arms and stared into the distance.

'Charles …' Alice put her hand on his again. 'We need your help.'

He stared at her.

'My help! You betrayed my employer, broke into her house and stole royal property! Do you know how much trouble I'm in when I get back?'

'Then you have two options,' Alice said. 'Call the police now, or go back to the castle and tell them – truthfully – that you were lied to and betrayed by two old friends who stole your security pass. They already know our names so you won't be telling them anything they don't already know.'

Charles gazed at her hopelessly.

'Call the cops on you ... you know I couldn't do that, Alice! Well, not on *you*,' he added, with an unfavourable sideways glance at James.

They sat and waited silently for him to make his decision. Then he held his hand out to James.

'I'll have my card back, thanks.'

James silently passed it over. Charles sighed.

'Okay. And what help do you want?'

'Just help us get away. Then tell them whatever you like at the castle.'

'I'll tell them you're insane,' Charles muttered, 'and suffering some weird kind of persecution delusion, which I think you are. But I'm convinced you believe it, and the only way you'll be cured is to work out for yourselves that it's all a fantasy – so, okay. You'd better have my car.'

*

'Does this still drive?' Alice asked in disbelief, soon after. 'How old is it? I remember it from university!'

Charles had settled up the bill and led them back through Eton to a parking lot. In the shade of some trees sat a small, old-style Mini. Once, it had been blue.

Charles bridled.

## CHAPTER 19

'Of course she's still driving! She was my first car after I got my driver's license. Okay, she has a few quirks but she's never let me down.' He unlocked the driver's door and tugged at the handle. ''Um, yeah, the door's a little wonky, but usually I can get it open …'

Charles tugged harder, and then harder again until James feared the handle might come off. He wasn't worried for Charles's sake but he didn't want their getaway vehicle to be ruined before they had a chance in it. Eventually Charles clenched his free hand into a fist and thumped the upper door frame hard, at the same time as yanking on the handle. The door opened.

'See?' he said proudly. 'She's a collector's item!'

'Anything else we need to know about our luxury conveyance?' James asked dryly.

'Yeah, you can start walking now if that's your attitude!' Charles replied, irritated. 'Okay. She wobbles badly over sixty miles an hour, so keep the speed down. Unleaded petrol, premium is best. Uh – that's it. And I promise not to report her missing for forty-eight hours.'

'Thank you, Charles, for everything. When the case is solved, I'll bring the car back to you personally,' Alice promised with a hug. To James, she said; 'I'll drive. Just in case they're looking for a car driven by a man with your description.'

James and Charles settled for a more impersonal handshake.

'I think we'll be done soon,' James said. 'We have the file – now all we have to do is evaluate it.'

# JACK

'Please don't remind me you're driving off with stolen Crown property,' Charles muttered. 'Just surprise me by bringing everything back in good order.'

But he managed a faint smile as he waved them off.

The Mini bumped and lurched as Alice drove it carefully out of the uneven parking lot and on to the well tarmacked road. Even then the ride wasn't exactly smooth. James shifted in his seat, while in the rear-view mirror the lanky figure of Charles became smaller and smaller.

'One thing he forgot to tell us, the suspension is also pretty worn out. This is going to put my back out,' James joked.

'It's a ride, James. Better than nothing! And a lot more than Charles owes us. But that's him to a T, always helpful and nice. So …' She tapped her fingers on the wheel. 'Where to?'

# CHAPTER 20

William Johnson kept a cap on his boiling temper. He had tried snapping at the soldiers, but underneath the fancy red uniforms and bearskin caps they were professional fighting men, veterans of the Gulf and not going to be frightened of an angry civilian.

So instead Johnson unvented it all on the man in charge of the cameras.

The little control room was opposite the entrance to the Round Tower. The screens were ranked in rows in front of the man's console and showed images from all around the castle, apart from the one that was incriminatingly blank. Johnson had already investigated the camera in question and found the cable severed – he guessed with a pair of common garden secateurs that James Kent could have picked up in any hardware store in town, along with his smoke bomb.

'So why didn't you raise the alarm the moment the screen went blank?' he raged.

'Sir, cameras are always going on the blink! It's the budget, sir.' The man was pale, maybe sensing that career suicide was just around the corner. 'And the camera points at a secure door – no one's meant to be able to get in without a proper pass – so it's not deemed high security.'

'Well, show me the recording from before it went out,' Johnson grated. He winced as he saw the man hesitate. 'Let me guess. You can't because of budget?'

'Only some of the cameras actually record, sir. The most important ones. The others are direct surveillance only, or designed to be deterrents.'

'Fucking hell!' Johnson breathed. He chewed thoughtfully on his lower lip. 'All right, which cameras do record?'

'Well, all gates leading to the park or the castle. I can even point them manually, but most of the time they're set to automatic.'

'Well, then show me the camera for the tourist entrance. I can imagine he came through there today.'

'Right away, sir.' The guard turned in his chair and rolled it towards the console. After a few taps at the keyboard, the image appeared on the large main screen.

'This is the main gate live, sir.'

'So I see.'

The camera showed the hearse entering to pick up Monica. Amused, he noticed that he felt no pity at all for the woman. She had only annoyed him and she had not been useful either. Of course, she had been a better fit for his number two than Sean Miller – that man had been just a little too independent for Johnson's liking.

The hearse made its way past crowds of tourists being held back by barriers. It was like with the big fire of 1992 – everyone wanted to be there to see it live, even though they could get a much better picture on TV from the numerous cameras, drones and social media feeds that were already converging on the spot. The big plume of smoke that blew over the castle had been like a beacon saying, 'come to me'. Johnson was happy to leave it in the hands of the PR department. Let them and the police and the army miscommunicate at each other – no one but him knew what had really happened, and everything would get lost in the confusion. It bothered him that this would distress the Queen, as if her year wasn't bad enough already, but she had come through worse crises than this and it would soon be forgotten.

What mattered was stopping Kent and preventing that hidden knowledge from becoming public.

So, Johnson thought, if Kent had come in this way, it would have taken him a certain length of time to get to the Round Tower … maybe slowly, by a roundabout route … He did the calculation in his head.

'Show me the main gate images from twenty minutes before the camera went out.'

A few moments later:

'Stop, stop right there!'

And there he was, James Kent, hoisting a shopping bag, talking to one of the guards at the gate. He obviously hadn't bought a ticket. So why the hell had they let him in?

There was nothing more the cameras could tell him, so Johnson left the room.

He hurried to the main gate with long strides, past the firefighters who were rolling up their hoses and the policemen who were still questioning people about the incident. The hearse was waiting outside the Round

# JACK

Tower, for the scene of crime officers to do their work and release her body. He wasn't worried about what they would find: he had already perfected his story to show that James Kent had shot her, an ex-lover's tiff gone wrong.

The guard he had seen in the video footage was still on duty. Johnson took the offensive, striding up to him with ID in one hand, picture of Kent on his phone in the other.

'You let this man into the castle today without a ticket. Explain!'

The soldier immediately began to bridle at his tone, until Johnson waggled his ID a little more closely under his eyes and the man saw exactly who he was talking to.

'We'd already seen in the company of a member of staff. Sir.'

'Which member of staff?'

And then Johnson had his first genuinely pleasant surprise of the day. The guard looked up and pointed at a lanky figure in a suit, loping up towards the gate.

'Mr Brown, sir.'

Johnson looked thoughtfully at the approaching man. Then he looked coldly back at the sentry.

'You guard the Queen. Your lax conduct today is inexcusable and I will certainly be putting you on report.'

Then he went to meet Charles Brown. The man saw him coming.

'Mr Johnson —'

'Mr Brown —'

## CHAPTER 20

They spoke together, then stopped and waited for the other to finish. Johnson silently gave Brown the go-ahead with a gesture.

'I have a serious security lapse to report, Mr Johnson,' Brown said – the second pleasant surprise of the day.

'We'd better go to my office to discuss it, then,' Johnson said.

It wasn't his office. It was a disused room that in previous years had been an interrogation cell. Johnson had always wondered if it would come in handy. Brown stopped immediately he stepped through the door and looked back curiously at Johnson, as if to check this was for real. Johnson smiled encouragingly for him to go on.

Not a single window illuminated the room, just a long neon tube on the ceiling, filling the room with sterile white light. In the middle was a single aluminium table with two matching chairs. With another anxious glance at Johnson, Brown took his seat at the table. Johnson perched on the edge and gazed down at him. Brown swallowed.

'Yes. Well. Um. I was visited by on old friend today, and her ... boyfriend, I guess, I wasn't sure ...'

Then his eyes boggled as Johnson silently laid his phone with its picture of Kent on the table.

'Yes, that's him! How did you –'

'Just tell me how this wanted man came to get illegal access to the archives, Mr Brown?'

'Obviously I didn't know he was wanted! But that's what I came to tell you. The whole thing was a ruse. While I wasn't looking, he stole my pass and ...'

For the first time, Brown seemed to remember the things he had seen as he walked up to the castle.

'All those police, the fire brigade … was that him?'

Johnson ignored the question.

'How did he steal your pass? Did you just leave it lying around?'

'I left it in my home, here inside Windsor Castle!' Brown said indignantly. 'You'd expect it to be safe, wouldn't you? What else am I supposed to do? I don't expect my friends to steal from me!'

'You could have locked it in a drawer or a box.'

'Okay, next time I'll do that.'

'Where are they now!'

'I have no idea. They left me immediately after dinner.'

'Bullshit! You didn't think of asking?'

'Listen, if you remember, I was coming to you to report this! I'm not the bad guy here!'

'Just an incompetent one,' Johnson snapped.

'Well, fine.' Brown shrugged and started to get up. 'If you're going to take that attitude …'

He started to get up.

'Sit down!'

Full of anger, Johnson shoved him back into the chair, so hard that it toppled over backwards. Before either of them could react, the back of Brown's head had thudded into the cold stone floor. He gasped with pain.

'You son of a bitch!'

Johnson made no effort to help him get up.

'James was right about you. You're a bastard.'

## CHAPTER 20

'Oh, you discussed me?' Johnson asked with cold humour.

Brown started to wriggle off the fallen chair. Johnson put a foot on his chest to keep him still. The other man glowered sullenly up at him.

'You came up in the conversation.'

'You had better tell me, Mr Brown,' Johnson said pleasantly, 'because I know you helped them, I intend to make sure they go to jail for life for treason, and if you don't help me then you'll join them there. Do we understand each other?'

Brown looked at him in horror. Carefully he felt for the back of his head. When he looked at his hands, he found they were red. He took two deep breaths. Then he forced a smile.

'What, only jail for life? James is convinced you want him dead.'

'Really?'

'And that you killed his father.'

Johnson snorted.

'That's ridiculous.'

'I know. That's what I told him. But let's just say that if this is your normal behaviour, I can see how you don't make friends.'

Johnson had one last question.

'Did Kent say why he wanted to break into the archives?'

'No.' Johnson heard the ring of truth in Brown's voice: the weariness that comes with giving up and not trying to hide anything. 'He didn't.'

'Okay.' Johnson was thinking. If Charles Brown complained about his treatment here then that would be one more inconvenience to deal with. So, he would make nice and get the man out of here. He removed his foot from Brown's chest.

'You're off the hook for now, but I will make a report about that stolen card—'

'But it was to do with Jack the Ripper,' Brown added.

Johnson glanced at him sideways.

'How did you know that?'

'I saw the file number on the folder he was carrying. 1888, JtR – come on!'

Johnson looked at Charles with something as close to pity as he ever came. What he hated the most were people who didn't know when it was better to keep their mouths shut. He had got a long way in life following the simple rule: talking is silver but silence is golden.

'Let me help you up,' he said, holding out a hand. Charles Brown reached for it to pull himself up from the ground. Johnson let him get halfway. Then, without warning, he put his foot on Charles's chest and pushed down hard. Charles fell back to the floor and his neck smashed against the low stone ridge that ran around the room. There was a sickening crack of cervical vertebrae, and his body went limp.

Johnson checked for a pulse, then knelt beside the body and quickly went through the pockets.

No car keys. Interesting.

'Perhaps you were more helpful than you were prepared to admit, Mr Brown,' he murmured.

## CHAPTER 20

Then he drew a deep breath to fill his lungs.

'Guard! Help!'

The guard rushed in immediately.

'Call an ambulance!' Johnson shouted. 'He was leaning back in that chair, he fell over backwards and hit his head …'

The man took in the scene at a glance, and whipped out his radio to start calling for medical help.

Johnson left the cell at a leisurely pace, taking his phone out as he went. He put a call through to Berkshire CID and identified himself.

'I need to know if a particular individual owns a car. Make, colour, number.'

# JACK

# CHAPTER 21

The sentry that Johnson had bawled out had had his fill of pushy civilians for that day, so he wasn't in a receptive mood when the black Land Rover with tinted windows pulled up in front of the gate and a brawny, broad-shouldered man got out.

'Hey, you can't park here! Park your vehicle in the marked places,' the sentry barked. The man looked as unimpressed with him as he felt about the newcomer, and flashed him a badge. The sentry's heart sank. *Oh, Christ, another one!*

'Miller,' said the newcomer. 'MI5.'

\*

A few minutes later, Sean Miller was being briefed on the day's events by someone higher up the security food chain.

His brief from the mysterious stranger in the Jubilee Gardens, to amass evidence that would lead to the downfall of William Johnson, had not got off to the best start when Johnson had appeared to disappear from the scene. Unfortunately a man with his kind of clearance and authority could go pretty well wherever he liked without having to explain himself to anyone. You couldn't track him by facial recognition or automatic number plate detection because the system automatically deleted him, and it would be very hard for someone like Sean to make his own enquiries without Johnson hearing of it and being alerted.

Then the rumours of deaths, more than one, at Windsor Castle had started circulating. Johnson's duties on behalf of the Queen included Windsor, her favourite residence, so it had been as good a place as any for Sean to start looking.

And, bingo! The sentry had called a young officer, who had confirmed that yes, Mr Johnson had been here today, and had been the one to call in both the fatalities. Apparently one of them had already been taken away to the mortuary but the other was still lying where he had fallen, awaiting the attention of the suddenly overworked scene of crime officers.

As Sean was led down to the interrogation room where the second fatality had occurred, they passed a row of cars – and there was the blue Rover he remembered from New Scotland Yard. So, Johnson was around. He would have to keep his head down.

Now Sean squatted down and looked thoughtfully at the body of a lanky man in his thirties. What did he know? Why did he have to die?

The angle of the man's head suggested his neck had been broken. It certainly looked like his chair had overbalanced, but Sean knew at least a couple of ways to achieve the same effect deliberately. A skilled coroner might be able to detect it – if was he looking for it.

'Obviously, sir, we have to leave him like this until the scene of crime chaps can —' the officer began.

## CHAPTER 21

'I understand.' Sean straightened up. 'Who is he?'

'His name is Charles Brown and he worked in the royal archives here.'

'And Mr Johnson was with him when he died?'

'Yes, sir. He had just questioned him about the intruder who caused the chaos earlier. During the interrogation, Mr Brown fell off the chair because he was so nervous. That's how Mr Johnson reported it.'

Sean didn't believe a word of it. He was pretty sure that Johnson had killed the man to keep a dangerous secret. That seemed to be how Johnson worked. He remembered his conversation on board H.M.S. *Belfast* with James Kent – the claims the man had made. At the time Sean hadn't believed a word of that either, and Kent hadn't helped his case by clouting him on the head, kneeing him in the balls and generally making him look ridiculous.

But since then, Sean had learned a few more things about Johnson, and now he was at least prepared to listen to what Kent had to say – if he could find him.

But what could the secret that got Charles Brown killed have been?

'All right,' he said with resignation, 'let me have it. Who was the other fatality?'

'Ah. A woman, sir. Mr Johnson's assistant, I think …'

Sean looked sharply at him.

'A, um, Monica Leapman, her name was …'

The name hit Sean like a blow to the gut. The young officer looked at him in concern.

'Are you all right, Mr Miller?'

Sean realised he wasn't exactly projecting the ideal image of the Security Service's finest. He was clutching at the aluminium table. His legs felt weak and he had probably gone pale. He took his hand away and stood up a little more straight.

'Monica Leapman was a former partner of mine,' he said.

'Oh, I am sorry, sir —'

'No, go on. What happened?'

'According to Mr Johnson, shots were exchanged in the archive building between Leapman and the man they were pursuing.'

And now Sean was convinced. James Kent had had every chance to kill him, and he hadn't. He was tough, he could fight his way out of a corner – but he didn't apparently kill even strangers like Sean Miller. Kill his ex-girlfriend? Never.

'Mr Johnson is still on the premises somewhere, sir,' the officer was saying. 'I could call him and ...'

'No. Thank you.' Sean held up a hand. He did not want Johnson to hear he was poking around in the man's trail. 'If he asks, just say MI5 routinely despatched an agent to investigate Leapman's death, and that Mr Johnson's account is accepted as the official one.'

And that, Sean thought, would probably be believed by Johnson. It would appeal to his ego, to think that he still had such power that his word was enough even in a double homicide.

## CHAPTER 21

The officer looked puzzled, but agreed. One thing about the army, Sean thought: they know how to take orders without questioning.

'I'll see myself out,' he said, 'if you could just point me to the gents first?'

*

In a toilet cubicle Sean quickly felt around in his pockets for the device he needed.

He had already made his plans.

He needed to amass evidence on Johnson. Johnson wasn't going to do anything more here. He would be looking for James Kent. So, Sean just had to follow him.

And finding Kent might also help answer the question that Sean knew he wasn't meant to be asking: what the hell was all this about?

Sean flushed, washed his hands and then half undid one of his shoelaces. After that he walked quietly to the exit. Next to the blue Rover he stopped to retie his lace properly.

And slipped the small metal bug in his hand inside the wheel arch.

He stood up again and carried on walking back to his own car.

*

William Johnson believed in the paperless office and the power of the cloud. Desks covered by paperwork were the sign of laziness, he believed: incompetence, a disordered mind.

The drawback was that as long as you were anywhere near a computer – one that was suitably secure, in his line of work – then there was no way of leaving the office behind. And he had to admit, given his recent preoccupation with James Kent and matters arising, that the virtual paperwork had been piling up.

And so, while he waited for the reports to come in from the traffic cameras – which, given enough time, was inevitable – he passed the time by retreating to the cell of Windsor Castle that he used as an office and logging on to deal with the backlog of emails.

He was just drafting instructions that, for obvious reasons, Her Majesty's visit to Windsor that weekend was to be cancelled when his phone rang.

*Excellent!* He thought. *Traffic are quicker off the mark than usual.*

'Johnson,' he barked into the phone, while his other hand held a pen poised over a notepad. 'What have you got?'

'Mr Johnson.'

He knew the dry, male voice very well, but it was so not what he had been expecting that it took him a moment to place it.

'Yes,' he snapped. 'Look, I'll have to call you back. I'm expecting an important report –'

'It will only take you a moment, Mr Johnson, to note that Her Majesty expects your attendance at ten o'clock tomorrow morning. Here.'

## CHAPTER 21

'What on earth for?'

'Two bodies at her favourite residence, Mr Johnson?' The voice sounded amused. 'And you have to ask that?'

'Obviously I will present a full report as soon as I can, but in the meantime I am engaged on a matter of national security and –'

There was a slight muttering at the other end, and then another voice spoke. Older. Female. One that Johnson could no more disobey than he could fly.

'Mr Johnson.'

He swallowed.

'Yes, ma'am.'

'Ten o'clock tomorrow morning, here. Good night, Mr Johnson.'

\*

Sean Miller drove just far enough from the castle that Johnson wouldn't spot him if the man suddenly appeared. He pulled over at a petrol station and got his phone out.

He authenticated himself with his fingerprint and called up an app that very definitely could not have been downloaded from any of the usual online stores.

After a moment, a map appeared on screen with a dot.

It was moving.

In fact, it was very close …

Sean looked in his wing mirror, just as the blue Rover came into view. He watched it pass by and disappear towards the M4.

So, Johnson was on the move. He would give the man five minutes, then trail him, being careful not to come into actual view. Sean stuck the phone into its mount on the dashboard and watched the dot join the M4.

He turned on the engine and pressed the accelerator.

The dot vanished and a message popped up on screen: 'Signal lost.'

'Fuck!' Sean bellowed. 'Do we really have this crap in the company?'

He took the phone from its cradle and shook it vigorously. The dot flickered back into life, then vanished again.

And now the whole phone seemed to be bricked. Sean had no choice but for a hard reboot. He started driving while the phone did its stuff to bring itself back to life.

A minute later the phone was on again and the dot was on screen, moving towards the M25. Sean had reached the slip road for the M4 and was gunning up towards the motorway when the dot vanished again.

Angrily, Sean Miller roared out loud.

'Damn it!'

Okay, until and unless the phone deigned to work, he could write it off as a reliable source.

He drummed his fingers on the wheel, thinking.

Johnson was after the same thing as he was: James Kent. Find Kent and he would find Johnson. Johnson was ahead of Sean when it came to information on the fugitive. In fact, he might already have put a search in place …

## CHAPTER 21

Sean quickly used a voice command to call up traffic control and see if they had been instructed on any urgent searches within the last hour.

It turned out they had. A blue Mini. Not spotted yet.

Sean gave instructions that he too was to be alerted if they found it.

Once he knew where the vehicle was, he was sure Johnson wouldn't be far behind.

# JACK

# CHAPTER 22

'Arundel,' Alice said, jerking James out of a fitful sleep. Despite the discomfort of the Mini, James had been so exhausted by the events of the day, not to mention running a couple of miles around Windsor and the sheer mental fatigue of his experiences, that he had slept the whole way, pillowing his head against the vibrating door pillar.

'What, already?' James mumbled. A glance at the dashboard clock told him that it was shortly after midnight. He could already picture his uncle's face when he got rung out of bed at half past twelve. Well, Uncle Howard was a very understanding man.

From Windsor, Alice had quickly slipped south-east and reached the M25 without any problems. It was late enough for traffic on the great circular highway around London to have dwindled. On a bad day during rush hour, the M25 could be London's largest car park but now cars could move freely.

Soon she had turned on to the A24 where she saw signs leading to the seaside resort of Brighton, once the favourite resort of a long-ago king. After an hour she started to follow signs to Arundel, turning on to the A27. From the luxury of four lanes on the motorway, now she was down to just one either way.

'You'll have to give me directions.'

'Ah, there we are!' James said and pointed his finger into the night. Alice could only see darkness, until they drew closer and she could make out the shape of a large castle towering over them.

'That's not your uncle's, is it?' she asked. He laughed.

'Not, it's been owned by the Dukes of Norfolk since the sixteenth century. They're the Howard family but no relation to Uncle Howard. Though Uncle is a friend of the Duke's. Mind you, after forty years at the Home Office he's a friend of most people's. But I'm sure he'll tell you all about himself.'

'And you're sure he'll help us?' Alice said cautiously.

'Totally. He's all the family I have now.'

'Will you tell him what you've learned about his brother?'

'In other words, my father?' James paused. 'I'd like to. But, same principle as telling Charles—'

'We don't tell anyone anything that could get them killed. I understand.'

They drove over a bridge that spanned the river Arun and came to a roundabout.

'Right,' James said, and they drove into town. And soon after: 'First up the hill.'

Alice had to engage second gear and drive slowly up the steep road. On the right they passed several outbuildings that seemed to be connected to the castle. A little further up they passed the parish church of the town, looking like a small cathedral.

## CHAPTER 22

'Now slow down, we have to turn left in a moment.' James looked out for a small side street. 'Okay, there. Drive in!'

Alice turned into a narrow alley. The houses were all grand mansions, some stone, some original half-timber.

'Find any space you can,' James said. 'It's first come first served, here.'

They came to a space that had only been left because it was too small for any modern car, but Alice was able to squeeze the little Mini in with centimetres to spare.

'Thank Charles never upgraded to a Mondeo,' she said as she clambered out, wincing. The Mini's cramped interior and rickety suspension had not done her back any favours. 'Or a modern 4x4. We'd never have made it down the street this far!'

James smiled as they walked a short distance to a large stone house with a pillared porch.

'These houses are all enormous, but when this place was built, no one parked in the street.'

He rang the bell and they heard it echo inside the hallway. Soon they heard someone approaching the wooden door from inside. The light came on over the porch and a chain was pushed to the side, then a grey-haired man dressed in a red bathrobe opened the door. He was slim for his age and round cheeked, and his grey-green eyes blinked tiredly at the couple outside the door.

'What on earth is this all about? Do you know what time it is?'

'Yes, I know what time it is, Uncle Howard, but we really need a place to stay,' James said.

The tiredness dissolved as the eyes widened and a huge smile split the man's face.

'Oh my, can this be true? James! I haven't seen you in so long. Last time was … Ah,' The last time, they both knew, had been at James's father's funeral. 'Anyway, come in, come in!'

The man opened the door and Alice and James entered a small lobby. The floor consisted of large stone tiles, most of which were covered by an old Persian carpet.

'And you have a truly gorgeous lady with you,' Uncle Howard went on. 'I hope my wife won't get jealous!'

'Oh, yes, Uncle, I'd like you to meet Alice Gull,' James said.

Alice offered her hand, a little unsure, still knowing the massive liberty they were taking. Howard grabbed it and pumped it up and down.

'I'm delighted! Howard Kent, but you can call me Howard, as can any friend of James's,' Howard said, with a big grin. 'Well, given the time, I'm sure there's an excellent reason for your turfing me out of bed but I'll show you your room now, and tomorrow we can talk about everything.'

'Thanks, Uncle,' James said gratefully. 'We owe you big time.'

Howard snorted.

'Nonsense. You're welcome any time, day or night. Just … try to make it more day next time, hmm?'

He led them up the old stone stairs, then down the landing and up a further flight to the guest suite James

## CHAPTER 22

knew so well, a cosy little room with an en-suite bathroom tucked away in an attic conversion under the eaves.

Alice smiled as Howard withdrew.

'He's a dear, isn't he? And he tactfully didn't say a word about whether we wanted one room or two.'

James laughed.

'He knows I could find any of the other spare rooms if I wanted.'

'And here you are.'

'Dog tired.'

'Likewise. So let's get to bed.'

They cleaned their teeth with the new toothbrushes they found in the bathroom. Back in the room, James undressed all the way up to his boxers. Alice took off her shirt and stopped in the middle of the movement. She turned her head to James.

'What's the matter?' James asked, pausing just as he was slipping under the duvet. Then he laughed. 'I've seen a lot more of you.'

'True.' She quickly removed the rest of her clothes. 'And I've seen more of you.'

James wriggled under the duvet and produced his boxers, which he dropped on the floor.

'Better?'

'Much.' She slipped into bed next to him and snuggled into his arms.

He didn't kiss her immediately. Just looked at her.

'Have I told you I'm grateful to God?'

'For what?'

'For every second he gives me with you! I could never have imagined meeting a woman as amazing as you.'

Alice smiled, and began to kiss him gently.

'And I could never have imagined meeting a man who has turned my life so completely upside down as you.'

'So? You came into my life first. Well, you spoke to me, not me to you,' he teased.

'Oh shut up!' she laughed and rolled on to his stomach. Her kisses grew harder as she moved them down to his body. She backed down beneath the duvet and kissed on. James closed his eyes with bliss.

\*

James woke up with the sunbeams shining on his face. He lifted his head to peer at the clock radio next to the bed: eight o'clock. He let himself fall back to the pillow and looked at Alice. She was still fast asleep, her blonde hair ruffled over her face.

James smiled as he thought back a few hours. He had never had an experience quite like that with a woman before.

There had been a time when he had thought Monica might be the one. After they split he had had to face it: all that amazing sex, which he had thought might be love, had just been about control.

Maybe that was the test, he thought. He had never been able to imagine getting into bed with Monica and *not* having sex. But Alice ... sex or not, he wanted to be able to wake up next to her every day for the rest of his life.

## CHAPTER 22

That had to mean something, right?

But, enough of this, he told himself – priorities! He gave himself a jolt to shake away the dreams and went into the small bathroom.

After a shower and brushing his teeth, he went back to the bedroom. There was a small table with two chairs next to the bed and a large wooden closet. He sat down at the table and let his gaze wander out the window. The house was overlooked by the mighty walls of the castle. For all its size, its days as a medieval fortress and centre of military might were behind it. The restored walls looked like an immaculate stately home with a dodgy vertical hold, taller and slimmer than they should be.

Then it was back to the table – and the file had left there last night. A layer of dust puffed away as he blew on it. He opened it, and started reading.

Most of the notes were typewritten, in the old, blocky typeface of Victorian typewriters that he remembered from the documents George Anderson had left him. Some might be original reports, some might be copies of handwritten originals. There were some black and white pictures, photos and lithographs, showing the disfigured bodies of the women, and also a few handwritten notes among the papers, which seemed to James to all have come from the same person.

James thoroughly studied every sheet of paper, every picture, taking in every detail before carefully laying it face down next to the file, to keep it all in the same order.

After about an hour, he sat back with his hands behind his head and stared at the ceiling.

'Shit,' he muttered.

'What's the problem?' Alice asked from the bed. He glanced over at her.

'Have you been awake long?'

'I didn't want to disturb you. So ... shit?'

James waved a tired hand at the pile.

'It's all the Ripper cases – all the notes, the evidence, the investigations, the conclusions. Everything you could possibly want ... except the bit that ties it all together and says who they think the Ripper was.'

He slumped, disconsolate, in his chair.

'Please don't say it was all for nothing!' Alice begged.

James grunted. Had it been? Not just everything he had put himself through, turning himself into a wanted criminal along the way, but also dragging the woman he was now sure he loved down with him?

'There's not a trace of the Ripper in the entire file,' he said dully. 'I think there was, once, but it's like someone has removed the most important pages.'

'Johnson?'

'No, I don't think so. There was still thick dust on the cover – I don't think he ever got round to reading this. No, I think the trail was destroyed in 1888.'

Alice stood up and wrapped the blanket around her slender body. She took the chair next to James's.

'Let me see?'

James pushed the file over and Alice began to leaf through the papers herself. James looked out of the window again, lost in his own thoughts. Downstairs he

## CHAPTER 22

could hear the quiet clattering of pots in the kitchen. His uncle and aunt were already preparing breakfast.

No, it couldn't all have been for nothing, he thought. Something in those papers had to tell him the answer. He couldn't see it, but maybe she would.

He decided to let it rest for a while. Then he could concentrate better later. When he was less hungry.

'I'm going to go downstairs and see if I can help.'

'I'll be right behind you,' Alice said without looking up. James left her alone with her thoughts and went downstairs.

Two floors down, the little stone-floored kitchen was bright with daylight shining off its yellow walls. On the right was a large old cooking range, with the sink and washing machine opposite. In the middle stood a heavy, battered table that was both a work surface and a dining table. Uncle Howard was sitting there, absorbed in the newspaper. His Aunt Mary was half hidden by the open door of the big American fridge.

'Good morning, Uncle, Auntie!'

There was just a grunt from behind the newspaper.

'Good morning, honey!' His aunt emerged from behind the fridge with some eggs. She was a tall woman with long red hair and James was already picking up the delicate scent of her perfume. She came and kissed him. 'Well, how are you? It's been ages since we saw you.'

'Yes, a long time. I'm fine, thanks.'

Mary beat the eggs into a cast iron pan and added sliced bacon while she continued the conversation.

'And Howard told me that we have another guest. What's her name? How long have you known her?'

'Name, rank and number. That's all you're meant to give in an interrogation, isn't it?' James joked.

'Well, dear, I just want to know everything so I don't have to worry anymore.'

'Oh, please don't.'

'So, will she be the woman for life?'

'Mary!' Howard protested. Then he looked at James. 'Just tell us everything now, boy, and put her out of our misery.'

James smiled and sat down. They were joking, but he also knew Mary would not rest until she had every scrap of information. James had grown up without a mother and Mary had always made it clear that she saw herself as a substitute.

'All right, then. I met her at a party. We talked about stuff we were both interested in. The next day we met again. Yeah, she's kind of like my dream girl. We just get along great and complement each other in every way.'

'I think that's beautiful! It took you long enough. My mother always said that every pot finds its lid and every lid its pot.'

Howard smiled approvingly.

'Good starter, boy, nicely dodging around why you turn up out of nowhere after midnight badly needing somewhere to stay. Don't worry, Mary will sweat it out of you – and here she is!' He beamed and stood up as Alice came into the kitchen. James introduced her to his aunt and they sat down together. When Alice wasn't looking, Mary winked at him and gave him the thumbs up.

Alice's eye fell on the newspaper that Howard had laid down on the table. James hadn't got around to looking at it yet.

'May I?' she said as she picked it up. There was something ominous in her tone that only James heard.

'Of course,' Howard agreed. 'Had you heard about that business at Windsor? Shocking stuff.'

Alice unfolded the paper. With a sinking heart, James nestled close to her so that they could read it together.

### Back to 1992?

Two people are confirmed to have died in yesterday's fire at Windsor Castle, which reminded many local residents of the devastating incident of 1992 that destroyed large parts of the state apartments. Castle officials have emphasised that yesterday's fire was on nowhere near so great a scale, and it was extinguished by the local fire brigade in good time. The casualties have not yet been identified, pending notification to their families.

The castle administrator expressed his deep regret about the incident and the deaths, and would neither confirm nor deny rumours that the two dead had died in circumstances unconnected with the fire. Nevertheless, several eyewitnesses have said they clearly heard shots within the castle. The Queen, who will spend the weekend at Buckingham Palace, is said to be taking a close interest in the investigation and has passed on her condolences to the families of the dead people.

Beside the text was a picture of the castle with a column of smoke billowing up from the base of the Round Tower.

Alice and James gazed at each other. Both were thinking the same thing: who could have died? They knew nothing about that!

James thought back to the only gunshots he had heard. Three, wasn't it? When Johnson dropped the gun, when Johnson fired at him and missed, and just as he was throwing himself away from Monica …

Who, he suddenly realised, he hadn't seen since. The sudden suspicion hit him like a physical blow that made his jaw drop. It couldn't be her …!

Could it? He remembered Johnson firing wildly, blindly …

'What's the matter with you?' Howard asked, taking in their horrified expressions.

'We have a friend there and hope nothing happened to him,' Alice replied quickly.

'Well, give him a call and ask how he's doing,' Howard suggested. 'You can use the phone in the hall.'

'Yes, thanks, I'll do that.' Alice left the kitchen and James took the paper, quickly reading the rest of the story. At the bottom was a link to the editorial pages, so he flicked it open and continued to read.

### What's going on in Westminster?

### Investigations initiated

A Committee of Inquiry has been officially convened to investigate reports two days ago of gunfire near Buckingham Palace. Unconfirmed reports state that a high-ranking member of the Queen's security retinue authorised the use of deadly force despite the proximity of unarmed civilians.

If this is true then immediate questions are raised about the competence of the security forces responsible for safeguarding the Royal Family. A spokesman has confirmed that no individual should have the authority to take steps that would normally require approval by the Home Office. The Home Office has confirmed that no such approval was given.

This further domestic political mishap increases the pressure on a Prime Minister already dogged by scandal, and opens up a new front of attack for the Opposition as well as internal party critics. A Downing Street spokesman confirmed

> the Prime Minister's full support for the Royal Family and stressed Buckingham Palace's determination to investigate the incident without cover-up. Meanwhile, republican factions across the political spectrum have stepped up their call for the abolition of the monarchy, but this is only supported by a small minority in the House of Commons ...

James hadn't realised how long it had been since he had actually read any news. His phone was still in his apartment so he hadn't seen the internet or any social media. He hadn't had time to listen to the news or watch the TV.

All this had obviously been boiling up ever since their chase through London. Was this why Johnson was so fired up about the case? He must have known his own job was on the line.

And then Alice came back into the kitchen, with tears in her eyes.

'It was Charles. He's dead,' she sobbed.

Mary rushed to her and took Alice in her arms. Howard looked bewildered.

'Prince Charles? We'd have heard!'

'No, an old friend of Alice's. His name was Charles Brown and he worked in the castle. We saw him yesterday,' James explained, dazed. How the hell had anything led to Charles being hurt? To Alice he added, 'What exactly did they say?' He quickly got up and

## CHAPTER 22

helped her to a chair, then sat down next to her, holding her hand in both of his.

Alice just sat down and took two deep breaths.

'Charles fell from his chair and broke his neck. He was dead on the spot.'

'How did he fall off his chair?' James asked, baffled.

'The officer said he couldn't say.' Her voice went cold. 'He just said it was a tragic accident.'

Their eyes met and James knew they were both thinking the same thing.

Charles had said he was going to own up about his stolen pass. He must have said something that made Johnson decide to eliminate him.

'If we'd had the slightest idea …' James murmured. The rest of the sentence went unsaid: '*then we would never have let him report himself.*' Alice knew what he meant and she just nodded. Johnson was the kind of man who could be dangerous and unpredictable when his back was to the wall. They should have realised earlier, and it was all the more painful to have to do it now.

Howard hadn't missed the silent exchange. He coughed and laid his hands flat on the table.

'I have no idea what is happening,' he said quietly, 'but you know I would trust you with my life, James, and I hope you know you can trust me with yours. Is there anything I can do?'

James shook his head gently. He couldn't involve his uncle and aunt in this. Not with that madman on the loose. He just couldn't.

'That's really kind, Uncle, but I don't think—'

'You can help us track down the descendants of someone called Frederick Abberline,' Alice said.

James and Howard both stared at her.

'But,' Alice added quickly, 'without attracting any attention – because that's what we've been doing wrong. James mentioned you did forty years at the Home Office. You must have made some contacts?'

'I did, before a happy retirement.' Howard confirmed. He glanced at her sideways. 'That's not a common name so it shouldn't be hard. Who is this Mr Abberline?'

'He was a Chief Inspector at Scotland Yard who died in 1929 at the age of eighty-six. We need more than what you can just find on Google. We need names and places.'

'I'll make a few phone calls,' Howard said simply. 'I still have friends at the old place who will be able to be very discreet.'

'Thanks, Howard,' Alice said warmly. 'You're a real sweetheart!'

Howard visibly melted under the compliment as he got to his feet. Mary rolled her eyes.

'You've never looked at me like that, dear.'

'Oh, come on, Mary, you know I love you.'

'You always say that.'

'Well, then it must be true …'

The good-natured bickering carried on as they left the room, leaving James and Alice together at the table.

'What was that about?' James asked. She answered with a smile.

'Doesn't the name Abberline mean anything to you anymore, James?'

## CHAPTER 22

'Sure. The detective in charge of the Ripper case ...'

'And who wrote all the handwritten notes in the file.'

James frowned.

'They weren't signed or anything.'

'No, but I recognised the handwriting from the exhibition. It was definitely him, James.'

'God, that seems ages ago,' James muttered, thinking back to the night he had met Alice ... all of four days ago.

'And if he also removed all the really incriminating stuff, he must have had someone he trusted – *really* trusted – to hand it on to.'

'So you think he might have left something with his children?'

'You've hit the mark.'

James grinned.

'God, you're brilliant!'

Mary came back into the room, oblivious to the smiles between them.

'Oh, that man. He's impossible,' she said fondly. 'Alice, dear, why don't we go into the living room and wait for Howard there? It's more comfortable than the kitchen.'

The living room was furnished with a large inviting sofa and a small side table, with several magazines about better living or fashion tips spread out on it. Two comfortable wing chairs stood in front of the open fireplace. Over the mantelpiece hung a large painting of Mary as a younger woman. Mary saw Alice studying it.

'Howard gave me the picture for our tenth anniversary. He wanted to show me that I was still the most beautiful woman in the world for him. Please have a seat.' Alice and James gratefully accepted the offer and sat down on the sofa. James took one of Alice's hands in his, because he guessed what was coming: the nicest, politest interrogation any woman could have.

Mary took one of the armchairs by the fire and looked at them both with her big eyes.

'So, Alice, what do you do for a living, sweetheart?'

'I work for MPs in the House of Commons in London.'

'I see. Then did you study politics?'

'Yes, I studied international politics at King's, Cambridge. My father is the owner of a private bank in London but I realised that finance isn't the thing for me. I like to approach people, so I decided to study politics.'

James smothered a smile as Mary flashed him an approving look. He could tell she was already thinking: *She's rich! Don't let her get away!* But in fact, he would have wanted to be with Alice if she was dirt poor.

'What's your father's name, dear? Should I have heard of him?'

'Well, he's the Duke of Cardiff. Sir Thomas Gull.'

'Fancy! So you're a real lady!'

The two women chatted and bantered while James leaned back and supported himself with his free arm on the back of the sofa. He turned so he could look at Alice. He was pleased she could stand up to the interrogation so easily. Not everyone liked his aunt's pushy and curious nature. Many of James's girlfriends had been desperate to leave at this stage. It hadn't stopped him introducing them.

## CHAPTER 22

After half an hour Howard came in and looked around with a big smile. He dropped down in the other wing chair. After stretching out his feet, he started the report.

'Well, it wasn't that hard. First I called the Society of Genealogists in London. They are good at helping people find British ancestors.'

'And what did they say?' Alice asked excitedly.

'Not much, but they gave me the number for the Family Records Centre, which is also based in London. All birth, marriage and death certificates from England and Wales from 1837 onwards are kept there. At first they didn't want to give me any information, because they are only allowed to give it to relatives.'

'You made it, though, didn't you?' James interrupted him.

'Where do you think I'm going with this? Of course I made it. I ... *may* have given the impression that this was in some way connected with my civic duties as the mayor of Arundel.' He blinked innocently. 'I don't quite recall. After a while, they unbent enough to tell me that Mr Abberline's sole surviving descendant is called Thomas Joseph Hudson and he lives in a small village on Dartmoor called Buckland-in-the-Moor. As did his father, and his father before him, and so on – probably in the same house, I expect. They wouldn't go so far as to give me the house number, but don't worry. I already took the liberty of Googling it – I say village, it's more like a collection of houses. You could probably make door-to-door enquiries in less than ten minutes, or just ask at the local pub.'

'They haven't said they're going there, dear,' Mary pointed out. Howard snorted.

'No, of course not. No doubt they just want to solve a particularly difficult crossword clue. For God's sake, woman, of course they're going!'

'He's right, Auntie, and Howard, you're the best! Thank you so much! Alice, I think we have to go to Buckland.' James jumped up from the sofa, beaming all around them.

He noticed the three disappointed faces. Howard and Mary he could understand ... but Alice?

'Is there a problem?' he asked.

'Well ... no.' She smiled ruefully as she got to her feet. 'Just, how far is to Dartmoor? A hundred miles? Two hundred? Several hours in that rickety little Mini, not doing over sixty ...'

'What, that blue death trap parked in the road?' Howard asked in amazement, jerking his thumb at the window.

'Beggars can't be choosers, Uncle,' James pointed out.

'The Kents do not beg, m'boy. You're taking the jeep.'

James breathed a sigh of relief. He hadn't been looking forward to using the Mini either.

'Thank you, Uncle, that's very kind.'

'Will you at least have some lunch before heading off?' Mary volunteered. James laughed.

'Did you think we'd miss one of your legendary sandwiches, Auntie? No way!'

'I'm so pleased! Alice, love, why not help me get lunch together?' Mary suggested, in a way that wasn't a

## CHAPTER 22

suggestion but such a nice order that no one could turn it down. James knew Alice met with Mary's approval and she wanted to be friends. Their hands brushed together as Alice meekly followed Mary out of the room.

'I'll pour us all a sherry,' Howard called. He crossed over to the side table that was laden with decanters. James sat back on the sofa and watched his uncle.

Should he talk about the danger? If Johnson found out that Howard had helped them, it could be dangerous for him too.

But not even Johnson could afford too many bodies stacking up, could he? The two deaths at Windsor were already generating conspiracy theories. The higher up the tree you went, the harder it had to be to explain mysterious deaths away – and Howard and Mary were pretty high up.

There again, James realised he was thinking of Johnson as a rational human being, which he obviously wasn't.

No, James decided not to tell Howard anything more.

'Try this.' Howard offered him a glass. 'It's the same label that the Duke's pushing. It's really very good.'

'Thank you.' James took a small sip. The alcohol flowed down his throat and made a warm glow in his stomach. By the time he had finished lunch, there would be enough protein inside him to absorb it and he would be safe to drive.

Howard, on the other hand, took a good swig. Probably more used to it, James thought.

'So why exactly are you looking for Mr Abberline's descendant?' Howard began the conversation, as James had guessed he would.

'It's complicated. Very difficult to explain correctly. I'd just say this man has a connection with Alice's family.'

'It's none of my business, really, of course ... This Abberline – do you know what he was famous for?'

'Yes,' James said sharply, 'and you don't. Promise me, Uncle. Promise me you will not mention ... Inspector Abberline's most famous case. Not to Auntie, not to anyone. Just forget it. Entirely and completely.'

For the first time since they had roused him from bed, Howard looked taken aback. At last he just said, 'Fair enough'. Another drink, and Howard closed the subject by saying, 'You know you can always talk to me if I need to. Now, take these glasses out to the women, will you?'

'Sure thing.'

As James carried the glasses of sherry through to the kitchen on a tray, he wondered how William Johnson was spending his day.

# CHAPTER 23

'She is expecting you, sir,' the butler said with a bow. 'This way, please.'

'I know the way,' Johnson grunted, and started to walk forward.

The butler moved too quickly, barring his way.

'Even so, sir?'

It was said so politely as to make it clear Johnson was not being presented with an option. He would be escorted: he was not the one in charge here. He ground his teeth and followed after the man. This was the worst possible time for his employer to start taking an interest in what he actually did to look after her, but an order was an order.

The butler led him the familiar route, down the long corridor and through the small door hidden behind a tapestry, stopping finally outside the audience room on the next floor. He knocked, then opened the door without waiting for a reply. Johnson entered carefully, not quite sure of what he might find on the other side.

There were three people already there. On the sofa in front of the fireplace sat the Queen herself, immaculate in her choice of dress and her hairstyle. Opposite her was the Prime Minister in an armchair. A little further away was a man in a dark blue suit and a £100 haircut, whom Johnson didn't know.

Johnson pointedly ignored the two men. Only one person in the room mattered, and he bowed to her.

'I'm glad you could make it, Mr Johnson.' The Queen opened the conversation. 'Please have a seat.'

She pointed to the free armchair next to the Prime Minister. Johnson bowed again and sat down.

'Tell me, how long have you worked for us?' the Prime Minister wanted to know about him.

'I have given loyal service directly to Her Majesty for ten years,' Johnson replied calmly, barely looking at him. 'But first, if you'll forgive me, ma'am, before we go any further, I haven't been introduced to this gentleman.' He indicated the second man in the room, without actually taking his eyes off the Queen. The Queen gave the stranger a nod.

'Thomas Black,' the man said with calm confidence. 'Special Adviser to the Prime Minister.'

Johnson still didn't look at him.

'And is Mr Black authorised to receive information at our usual level of disclosure, ma'am?'

'He is. In fact, Mr Black has some questions to ask you on our behalf.'

Now Johnson couldn't very well not look at Black, so instead he smiled coldly at the other man and waited.

'Let's start with this.' Black smiled in satisfaction. 'I was contacted last night by a security officer based at Windsor Castle who told me about a fatal interrogation you conducted. Can you kindly tell us what exactly happened?'

Johnson shrugged.

## CHAPTER 23

'There's not much to tell, and I've already made my report to the scene of crime officers and the coroner's office. It was a tragic accident. I questioned the witness, and he was fidgeting about nervously, and he fell off his chair. I immediately tried to revive him, but tragically I could do nothing more for him.'

'And why was he nervous? Did he have anything to hide, Mr Johnson?' Black asked.

Johnson decided it was time to go on the attack. He was coming across as too defensive, and that was something people remembered.

'Since you're so well informed,' he said curtly, 'I'm sure you also know that another person died last night. My personal assistant! We attempted to seize a man who was burgling the royal archives and he murdered her in cold blood. Mr Brown, the man who died, had been a good friend of the burglar so obviously I had to question him.'

'I must agree with Mr Johnson.' Help came from an unexpected quarter: the woman that every man in the room ultimately worked for. 'It is his duty as my Security Counsel to investigate the matter.'

'Thank you, ma'am,' Johnson said heavily.

Black was unruffled.

'Fair enough,' he said calmly. 'And what exactly is being done to get this murderer caught? I don't recall any bulletins on the main news channels, for example, which seems rather an oversight. I understand he is connected with the recent exchange of fire outside the Palace, which surely makes it even more imperative he be caught. If he belonged to a known religious extremist organisation, for example, no stone would go unturned when it came to tracking him down. Why the relaxed attitude?'

'The attitude is anything but relaxed,' Johnson snapped. 'I have already explained my approach to Her Majesty. The police have a description of the man, his companion and his transport. No, I have not made these public. As we all know, sometimes the public is best left in the dark. Otherwise things they ought not to know have a habit of emerging into the daylight.'

'But surely the more reports the police can get on his whereabouts—'

'Then the more hoax calls and false leads the police will have to deal with. This is a decision I am entitled to make by virtue of my position. Trust me with it.'

Johnson sat back in satisfaction. He hadn't been bluffing: the Queen's Security Counsel did have that right, and it was so entrenched in history that it would need an Act of Parliament to take it away from him.

The Queen chose her words carefully.

'You've always had your own style, Mr Johnson,' she said. 'A quite effective one, too, but lately … the negative consequences of your work have been accumulating.'

'Can I ask what you mean, ma'am?' Johnson spoke innocently. He could guess exactly what she was getting at, but he wanted to hear it from her mouth.

Instead, the Prime Minister replied.

'Mr Johnson, do you really think we don't know what you're doing just because you choose not to tell us? We don't depend only on you for reports on your work.'

## CHAPTER 23

That did surprise Johnson, for a moment. Did they really know everything? No, he told himself, they couldn't. If they did then they would have had this conversation long before now.

'The escalation in recent events,' he said, making himself be calm, 'only reflects the escalation of the danger to Her Majesty. A pair of very dangerous terrorists —'

'Bullshit,' the Prime Minister snapped. Johnson couldn't quite believe someone had used that language in front of the Queen, but she didn't seem put out. He had to remind himself who she was married to: she had heard a lot worse from her ex-sailor husband. 'Thomas?' the Prime Minister continued.

'MI5 has received no reports that Her Majesty is in any kind of danger,' Black said calmly. 'There is no conspiracy, no alert. The whole affair seems to have been invented by you, Mr Johnson.'

The Prime Minister, the Queen and Mr Black all looked at him expectantly. Johnson felt himself flushing. Who had been blabbing inside MI5? That was supposed to be all sown up.

'Well, ma'am, perhaps they are not terrorists in the conventional sense, but they're people who can do considerable damage.'

'What damage?' the Prime Minister demanded, and for the first time Johnson began to feel worry. If any of them knew what this was really about then he had no doubt they would support his actions – but then, the genie would be well and truly out of the bottle and that was the one thing he could not permit.

'All I can say,' he told them, 'is to assure you all that I have always tried to cause the least possible damage to the Crown.'

From the corner where Thomas Black was sitting came a disbelieving snort. The monarch also raised her eyebrows slightly. The Prime Minister just looked at Johnson in disbelief.

'Mr Johnson, if the press goes digging, the trail will lead to you, and we can't let that happen.'

'I entirely agree. What approach do you suggest, Prime Minister?'

To Johnson's surprise it was the Queen who answered with a firm voice.

'Mr Johnson. We have discussed this in some detail and have come to the conclusion that it would be best to dissolve the connection between us. We will accept your resignation.'

'Ma'am!' Johnson felt a lurch as his world fell away. He would never have expected an attack from this direction. 'I've served you faithfully all these years and now you're going to drop me off, just because there's a little crisis?'

'I agree, Mr Johnson, you've served us very faithfully and I am very grateful. I am truly sorry for the choice I have made, but if you love this institution as you say, you will understand it. You have left a trail of bad decisions behind you that leads directly to the Crown.'

She really did look sad, Johnson had to give her that. The Prime Minister looked like he was working himself up to being tough.

## CHAPTER 23

The only person in the room who hadn't changed at all was the calm, collected Thomas Black. Johnson studied him through narrow eyes. *So,* he thought, *how did I let you slip under my radar? Who are you? The official state executioner?*

The Prime Minister coughed.

'You have two hours to clear out your office, Mr Johnson. Please hand over your weapon and credentials to Mr Black.'

Still looking as though this was all perfectly normal, the Prime Minister's Special Adviser crossed to Johnson's chair and held out his hand, palm up. Johnson met his unblinking gaze, then slowly handed over the requested items. Thomas Black left the room without comment, taking the items and Johnson's career with him.

This was it. It was slowly sinking in, only slowed down by the sense of denial that comes with any calamity. He was the sacrificial lamb. It was over. If you've been fired by the Queen, you are not going to get a good job reference for any other line of employment.

And there was no other line that he wanted.

'Leave us, please,' the Queen said – to the Prime Minister. He grunted in surprise, but stood up and shambled from the room, leaving the two of them together.

The Queen rose and held out her hand.

'Goodbye, Mr Johnson. And thank you again for your loyal service.'

Johnson grabbed her hand a little harder than usual. The Queen flinched slightly.

'You'll see, Your Majesty, what I'm protecting you from,' he said savagely. 'I'm sure you'll be thanking me even more when Uncle Jack is finally laid to rest!'

He looked her firmly in the eye. He couldn't tell exactly whether she had understood the allusion. Her unflappability was legendary – like the time when she had woken up one day in the 1980s to find an unemployed nutcase sitting on her bed. She looked deep into his eyes once again, then left the salon with quick steps.

The Prime Minister was waiting outside.

'Well, Johnson, you only have yourself to blame. Really sad, and so tragic. You'd better get to your office to clear it out.'

# CHAPTER 24

The jeep was covered with a thick layer of mud, though you could see the original colour beneath. Howard had said that here in the country, driving a dirty 4x4 was expected.

'You can tell it's a proper working car, not some Chelsea tractor driven by a yummy mummy!'

The brown seats were covered with of all kinds of unimportant items – rubber boots, crates of old bottles, even a dog blanket on the back seat. As far as James was concerned, it had petrol – though he would need to fill up within the next hundred miles – and it ran smoothly, wheels thrumming on the smooth tarmac as he piloted it down the M27. That was all he needed to know.

Apart from the way.

'So …' He frowned. His aunt and his uncle had both had different ideas for how to get to Dartmoor, and Alice's phone was now completely flat so there was no way of checking Google Maps. 'Where was it after the motorway again?'

'Hang on.' Alice rummaged around in the glove compartment. Under a lipstick, a few sweets and an empty bag of gummy bears she found the road atlas and started to flick through it.

'Okay. Going via Salisbury looks longer because it's further north but your uncle said it was quicker than the southern route. So, take the A36 when we get there, then the A303 all the way down to Exeter.'

'Got it.'

'Once we're on Dartmoor, we'll head to Princetown first. That looks like the nearest big town and it will help us get out bearings. Dartmoor Prison's there so we can assume it's going to be signposted, unlike Buckland.'

'Good plan.'

James signalled and moved over into the inside lane to leave the motorway. The landscape behind the window in this part of England consisted of lush meadows on which cows grazed. Here and there it was interrupted by individual villages or cottages. The sun, beaming through holes in the dense cloud cover, set it all marvellously in a golden light.

After a while Alice, looking out of the windows, said, 'Don't you think we live in a very beautiful country?'

'Yes. I tend it forget it, because there aren't many green meadows in London. At least not in Westminster.'

Alice laughed. 'So? You have St James's Park right opposite you!'

He chuckled.

'I haven't seen any cows there yet. Have you?'

'No, I don't think so.' They went on in silence.

'What do you think of all this?' Alice renewed the conversation with a question.

'What do you mean? Nature?' James asked, guessing what she actually meant. The silence had been a little too tense.

## CHAPTER 24

'No, that was just an awkward attempt to dodge the elephant in the room. I mean, what we're going to find in Dartmoor. Assume that Abberline did uncover something so amazing that it had to be hidden with his heirs. What could it have been?'

'That's the one thing I don't think. I've said before, he just wasn't in any physical condition to be the Ripper, and there's nothing in the file to make me think Abberline thought that – probably for the same reason.'

'So, who else is on the suspect list?'

'Let's assume it really was a royal conspiracy, for sake of argument. Then, it must have been someone who also had great influence at court. Or a person who had worked for the Royal Family. A doctor, that's for sure.'

'There's another possibility,' James said thoughtfully. 'Henry II and Thomas Becket. They had a real falling out, remember, and Henry II shouts, "Will no one rid me of this turbulent priest?" He's just angry and frustrated – he doesn't mean anything by it. But a couple of knights overhear it, and they take it as licence to go off and murder old Thomas.'

'You think the same thing here?'

James nodded.

'I think maybe there was some big secret in the Royal Family, some crisis, and they were discussing how to deal with it – just hypothetically – and someone, maybe like our friend Johnson, takes them at their word and assumes it's an instruction.'

'Okay.' Alice thought. 'And the crisis people talked about was that one Queen Victoria's grandsons had married in church and had a child who would be in line to the throne, right?'

'Right! And even if the mother agreed not to say anything, she could have blackmailed the Royal Family for a fortune. So, she and the witnesses had to go.'

'What I keep wondering is, why didn't they just kill the kid?' Alice wondered.

'Why bother? Stick a little baby in an orphanage and it would never remember anything about its origins. Whereas the adult witnesses – well, they have memories, so they were the ones to take care of.'

'So, if the child survived, then perhaps there would be descendants, and they would be entitled to the throne, ahead of George V and his descendants, which includes the present Queen and – oh, my God!' Alice stopped in the middle of the sentence and turned her head to James.

'Go on?' he said.

'James, that's what this is about! It's about making sure that the kid's descendants never find out. I mean, if your great-grandmother was the legal heir to the throne, and so you were too, but your ancestors had lived in poverty – wouldn't you at least expect an absolutely massive payout as compensation?'

'You think there are descendants of this child?' James puffed out his cheeks. 'Okay, that would be huge. A lot of things would fit together … but it's still not proof, by a long shot. As long as we don't have proof, we can't use that.'

'DNA testing!' Alice said. 'Something the Victorians didn't have!'

## CHAPTER 24

'DNA testing shows who you're descended from but it doesn't prove they were married.'

'That's true again. Oh, damn it. You know, if we don't find any evidence with Thomas Hudson then we're lost.' Alice sighed out loud. All of a sudden it became clear to the two of them just how small a straw they were clinging to. If they failed then they would have nothing to show for their efforts, and Charles Brown and James's father would have died for nothing. There had to be some kind of justice in this world.

And meanwhile, William Johnson would still be on their tail. James thought about their conversation in the Windsor Castle archives and a slight shiver came over him.

'Are you cold?' Alice asked.

'No, no, no, no. Everything's fine. I was just thinking that Mr Johnson is exactly the kind of person we're talking about. He believes in the system, he doesn't want to lose it and he's willing to kill for it. I can't get rid of the feeling that he won't rest until we're both dead!'

\*

Ingrates. Meddlers. Fools!

William Johnson paced up and down in his office.

It was all the fault of that little man, Thomas Black! It had to be. The Queen had always abided by his decisions and the Prime Minister never knew what day of the week it was until someone told him.

And someone had. Someone had whispered poison into his ear and it had soaked all the way through to his brain. How he would have loved to put a bullet into the little man's head!

Eventually Johnson could put it off no longer. He started to throw his personal belongings into a large box he had taken from the cupboard. Actually, it wasn't much. A few books and odds and ends. After giving his whole life to the Royal Family, he hadn't had much time to collect souvenirs.

And this was how they rewarded him, he thought savagely. Well, they could throw him out but he would never desert them, never abandon them. One way or another he would continue to serve, with or without their knowing ...

His computer pinged.

Johnson automatically glanced at the pop-up on the screen, fully expecting some notification from a random mailing list that he would soon be taken off.

But it wasn't. He saw the registration number of Charles Brown's Mini.

'Oh, great timing!' he muttered, but he quickly clicked on the message.

The Mini had been spotted parked in a back lane of Arundel. It didn't have a resident's permit and a sharp-eyed traffic warden had entered it on their system. The registration number had automatically made its way to Johnson's inbox.

'Arundel?' he murmured.

How much longer would he have access to the system? How soon would they rescind his credentials? Johnson didn't know how fast Palace IT moved and he wasn't

## CHAPTER 24

going to wait to find out. His fingers tapped on the keyboard as he called up a list of residents in that road.

They included a couple called Kent.

He thumped the top of his desk in triumph.

Okay, he had this information – what should he do with it? For the time being he still had the resources of every police and intelligence computer in the country at his fingertips, if he could just think of the right questions to ask ...

The Mini appeared to have sat there for some hours. He didn't think James Kent and Alice Gull would just be hanging around for some hours. Not in Arundel. William Johnson knew just about everything there was to know that was connected with Jack the Ripper, and he was certain there was nothing for them in Arundel.

Conclusion: they had changed transport.

Did the Arundel Kents have a car?

*Click ... click ...*

Yes, they did. An eleven-year-old jeep.

And that was when another notification came in. Alice Gull had used her debit card to buy petrol at some services on the A303, westbound-side.

The screen went blank and a fresh box appeared.

*'You are attempting to access information for which you are not currently cleared ...'*

Johnson snorted. So, he was officially off the system. He threw his last valuables into the box, clamped it under his right arm, and walked out of the office and along the long, tall corridors of Buckingham Palace for the last time.

# JACK

His blue Rover stood in the gravel yard outside. Carelessly he threw the box on to the passenger seat and sat down at the wheel. The engine howled as he turned the key.

*The A303, westbound?*

Lost in thought, he drove out on to Buckingham Palace Road.

It could only mean one thing.

*They're on their way to Dartmoor.*

He chuckled at the back of his throat as he wove his way between two black cabs.

*Good luck to them!*

He was so lost in thought that he didn't notice the black Land Rover following him – but then, its driver had been trained to avoid detection.

# CHAPTER 25

The wild and foggy moorland had lived at the back of James's mind ever since he read Conan Doyle's *The Hound of the Baskervilles*. It had been the eerie backdrop to his thoughts for so long that the barren and gloomy landscapes made him shudder.

Tired and exhausted, James finally pulled the jeep up in Princetown. As Alice had predicted, just following the signs to HMP Dartmoor had done the trick to get them there. Slowly James drove along the high street and looked for a pub. He was bursting for a pee, he was hungry and he wanted to stretch his legs after their marathon drive, and a pub seemed the best bet for dealing with all of those options before they pushed on to the end of their journey, Buckland.

Finally, he found exactly what he was looking for. The Railway Inn looked like a cosy pub: the sign suggested it had once been the railway station of a horse-drawn railway. James parked in one of the few spaces at the front of the house and gently woke Alice up.

'What? Where are we?' she asked with a startle.

'In the mire of horror!' James intoned. Alice looked at him confused.

'We're on Dartmoor. Princetown,' James quickly added.

'Aha!' Alice climbed slowly out of the car, her limbs looking as stiff as James's felt. The sun was low in the sky, just thinking about turning red in time for sunset, and there was no sign of the infamous fog.

They stepped into the little pub together. The dimly lit taproom smelled of stone and wood, and was completely empty apart from one very old fogey in the corner and the landlord, who gave them a cheery greeting.

'What can I get you?' he asked.

'Can we have the card, please?' James asked carefully. He wasn't sure if there was such a thing in a pub in the country, though most pubs in London served food.

'But of course.' The man reached under the wooden counter and laid a pair of glossy, laminated menus in front of them. James quickly learned not to prejudge the countryside. The choice of food was just as wide as in London, and cheaper with it. James ordered a pasta dish and Alice chose a juicy steak. Then they sat with their drinks and pondered their thoughts. Alice looked out through the little old glass panes. The sun bathed the Dartmoor National Park in red light.

'Strange that this area is so famous for its ghost stories,' she said. 'It all looks so peaceful.'

As they were the only three in the room, apart from the old guy in the corner, the landlord took this as an invitation to join in the conversation. Another quaint country custom, James supposed.

'Oh, there's some great ghost stories around here all right. Some may even be true.'

## CHAPTER 25

'Such as?' James asked sceptically. The landlord propped his elbows on the wooden counter.

'Well, there was a criminal, his name was David Davis, who was locked up in the prison in 1879. He served his sentence until his death in 1929, a full fifty years of his life. During his imprisonment David worked as a shepherd on the moor, a job he loved very much. When he was finally released, he deliberately committed another crime to get back to prison and his sheep. They say he never broke up with the animals, not even after his death. Sometimes you see him as Spirit Shepherd, a fleeting phenomenon in the fog. Just ask John Tucker, there.' The landlord raised his voice towards the man in the corner. 'Isn't that right, John?'

'Aye, I seen the dead shepherd with me own eyes,' the man said, with an accent so thick that James was certain he put it on for the tourists. 'He were wearin' a long, dark, hooded coat. I just got back from Moretonhampstead and I stood about an 'undred yards from him. Suddenly he noticed I were there and he turned around …'

'And then what?' James asked with false curiosity.

'Then I could see his face! His eyes were fiery red and his skin were lime white. I were so scared, I just drove off with my bike. You must, because otherwise the devil will drag you on to the moor and you will never come back!'

John Tucker knocked back the rest of his pint in one go, set his empty glass on the counter and staggered off to the back room, while Alice and James struggled to keep straight faces.

'I can see you don't believe us,' their host said. They couldn't tell if his apparent offence was real or put on.

'Have you ever seen anything yourself?' James asked.

'Well, since, you ask! Yes, I have indeed!' The landlord took a deep breath and began his story. 'Jay's Grave, between Hound Tor and Heatree Cross. It is said that the grave discovered in 1860 is that of Kitty Jay, a girl who committed suicide at a young age. Until 1823, it was customary to bury suicides with a stake through the body at crossroads outside the village so that their confused souls would not find their way into the village. Since the discovery of the tomb, flowers have always been lying here, without anyone ever being seen laying them down. And I know that, since I walk by there every day!'

'Amazing,' Alice said sincerely, gently kicking James's shin bone, just in case he was going to disagree. But he had already seen something to change the subject.

The pub had a dartboard on the wall next to the large open fireplace, and names were chalked up on the scoreboards on either side. One, he recognised.

'Thomas Hudson,' he said, with a grin. He nodded towards the board. Alice spun around quickly to see it, and a huge smile spread over her face.

'The very man!'

'Oh, aye?' The landlord followed their gaze towards the board. 'You know him?'

'He's the reason we're here,' James said. 'We're on our way to Buckland-in-the-Moor – do you know it?'

'Well, well. Small world,' the landlord said sadly. 'Aye, I know Buckland – but you've had a wasted journey.'

## CHAPTER 25

Alice and James's smiles slowly froze. Not again! Not another setback!

'And why's that …?' Alice asked. James already had a bad presentiment.

'Well, he died a week ago.'

James closed his eyes and hung his head.

'No!' Alice exclaimed.

'Yes, unfortunately. Took us all by surprise. He was playing cards with us the night before, wasn't he, John?' the man said to John Tucker, who had come back into the room. The old man nodded his head slowly.

'He were a good man,' Tucker agreed. 'Always helpful and nice.'

'Are there relatives or heirs?' James wanted to know. He could not come to terms with the thought that they had come all the way for nothing.

'Not that I know of. Thomas was a loner.'

'So, what happened, if it took you by surprise?' asked James.

The landlord looked like he was chewing on a wasp.

'Suicide, mate. With a hairdryer in the bathtub. He didn't seem depressed last time I saw him. I'd say more of a joie de vivre. But that was the verdict.'

'Strangely popular, all of a sudden, too,' John Tucker added. 'You two today and t'other guy last week.'

James had been reaching for his glass. His hand froze.

'Other guy?' he asked, as casually as he could, though he felt sick with realisation that he was going to recognise the description.

'Long hair,' John Tucker. 'Youngish, bit older than you. Black suit.'

'Ah, yes!' Alice said significantly. 'He must be the family lawyer we met, remember, James?' She held his gaze steadily, though he just wanted to scream, with rage and frustration that Johnson had notched up another killing and they hadn't been able to do a thing about it. Not that they could have. This must all have happened before he had even got involved with Jack the Ripper.

'Yes,' he agreed. 'The lawyer.'

He suddenly realised it was getting difficult to see inside the taproom. The light through the windows had almost vanished.

'Is it going to rain?' Alice asked. 'It didn't look like it earlier.'

'No, my dear, it's the famous fog,' the landlord said cheerfully. 'If you're lucky, it'll clear up as soon as it came. If you're unlucky you won't be able to see three metres.'

'Will we be able to drive to Buckland?' James asked.

'Sure,' the man shrugged. 'Just go slow and keep your lights on. From time to time there'll be small gaps in the fog, where you can see a little further, but the moment you step on the gas, the next wall of fog comes down. Drive out of town, then at Two Bridge turn right. Follow your nose and then you're already there. Your man Thomas's house was first on the left when you enter the village, after the bridge.'

## CHAPTER 25

*

'Out of interest, what are we looking for?' Alice asked.

James drove slowly through the fog. It was still daylight, technically speaking – the sun was still up, somewhere, which meant they drove through a light grey haze. He could see the sides of the road on the left and the right, because the lane was sunken between steep banks crowned with bushes, but ahead it just disappeared into more grey. If there was a sharp turn ahead then he would never know until he hit it, and so he crawled along at twenty.

'We'll see when we get there,' he said flatly. 'I'm not going to have come this far and just head back home again without at least setting eyes on the place. Maybe something will turn up. There's only one way to find out.'

Alice was silent for long enough that he thought she might be coming up with a really good argument against that point of view. But in the end she just agreed, 'Fair enough.'

They turned off the main road at the first turning the landlord had described, and very quickly had to slow down even more as they hit their first pothole. The jeep lurched as James slammed it into an even lower gear.

'Thank God we borrowed Howard's jeep. I'm sure it would have been a lot of fun with the Mini,' he said. From Alice came a snort of agreement.

The road ahead began to slope upwards into the murk and a pair of low stone walls appeared on either side. They were crossing the bridge into Buckland-in-the-Moor. James pulled over on the left side of the road.

'He said first on the left after the bridge, but I suggest we do it on foot. We could just drive right past it in this.'

They climbed out of the jeep into the clammy air outside. It didn't take long to find the low wall on the left, next to the car. They followed it and very soon came to a gate.

'Bingo,' James murmured. A brass plate was fixed to it, with an engraved name: 'Thomas J. Hudson.' They had reached their goal.

They walked up the gravel drive to the house. It was a cute little cottage, single storey, thatched, with white, narrow windows that stood out from the grey granite stone. The part of the garden they could see through the dense fog was quite wild. Wildflowers and weeds grew everywhere.

A bell pull hung on a chain next to the dark, wooden door.

'So, do we ring?' Alice asked.

'I suppose.'

'Your uncle said Thomas Hudson was the sole descendant, and he's dead.'

James grunted.

'Being sole descendant doesn't mean he didn't have a wife, or partner, or kids of his own who are too young to show up on the electoral roll, or … whatever. Maybe a housekeeper or cleaner. Anyone he might have said something to. And if none of that works then put it this

## CHAPTER 25

way – this place may be the end of the road, but we've got to go all the way. Haven't we?'

'So, ring the bell already.'

James pulled on the chain and they heard a bell chime inside, sounding far too cheerful for this dank day. After they had waited a while, James pulled the handle again.

'Nobody seems to be here.'

'I could have told you that, but you never listen to me,' Alice joked.

'Honey, I always listen to you.' Tired and exhausted, James turned to Alice and leaned against the wooden door. 'So, shall we try the neighbours—'

The door flew open under his weight and he toppled backwards to land on a cold stone floor.

'Oh, that hurts!' Alice said as she helped James, groaning, back to his feet.

They looked around, James still rubbing the back of his head. The hallway was dark. James fumbled around on the wall by the door for a light switch and flicked it. Nothing happened.

'If the power's off, that doesn't look good for our thinking someone else might live here,' Alice said.

'Or maybe this is normal for Dartmoor. Have you got a lighter?'

'I think you've worked out I don't smoke by now – but I'm pretty sure there was a torch in the car.'

Alice disappeared back into the fog. James peered around the hallway as his eyes adjusted to the gloom. It wasn't big – just a couple of metres wide and maybe three long. He could see a coat stand next to the door, and an umbrella leaning against the wall next to it. There were three doors – ahead, left and right. The floor was paved with large, rough slabs of Dartmoor granite, as the back of his head had already told him.

After a few minutes Alice came back with the torch.

'The fog has gone mad. I could hardly find the car if I didn't have the wall to follow. Here's the lamp.'

'Thank you.'

James turned it on and scanned the hall with the cone of light. The door to their left led into the kitchen. As they stepped in, they realised with sinking hearts that they were not the first to come this way.

'Poltergeist?' Alice said. All the kitchen utensils had been tipped into a pile on the table in the middle of the floor. The drawers had all been yanked out and piled up in one corner.

Alice quickly confirmed that the cupboards were all empty too.

'I know there are companies that clear out the houses of dead people with no families,' she said. 'Do you think this is something like that? They'd need to do an inventory.'

'I think they'd be neater. Let's try the other rooms,' was James's only comment, made without hope.

The bedroom was through the middle door in the hallway, straight ahead of the front door. It, and the small bathroom beyond it, were an unholy mess. All the cupboards had been opened and the contents thrown to the floor. The pillows and even the mattress had been

## CHAPTER 25

slashed. There was a coal stove in the corner, with the door hanging open and the ash grate tipped out.

'Still think this is estate clearance?' James asked. Alice gently kicked him.

'I think Mr Johnson was looking for something.'

'And he didn't find it,' James said soberly. He wandered into the middle of the room, his arms hanging limply by his side. 'Shit.'

Depression hovered at the edges of his mind. He knew that if he dropped his guard against it then it would come rushing in and crush him. The room looked as desolate as he felt. Ripped up and torn apart.

There was nothing here, and never had been.

'How do you know he didn't find it?' Alice asked.

'Think it through. We're only here out of desperation, *just in case* Abberline passed something on to his descendants. But Johnson, who knows much more about this than we do, was certain Abberline *did* pass something on – and if he'd found it, then he'd know we don't have it and therefore we're no threat and he wouldn't be trying to kill us.'

Alice groaned.

'Poor Hudson. Tortured and killed for nothing.'

Despite everything, James's spirits lifted – slightly. Not at what had happened to Hudson, but because he was with a woman whose first thought was for the poor man, not for the failure of their own quest.

'I doubt that bothered Johnson.'

# JACK

'We should keep looking,' Alice said. 'There's a third room. Just in case. Nil desperandum, as my father liked to say.'

'Never despair,' James agreed glumly. 'Whatever. Lead on.'

The third door from the hallway led into the small living room. It had a patterned sofa and two matching armchairs in front of the fireplace, and they too were slashed. The books had been thrown off the shelves and what looked like a couple of expensive vases lay in ruins. Like the other rooms, all the drawers were pulled out and their contents tipped into a pile.

Carefully, Alice and James climbed across the room. Even the pictures had been pulled off the walls and lay in the ruins of their frames. They looked helplessly at each other. Where would they start their search?

Alice kneeled down and picked up a book at random from the wooden floor.

'A biography of Gandhi. That will be helpful.' She flipped through it.

'And over here we have science and technology.' James poked through some of the discarded books with his toe. He was standing in front of the large stone fireplace opposite the door. Lumps of coal had been tipped out of the scuttle on to the carpet, and the cinders that were all that was left of the last fire had been kicked apart.

'I haven't seen a good coal fire since my grandparents were alive. Grandma always let me build it up and get it going. They're probably illegal now.'

## CHAPTER 25

They poked around in the room a little more, but even Alice's optimism seemed to be waning as they drew another blank. She pushed a couple of torn-up pictures away and sat down on the sofa.

'Remember your uncle said this place was probably in Hudson's family for generations? If there was something hidden here then he might not even have known it.'

'That would still have occurred to Johnson. He would have already looked everywhere we can think of. Do you think this place has outhouses?'

'Probably. Or an attic, or …'

James's eyes flew wide open as the thought hit him. He slapped his brow. 'Of course!'

Alice stared at him as he turned a slow circle, looking intensely at the floor.

'No, not in here – not anywhere there's a carpet …'

James strode out into the hallway with a few quick steps. Alice hurried after him and found him crouching down, peering at the stone flags.

'And here we are!'

'Here we what?'

James grinned up at her.

'Coal fire in the living room, coal stove in the bedroom – where does the coal come from?'

'Um …'

'Coal cellar! Just like my grandparents used to have. Look, here, and here.'

He quickly indicated small holes at either end of the slab. At first glance they just looked like uneven weathering, like all the other slabs, but they were positioned symmetrically.

'You take that end …'

Alice knelt on the cold stone floor and slid her fingers into the nearest opening. James did the same at the other end.

'Ready?' he asked.

'Ready!' With all their might they pulled on the stone slab.

It flew open so quickly that they toppled backwards in surprise. The slab was a counterbalanced trapdoor – after all, Alice reminded herself, an old man living on his own had had to be able to open it …

A few small steps led down into a brick-lined room. James grabbed the torch and went first.

The cellar was as wide as the hall, and as long as the house above it, but not much more than one and a half metres high. They couldn't stand upright. In one corner were some brown wooden boxes and the far end was taken up with a pile of black, glistening coal. The smell of it was thick in the air, and the brick walls and stone floor were covered in a thin layer of coal dust.

But there were no recent footprints, and the coal and the boxes were still neatly stacked.

'No one's been looking down here,' James breathed with mounting excitement.

'I guess Johnson's grandparents didn't have a coal cellar. Let's have a look in the boxes.'

They started to rummage, mindless of the dust that smeared across their hands. The first box was old

## CHAPTER 25

newspapers, dry and yellow – but from the sixties onwards, all too recent to be anything to do with Jack the Ripper. The next was empty jars, then empty bottles ...

James felt his pounding heart beat faster and faster at first, as every box without anything useful suggested that surely the next one would be it! And then the next, and the next, and slowly he began to face up to the terrible possibility that they were *still* going to find nothing.

And nothing was what they found.

'One place left,' he muttered despondently as he let the last box drop to the floor. They looked together at the pile of coal. James had a feeling it was looking back at them.

'I do *not* want to go digging in there,' Alice said.

'We might not have a choice.'

Alice very slowly and reluctantly reached for the shovel resting against the wall. Hiding something under all that coal, they both thought, would be a very good place indeed. Any thief would have to be really motivated to go looking for it.

But Alice's eye followed the shaft of the shovel down towards the floor. She paused.

'Would you say Mr Hudson was a modest guy?' she asked.

'He didn't live very grandly,' James agreed.

'No ostentation, not even a family crest anywhere in the whole house?'

'Not that I saw.'

'Except here.'

# JACK

There were faint outlines in the floor visible beneath the ever-present layer of dust. They seemed to be part of a design that poked out beneath the front edge of the coal pile. Alice scraped the coal away with the tip of the shovel, then scrunched up one of the old newspapers from a box and wiped at the dust that was left behind.

Slowly, a very familiar design emerged, monochrome, lines of coal dust filling grooves etched into a stone slab that had been mortared into the brick floor. They both recognised it even before they had cleared away much more than the hind feet of the heraldic lion and unicorn. It was Britain's most famous coat of arms – the royal arms of the monarch.

'Why would Mr Hudson put that there?' Alice asked.

'Maybe he didn't. Maybe it was his grandfather or great-grandfather. *X* marks the spot!'

James set the torch down so that it shone on the crest, and tapped at the stone slab with the tip of the shovel. The sound that came back was hollow.

'There are no holes in this,' Alice pointed out. 'Maybe it's not designed to be lifted.'

'Or, only once in a lifetime – in an emergency,' James said.

He raised the shovel high and smashed it down on the slab. And again. And again. The mighty *clang* echoed around the cellar and Alice had to clasp her hands over her ears.

James reversed the shovel in his hands and thumped down with the handle, like a pile driver.

## CHAPTER 25

A crack appeared in the stone and a small chip fell away to reveal a dark hole. James worked his fingers into the hole and heaved.

The slab lifted up. He laid it to one side and peered eagerly in while Alice shone the torch into the cavity underneath.

It was no more than a small, brick-lined trench – just deep enough to contain a bundle wrapped in leather.

*

They handled it very carefully, as though it were a sacrament. James wanted to tear it open there and then, but they took it up to the kitchen and wiped the thin layer of dust away with a moist cloth. Then they washed their hands, making them as clean as possible.

But it was still too dark to read the dense handwriting of the papers, even by torchlight. They returned to the car and drove through the clearing fog back to the Railway Inn. They ordered sandwiches, to keep the landlord happy, and then borrowed a quiet alcove off the main taproom.

They sat side by side at the table with the bundle in front of them. James carefully undid the buckles on the strap that held the whole thing together, then peeled away the folds of leather to reveal a pile of yellowing papers.

The first item was a small note, handwritten with smart, old-fashioned calligraphy. James held it so they could both read it together:

Dear Inspector Abberline,
Here is the truth about the case you've been working on for so long. Now that my master has passed away, I see no reason to keep the secret any longer. Use this information wisely. Too many people have already died for this.
Respectfully
A friend of the truth.

'What does that mean?' asked Alice.

James just shook his head and picked up the next paper. It was a letter again, but on a larger sheet that felt much heavier and more expensive. At the top was the royal coat of arms. They began to read it together again, though James's hands began to tremble and Alice had to steady it with a hand of her own.

London, 10 August 1888

Dear Dr Acland

James stopped, and looked at Alice.

'Wasn't an Acland one of your ancestors?'

'Sir Theodore Dyke Acland,' Alice said tonelessly. 'My great-great-grandfather. He married Sir William Gull's daughter.'

They went back to the letter.

Dear Dr Acland,

## CHAPTER 25

> As you are one of the most experienced doctors known in the field of brain research, we ask you for a favour. I enclose details of one Mrs Annie Elizabeth Crook. This person suffers from delusions and disturbs the public well-being with her absurd stories. We therefore ask you to undertake the treatment of this individual so that she can live in peace again and the public no longer be harassed. We will show our gratitude for your work. We also ask that you treat this case as discreetly as possible to avoid creating even more difficulties.
> Respectfully,
> Salisbury

'Just, Salisbury,' James said.

'It must be Lord Salisbury. Lords don't use their titles when they sign something. He was prime minister at the time.'

'So, what does this tell us?'

'Let me see.' Alice took the paper and read the letter again quickly. 'James – Annie Crook, that's the prostitute Prince Eddy is meant to have married!'

'It says she's delusional. Maybe she really did think she had?'

Alice shook her head.

'I don't think so. There are nutcases in every generation, and if she was one of them then she would just be ignored until the next one came along. But for the prime minister to get involved? No, she must have had something on them.'

Alice's mouth fell open as the truth finally sank in.

'Oh, my God, then that part of the conspiracy is true!'

James took up the next sheet of paper.

>
> Guy's Hospital, London,
> 12 August 1888
>
> My Lord,
>
> Enclosed you will receive confirmation of the work carried out. I would like to take this opportunity to thank you very much for the cheque for 10,000 pounds. Rest assured, the money will be well spent.
>
> Respectfully,
> Dr T. Acland
>
>
> Patient files 23/08/1888
> Annie Elizabeth Crook
>
> Diagnosis: Delusion and severe mental instability.
> Treatment: Separation of the anterior hemisphere.

## CHAPTER 25

> Although the patient has been cured by the operation, she is unfortunately no longer able to participate in public life. She has therefore, for her own safety, been taken to the insane asylum of St George.
>
> Signature of the attending physician:
> Dr T.D. Acland

They studied the paper together, letting it sink in.

'I'm betting "Separation of the anterior hemisphere" isn't a nice thing,' Alice said eventually. James remembered what George Anderson had told him about the fate of Annie Crook.

'It's a lobotomy,' he said eventually. 'They cut her brain up while she was still alive, and turned her into a living vegetable.'

Alice's voice trembled and there was the faintest hint of tears in her eyes.

'All so that she could do no harm to the Royal Family. How cruel and heartless!'

She blinked furiously and stared into a corner of the room while James silently read the next item.

He laid it flat on the table.

'This is the one,' he said quietly.

Now it was his turn to look away while Alice read it.

JACK

Scotland Yard, London
20 August 1888

Dear Dr Acland,
We are very satisfied with your work to date on the matter that is known to both of us.

We have a further favour to ask.

It has come to our attention that some of the allegations made by Mrs Crook were not without an element of truth. We had assumed the relationship between her and the Duke of Clarence to be of a purely physical nature, which was displeasing to Her Majesty but not of itself illegal.

We now learn that His Royal Highness, with no thought for the consequences, secretly underwent a marriage ceremony with the woman in question. Naturally, there are a number of legal obstacles that prevent this marriage from being valid. It was performed without the consent of Her Majesty, no bans were read and it is possible the ceremony was performed according to the Catholic rite, which would immediately render it void

## CHAPTER 25

for a man in the line of succession to the throne.

Nonetheless, the ceremony took place and was witnessed by the five individuals whose names are affixed. Their testimonies are every bit as explosive as was Mrs Crook's. Since you already have experience in this area, we ask you to take effective action cleanly and quickly.

Respectfully
Sir Robert Anderson

'The names are listed alphabetically,' James said quietly. 'Care to guess what they are?'

'Without even reading them,' Alice agreed grimly. 'Annie Chapman. Catherine Eddowes. Elizabeth Stride. Mary Ann Nichols. Mary Jane Kelly.'

Only then did she glanced at the end of the letter.

'Correct.' She sat back and puffed her cheeks out. 'Wow. There really was a royal conspiracy. And he didn't just lobotomise them, he ...' She trailed off for a moment. 'He slaughtered them,' she whispered. 'My great-great-great-grandfather wasn't Jack the Ripper' – Alice paused – 'But my great-great-grandfather was.'

James watched her closely, wondering how she would take it. Suddenly she gave a little shudder, like a dog shaking off water.

'Okay, so I'm descended from a slimeball. We all probably are if you go back far enough. Are you bothered?'

'Not if you're not,' he said with relief. He studied the bundle. 'So, what do we do with it?'

'Publish it,' she said promptly. 'Far and wide. We have proof the prince married Annie, so any kid they had would be in the line of succession.'

'Unless it really was a Catholic wedding,' James pointed out. 'Catholics were automatically disqualified from the throne. I'm pretty sure they still are.'

'Even so, there might be someone walking around out there with an absolutely massive grievance and claim against the Royal Family, and Johnson cares enough to kill anyone who might know it. So, we make sure that so many people know it that he can't go slaughtering everyone. You need to get on to your client, the guy who hired you to start all this, and let him know, for a start. Then send it to every paper and news channel you can think of.'

'Let's get the rest of the story first,' James suggested. He moved on to the next document. A slow grin spread across his face. 'Guess what. Your double-great-grandfather was a demented murderer, but your triple-great-grandad was okay.'

Guy's Hospital London<br>25 August 1888

Dear Lord Salisbury,

## CHAPTER 25

> I wish to express my severest displeasure at events that have come to my knowledge. The patient Annie Crook was in the best of health until without any reason a most questionable treatment was performed on her, apparently at your instigation. Please be informed that I have ordered the hospital management to conduct a full investigation of this affair. I have taken Mrs Crook into my care and will continue to treat her as best I can in her sadly and preventable debilitated condition.
>
> Respectfully,
> Sir William Gull

'I knew he was innocent! That's really great news.' Alice smiled full of joy at James and he couldn't resist a smile back.

'Not only did he not murder the prostitutes, he even tried to make things better!'

'Exactly. Well, as best he could. And a week later, the murders started ... Oh, dear God.' Suddenly her eyes were filling again. 'Was he why it happened? Because he was getting interested in the case? They couldn't move against someone as prominent as him, so they ...'

'Let's keep reading,' James said quickly.

London, 28 January 1890

# JACK

Dear Theodore,

It took a long time, but I have finally learnt your terrible secret. For my daughter's sake, I ask that we meet and settle this matter.

William Gull

'Well,' James said, 'that obviously didn't do him a lot of good.'

'No,' Alice said tonelessly, 'because he died on January 29th 1890, exactly one day after this letter. Apparently of a stroke – but I think a fellow doctor would know enough to fake one of those, don't you? Especially in a man who was already known to be unwell.'

James whistled.

'You mean he was murdered by his own son-in-law?'

'Hey, James, we're talking about Jack the Ripper. I think this murder was the easiest of all. The death certificate was issued by Dr Acland himself, which was unusual because normally relatives don't sign death certificates. There's always the suspicion that they want to enrich themselves by the death of their relative. But Acland could get away with it, of course, because he was a *gentleman*.' She spat the last word in disgust. 'And he was backed up by the prime minister and the chief of police – who was going to question it?'

## CHAPTER 25

James quietly placed Sir William Gull's last letter face down on the pile of all the other items. As he did so, a smaller note fell to the table. It was only on a scrappy piece of notepaper and the scribbled writing in smeared ink was barely decipherable. Maybe the poor quality of the ink had made it stick to the back to the back of Gull's letter.

> Mary, I don't think they'll let me live in peace much longer. Please take care of my child and bring her to the children's home of St Anna. She'll be safe there. Please hurry and keep it a secret.
> Annie

'Oh – my – God,' he breathed. 'There *was* a child.'

'And since Prince Eddy died before his father – that kid rightly should have been the next Queen when Edward VII died. Not George V, so, not any of George's descendants. Right down to the Queen we have now.' She studied the letter. 'I wonder who Mary was? Mary Kelly, the Ripper victim?'

James frowned, deep in thought.

'You know, we haven't got the whole story. Now we know there was a child, we need to know if she lived and had descendants.'

'And where do we find that out?'

James tapped the letter.

'St Anna's children's home, wherever that is.'

Alice closed her eyes.

'God, I'm tired, and I thought we were at the end – but you're right. What do you suggest?'

James began instinctively to reach for his pocket, the instinctive gesture of someone about to look up something on Google – then stopped with a grimace. Alice interpreted it correctly.

'I saw a payphone as we came in. Is there anyone you could ask?'

James thought.

'I don't want to call your family. Johnson might have their lines bugged by now. Ditto Uncle and Auntie …'

'You're a journalist. You must have heaps of contacts!'

Now James laughed.

'I'm a part-time food hack. I don't know …' Then he groaned and slapped his head. She looked at him.

'Yes?'

'My client!' he called, over his shoulder, as he was already hurrying out of the alcove to find the phone. 'He must have contacts coming out of his ears! And he'll need to know this eventually anyway, so I might as well bring him in now. Back in a moment!'

Alice nibbled her sandwich while she waited, though she was more tired than hungry, and leafed through the folder again. There was other stuff there further down – receipts, memos, notes, but the important material was the stuff at the top of the pile which they had already read.

James came back in five minutes later, looking pleased with himself.

## CHAPTER 25

'He's going to do some digging. Meanwhile he suggests we start back to London. We can find a Travelodge or whatever on the way and sleep there, and give him a call, by which time he should have something. Then we arrange to meet in the morning!'

Alice smiled weakly, but even bone tired as she was, she could feel a little more enthusiasm stoking up inside her.

'Every time we think we're there ... there's always something else, but it also always feels a little closer. Like Zeno's paradox.'

'Well, I'm going to get a double espresso before we go. It'll keep my eyes open at least till Exeter.'

Alice put all the paper back into the folder and buckled it back up, then took it with her as she went to join James at the bar, waiting for the coffee machine to do its job.

'I just realised, she said, 'you never told me who this client of yours actually is.'

'Oh, yeah.' James took the coffee and gave the landlord a grateful smile. 'No point in keeping it secret, I suppose. He's another of the Ripper descendants – Sir Robert Anderson was his great-whatever father. His name is Lord George Anderson.'

He raised his mug to his lips and took a grateful drink, before he realised she was staring at him.

'Problem?'

'James, you can't work for Lord George Anderson.'

'I was just talking to him on the phone.'

'No.' She shook her head brusquely. 'You weren't.'

'And why not?'

## JACK

Alice brushed her blonde hair back off her face. 'Because he died almost a month ago!'

# CHAPTER 26

The most famous London street in the world was lined with tall buildings, and although it ran from east to west it also angled slightly towards the north. So, as the sun set, a wing of the Foreign and Commonwealth Office blocked it off and the street was cast into shadow.

The street's most famous resident lived in what anywhere else would have looked like an inconspicuous Georgian terraced house. You couldn't tell from its simple exterior that inside the original property had been knocked through and combined with other houses, creating a warren of over a hundred rooms: offices, meeting rooms, reception rooms, sitting rooms, dining rooms, bathrooms and a kitchen – and, on the top floor, a rather meagre two-bedroom private apartment for the official occupant. Its bricks, originally yellow, had been blackened by centuries of pollution. When London was finally cleaned up, the bright yellow paint had been repainted black, such was the reputation and image that the building had acquired.

The house had the most famous front door in the world, austere and black, with a door knocker shaped like a lion's head, and the house number – 10 – and a brass plaque with the occupant's official title, First Lord of the Treasury. The house had been lived in by the holder of that title for over three hundred years.

The current holder, also known as the Prime Minister of the United Kingdom of Great Britain and Northern Ireland, was looking impatiently at the clock. He was famously unflappable in public, but that exterior hid deep undercurrents of emotion and he was not looking forward to this conversation.

He had successfully headed Her Majesty's government now for ten years. During that time he had learned to love and appreciate the old woman and the system that she headed. She was a constant in fast-moving, fast-changing times. As far as the Prime Minister knew, she had never changed or altered her principles in all the years of her reign and he found that remarkable. Of course, she could seem very cold and unreachable because of her position, but she had nevertheless brought the old traditions closer to the people.

The head of her government looked thoughtfully out of the window, through which he could just make out the tips of the trees of St James's Park. Too much had happened lately. He had made some wrong decisions, though he had always been convinced that what he was doing was right. Concerns in foreign policy were now being joined by concerns at home. His most trusted minister had been caught with his pants down with his secretary, giving the tabloids a field day, and he knew it was only a matter of time before he received the inevitable resignation. Then there was the alleged donations scandal. As though he would ever let people buy their way into the nobility! He had too much respect for the institution to allow such a thing – but it did look like some of his subordinates had

## CHAPTER 26

been taking a more flexible view behind his back, and the buck stopped with him. It was a blow not only against his battered party but one against himself.

So many scandals, and even loyal colleagues were starting to whisper the 'R' word, *resignation* ...

The Prime Minister had always thought the British government's greatest strength was that it was essentially one big committee. It could always withstand the loss of an individual, even the one at its head. But if you happened to *be* that individual, suddenly a strength looked a lot like a major flaw.

He could not quite bring himself to face the thought yet. He had promised the British people that he would exercise the responsibility assigned to him until the end. Still, he knew that soon he would have to make a statement and it would certainly not be his finest hour.

And to cap it all there was William Johnson.

Let no one question it, Johnson had done a really excellent job for ten years. Who could have told he was an unhinged maverick? No one could have known he would turn out like this! Yes, Prime Minister, but you *should* have known, they would say ... The man was a ticking time bomb and *you* let him near the Queen.

It had been quite satisfying to see the shock on the man's face when he learned that he was being fired. The Prime Minister suspected he would have been even more shocked if he had known where the impetus for the firing came from. Not from Her Majesty but from the club.

# JACK

He had been introduced to the club only a few months after his first election victory. He had heard of it before, of course – it had many legends attached to it but he had never taken it seriously. Then, having just been elected into what should have been the most powerful office in the land, he had realised how little power he actually had without the club's say-so.

Contrary to popular belief, it was not a conspiratorial secret society. It was a global, humanitarian community. Its statutes, writings and rituals were open to public scrutiny. Its cornerstones were straight out of the Age of Enlightenment: freedom, equality, fraternity, tolerance, humanity. Those were values that had been the central message of the Prime Minister's own campaign.

But behind all that lay one key, overruling principle: protect the Crown. And the Crown – the firm, as the Queen and her husband liked to call it – had needed protecting. Not so much recently, but there had been times when members of the family behaved so badly that the idea of a republic received serious public consideration. They still spoke in whispers of the last really serious crisis, in the time of Edward VII, the playboy king who would not keep his nose out of politics. Diana's death had come a close second.

At those times, the club began to stir, and woe betide anyone who got in its way. Considering what had happened at the end of the nineteenth century, Johnson was lucky to have got away with being fired …

A knock disturbed the Prime Minister's thoughts.

'Mr Black, sir.'

## CHAPTER 26

'Show him in.'

Thomas Black didn't walk into rooms, the Prime Minister thought with distaste. He insinuated himself into them. Now, Black insinuated himself on to the sofa opposite the Prime Minister.

'Thank you for receiving me so quickly, Prime Minister,' he said, in a way which suggested he would have been very surprised if it hadn't happened.

'What can I do for you?' the Prime Minister asked cautiously. He wasn't quite sure what to make of the little advisor. All the signs – tailor-made suit, expensive watch, and of course Oxford-educated – were that he was the right sort of person to be perfectly anonymous in the Civil Service, quietly indispensable to a series of ministers until eventually he retired to the Shires with a fortune in his pension pot.

And until recently Black seemed to have been just that – until suddenly he emerged from his shadowed lair, rapier swift, the one man who could bring down William Johnson.

'I wondered, Prime Minister, what you intend to do in the Johnson case?'

The Prime Minister harrumphed.

'I don't quite follow you. As I recall, we've already done everything humanly possible. He's no longer an employee of the Crown or the state. Anything else is beyond our remit.'

'Really? I've heard he's still up to his ears.'

'We're a constitutional state, Thomas. If Mr Johnson causes any more problems, he'll have to stand trial.'

'Prime Minister.' Black's smile was thin. 'You know what will happen if half of what Mr Johnson knows becomes public knowledge. Don't you think it's time to get this problem resolved – without a trial?'

The Prime Minister looked at the little man in surprise. Did he just hear right?

'What exactly do you mean?'

Black stared coldly back.

'You know exactly what I mean. Haven't you discussed this in your little club?'

The Prime Minister hid his amazement. He was certain Black wasn't a member. How could the little gnome actually know?

'I'm really sorry, but I'm afraid I can't follow you. What exactly are you suggesting?'

'I believe the correct term is your *lodge*, Prime Minister, as if you didn't know. The people who want to protect the Crown more than anyone else. Don't they have views?'

'What if they do?' the Prime Minister snapped. 'We have the rule of law in this country! No secret cabal has more power than the courts! The Johnson case will be handled legally and discreetly, and I don't need you to advise me otherwise. This audience is over.'

The Prime Minister stood up and looked down on Mr Black. With a smile, Black rose from his own seat and despite the differences in their height, the Prime Minister felt that he was the one being looked down on.

'You haven't fully grasped the gravity of the situation, Prime Minister. You won't be in office much longer. You and I both know that. The question now is what remains

## CHAPTER 26

for you. Will you go down in history as the PM who acted, or as the one who stood by and let it happen?'

'Thank you for your philosophical advice, but I didn't hire you for it.'

'You didn't hire me at all, Prime Minister, and neither did your club. Please think about what I have said. Goodbye, Prime Minister.'

The little man stepped into the hall and disappeared. The Prime Minister stared after him, and was surprised to feel his heart pounding.

# JACK

# CHAPTER 27

The phone's ringing came as a relief to Sean Miller as he ploughed through the emails that had backed up the last few days. He sat back from the screen and picked the receiver up, gazing blankly out at traffic passing by on Millbank below his office window.

'Miller,' he said in a flat, routine monotone.

'Mr Miller, good morning. How is Millbank today?'

Sean rolled his eyes. He recognised the voice all right – the man from Jubilee Gardens. The tone was the kind of vague sarcasm that a certain kind of official just loved to use on subordinates, to make it plain exactly who was boss.

'Millbank is its usually lovely self and all the better for your asking.'

'I'm just wondering what you're doing there in your office.'

Sean smiled flatly. For all he knew, the man had the office bugged for vision.

'It's where I work when I'm not conducting goose chases.'

'A goose chase, Mr Miller? I thought I impressed upon you just how important your assignment was.'

'Oh, you did,' Sean agreed. 'And then I heard the news yesterday; just as I was tailing him, in fact. I see Mr Johnson has ...' – he made air quotes with the fingers of his free hand – '"For personal reasons, requested early termination of his contract". In other words, you had something on him that persuaded him to throw himself on his sword and it turned out you didn't even need the material I was collecting. So I naturally assumed the assignment was over.'

'Oh, no, Mr Miller not at all,' the voice chided, but with an undertone of threat that made Sean sit up and take notice. 'We need your evidence more than ever.'

'Really?' Sean asked warily.

'Oh, indeed. Have you ever watched a prize fight between two equally matched opponents? They spar, they jab at each other and then – wham! A powerful blow! The other man is down on the ground! But no. The umpire begins to count. One, two – and then he's up again until *wham!* The final knockout blow sends him down permanently.'

'A double whammy,' Sean said drily.

'If you like. The point is, Mr Johnson is down for the count but he will spring back unless he is put down permanently. See to it. Oh – and go to the BBC News website in, let's see, three minutes time. A story is about to break there that might be of interest. Good day, Mr Miller.'

'"A story is about to break there that might be of interest",' Sean mimicked after the phone was safely hung up. 'Pompous prat …'

But he still called up the BBC News site.

And yes, it was of interest.

CHAPTER 27

## PRIME MINISTER SET TO RESIGN

As a conference outside Number 10, the Prime Minister has just announced that he will resign from his post later this year. Her Majesty was informed of his decision at an unscheduled meeting first thing this morning. A precise timetable has not yet been set but it is believed he will work towards having his successor in place in time for the party conference in October.

Criticism is known to have mounted within the Cabinet of the Prime Minister's handling of a series of crises and scandals. His most likely successor, the Chancellor of the Exchequer, spoke of this being the right decision at the right time. Other leading party members also welcomed the announcement.

Rumours are flying that the move is also related to yesterday's resignation of the Queen's Security Counsel, William Johnson. When asked if there was a connection, the Prime Minister simply said that he would not endorse gossip. Mr Johnson's role has been taken on, in an acting capacity, by a formerly obscure junior member of the Home Office, Thomas Black. Mr Black is the first holder of the newly

> created position of Permanent Chief of Staff at
> 10 Downing Street ...

For a very brief moment Sean caught a glimpse of a short, familiar figure in a smart dark suit dashing into Number 10.

'Well, at least I know your name now,' he said out loud.

And then he thought.

*Obscure junior member? Bollocks. You, Mr Black, are anything but junior. This is just the face you choose to present to the world.*

And Mr Johnson?

Another ten seconds' thought, and suddenly Sean was on his feet and heading for the door.

If Mr Johnson was going to bounce back from this then it was going to be one almighty bounce – and that made him twice as dangerous.

\*

'That is definitely it?' Alice asked.

They sat in Howard and Mary's jeep in the shade of some plane trees and looked out at the mouldering red brick construction that was their destination. It was gloomy and Victorian and neither of them had any difficulty believing it had once been an orphanage. A small cobbled courtyard in front of the house was separated from the street by an iron gate. The front wall was lined with scaffolding and the windows were grey and dirty. Apart from the street lights and cars, and the

## CHAPTER 27

towers of the city poking above the roofline, this part of Whitechapel did not seem to have advanced much since the Victorian age.

'That's what he said,' James said quietly, not looking around. 'St Anna's, used to be part of the Royal London Hospital until it shut down. It's being renovated – probably going to be turned into flats.'

'And we believe your client ... why? When we know he's only pretending to be Lord George Anderson?'

James shook his head.

'I still can't believe that,' he murmured.

'I was at the funeral,' she reminded him. 'My mother talked me into going with my father because she couldn't do it herself. It was awfully boring. The only consolation was that William and Kate were there so I had someone to talk to.'

'But he seemed to know my father. He knew enough to convince me that he had. Why pretend to be Lord George? Why not just come to me in his own identity and hire me to do the same job?'

'Would you have taken it on if he hadn't pretended to have some kind of connection? You said yourself it's not the usual kind of thing you do. But this brings us back to – why do we believe him?'

They had followed the agreed plan the previous night. They had driven as far as Exeter and found a Travelodge to crash in, but not before calling the so-called Lord George Anderson. James hadn't mentioned anything about what Alice had revealed to him. He was curious to know just how far the man would go in the deception

– and the best way to get hold of him was to play along. You couldn't really do that over the phone. James wanted to meet the man whose play-acting had got him into a life and death situation, several times, face to face.

'Because why ever he did what he did, he obviously wants results, and this is how we deliver them. It wouldn't be in his interests to send us to a dead end now.'

'But that's no reason to sit quietly and let him turn up.' Alice pushed her door open and swung her legs out on to the pavement.

James waited a moment, then nodded and followed.

They crossed the road quickly to the building. James tentatively gave the gate a shake. It immediately gave way to the light pressure and swung open. They looked at each other, then walked through. A slight gust swept a few leaves across the yard. A skip full of builders' rubble and a pile of scaffolding lay over to one side but otherwise the place was empty. They were obviously there too early for the builders to have started work.

'I wonder where the orphanage kids are now?' Alice said.

'Maybe we can find someone who can help us look up the old records.'

Together they crossed the courtyard and stood in front of a large black double door. James knocked his fist on the wood. The only thing they heard was a *thud* echoing inside the house.

'No one home?' Alice commented after they had waited a minute. James looked thoughtfully at the old building, then at the gate, then at the builders' gear, then

## CHAPTER 27

back at the building. He stepped back and ran his gaze up and down and along the scaffolding that covered the facade.

'The builders wouldn't have just left their stuff here without locking the gate,' he said.

'So …?'

'Alice, didn't you wonder why the gate was open when the building is still locked?'

He could see her expression change as she realised.

'Honestly, no, I didn't. So, someone got here before us?'

'I think so, and I think they're inside.'

He nodded at the nearest window to the front door on the ground level. All the windows were covered with tarpaulins, but this one was bowed inwards as though it was being sucked in. James took hold of a corner of the tarpaulin and pulled it aside with a jerk. Behind it was an open sliding sash window. Its being open was no accident. Someone had smashed one of the frames to get at the latch inside, then slid the bottom half up.

They glanced at each other and read each other's minds.

There could very well be a man with a gun in there, waiting for them. He had turned up several times, always in unexpected places.

'It could just be a burglar,' James said quietly. 'Or Johnson. Or Lord George.'

'We can handle a burglar,' Alice answered, 'and Johnson's been sacked. We heard it on the radio. And as for George …'

He nodded. If it was the fake Lord George in there – well, as far as they knew, unlike William Johnson he wasn't a homicidal maniac. They were so close to some kind of resolution, they had to go on.

James hoisted himself over the sill and reached out a hand to help Alice climb in after him. Together they stood in the entrance hall of the children's home.

It was a big, bare room that smelled of dust and paint. The plaster on the walls was crumbling and the stone floor was covered with a large white sheet, held down with pots of paint. A scaffold tower stood in one corner so that the workers could reach the ceiling. To their left, a staircase curved up towards the next floor. A fallen paint bucket lay at the bottom of the stairs.

'I guess someone wasn't as careful as us,' Alice said. They could clearly see a trail of white footprints leading to the upper rooms. Quietly and carefully, they followed it up the stairs.

At the top was a high ceilinged grey corridor lined with grey steel doors to the left and right.

'This looks more like a jail than a home,' Alice murmured quietly.

A creak in the ceiling above them made them look sharply up. Someone was walking on the floor above.

The white footprints led along the corridor to a spiral staircase at the end. They sneaked carefully up the steps. At the top was another corridor, grey walled like the one they had just left but lined with old brown wooden doors. They crept towards the end, which would be where

## CHAPTER 27

they had heard the footsteps. The sign on the door said 'Archive'. Carefully, James pushed the door open.

He smiled grimly to himself as he recognised the bowed shape of the man who stood with his back to them, perusing the shelves. It was indeed the man who had claimed to be Lord George Anderson.

And so, he knocked loudly on the door and walked in.

'Knock, knock,' he said cheerfully – and froze.

The man had shouted loudly in surprise, and spun around – with a revolver in his trembling hand.

'Don't make a wrong move,' the old man ordered. 'Are we clear on that? Now, very slowly, come in.'

Carefully, Alice and James went into the room. It looked and smelled like an old library. On the walls there were old wooden shelves with files and old books heaped on them, presumably ready for putting into crates, though no one had got round to that stage yet. A few cupboards had been covered with white cloths because the painters had already erected a series of scaffold towers around the room for the ceiling. James and Alice stood in the middle of the room in front of one of the scaffolds.

'The gun isn't necessary,' Alice said calmly. The man smiled flatly.

'Perhaps not, but I have been following your progress and bodies have been accumulating, one way or another.'

'Not caused by us!' James said, outraged.

'Just say I want to be careful.'

'You're looking well, Lord George,' Alice commented. 'Given that I last saw you at your funeral.'

'Ah.' The smile grew wider. 'Lady Gull. I am pleased you two met – though that was one reason for getting you on the list for the Ripper Diary event, James. Well, I hired you as an investigator – I suppose I shouldn't be surprised what else you've found out.'

'So, would you be so kind as to tell us who you are and what you want?' James asked.

The old man nodded, released the hammer on the gun and laid it down on the table in front of him. He cocked his head at them, eyebrows raised. It was clear that he could still grab the gun more quickly than they could get at it, even if they tried, but it was a gesture of good faith.

'We're listening,' Alice said.

'I worked for Lord George Anderson,' the man said. 'My name is Roger Harris and I was His Lordship's personal assistant for many years. He was, quite frankly, not a nice man. He let me go for no reason at all a few years ago and I've been unemployed ever since. Do you know how hard it is for a sixty-five-year-old to find another job? Plus, I'm not in very good physical shape. I'm already very fragile and my legs are wonky.'

'Yes, and what does all this have to do with us?' Alice asked, already irritated by his self-pitying tone. He glared coldly at her.

'I'll get to that in a minute. I have a large family, and they are not well off either. All my children are unemployed and have families of their own to feed.'

His face turned red with anger.

## CHAPTER 27

'The system in England is just not fair!' he spat. 'If you are born into the working class then you have no chance of getting out. The good schools are reserved only for the children of the rich. The whole class system is a disgrace to this country!'

'And who do you blame for that?' James asked.

Roger Harris snorted.

'The system is so old you just can't tell who's to blame, but I know exactly who is at the head of the class system. As long as we have a Royal Family leading the way, nothing else will change.'

'That's bullshit!' Alice snapped. 'How many charities are they patrons of? How much good have they done for issues like the environment?'

'And how much more could be done if we all just pulled together instead of letting that lot take the lead?' Harris shrugged the point away. 'I came to fantasise about causing the first family in the country as much harm as I could. Making life so intolerable for them that they would run away like dogs and hide. But of course, it was just fantasy. What can one angry old man do? Then one evening, just before I went home, I heard His Lordship talking about the Ripper case. He had a theory, which if it was true … well. It would go a long way towards achieving my dreams. He hired your father –'

'Did Lord Anderson have anything to do with my father's death?' James demanded. Harris looked shocked.

'Oh, no! Of course not! Your father's death was very inconvenient for him because it left the case unsolved. Anyway, I decided to conduct my own investigations.

Even if I couldn't rid the country of the royals, I could do the next best thing for myself – blackmail them with what I knew, then after they had paid me the money, I would have sold the secret to the highest bidding journalist. So I would have won twice. But …'

'But you'd already guessed it would be a dangerous investigation, so you didn't want to do it yourself,' James stated with contempt. He felt the anger swell within him. Anger with himself, for falling for the old man's lies so easily, and anger with Harris for using him like a canary in a coal mine.

'And you very nicely confirmed His Lordship's theory. Jack the Ripper was Dr Acland, Sir William Gull's son-in-law, as you told me on the phone last night.' The old man's eyes were shining. 'His Lordship said he always believed Chief Inspector Abberline kept a copy of the key evidence, which Sir Robert Anderson couldn't get his hands on to suppress. So, I just need this evidence. Where is it?'

'In a safe place,' Alice said, 'which we have no intention of telling you about.'

'Really?' Harris glanced thoughtfully at his gun, still lying on the table. Then he held both hands up to show he didn't intend to pick it up. 'I could threaten and bluster – and maybe shoot you, James, because you are nothing to me. But I'll try persuasion.'

They both stared at him, not having the slightest idea of what he was talking about – and James wondering exactly what was meant about him not being important.

## CHAPTER 27

'I'm sure you found out that Mrs Crook's kid survived all these murders, right?' Harris asked.

Alice nodded.

'And that child was, arguably, the legitimate heir to the throne – and even if not, her descendants are arguably entitled to a lot of money,' James added.

With a broad smile, Roger Harris reached for the shelf behind him and produced a thick book. He placed it on the table next to the gun and opened it at a bookmarked page.

'You're so right. Now, in this book are all entries and exits for the year 1888. You have the honour of reading it. Here you go.' He turned it around and pushed it across the table towards Alice. She stepped forward and peered down to read the handwritten entry.

'Child: Alice Crook. Presented by: Mary Jane Kelly,' she read out aloud. 'So what? We already know –'

'Please read on, a little further down.'

Alice drew a breath and continued.

'Said child Alice Crook adopted on 20th January 1890 by …'

James stepped forward in alarm because Alice stopped so suddenly and her whole body sagged, as though she had just been hit by something.

'Oh, my God, that can't be right!'

'Oh, it's right. You've read it correctly, Lady Gull. Little Alice was adopted by Sir William Gull. But it gets better. As I'm sure you're aware, Sir William died just a few days later, on the 29th of January. So what happened to the little girl? Obviously, she was taken in by Sir William's other daughter, her big grown-up sister Caroline, who by that time was married to …'

'Theodore Acland,' Alice whispered.

'Perhaps he didn't realise who the baby was, perhaps he'd had enough of death, perhaps he just decided to raise the child in ignorance, because what harm could it do, he thought? Whatever the reason, the child lived. Your great-grandmother's name was Alice, wasn't it? You are the only heir to the love story of Prince Eddy and Annie Crook. And now, you are going to help me make my millions.'

Alice was too stunned to make any kind of reply.

'I don't think Alice is in on it with you,' James said cheerfully.

'Do shut up, James. As I have said, I have no use for you. I could shoot you at any time with no qualms.'

Roger Harris underlined his words by casually laying his hand on his gun. James looked at Alice, but she was lost in thought, still taking in what she had just learned. She was the rightful heir to the throne?

So, instead he studied Harris's hand carefully. It trembled – no question about that. It was just age but still, a trembling hand would not make a good shot. Could he get it away from Harris without getting hit?

It would just take one surprise, he thought, something Harris hadn't been expecting, to distract him. The old man moved more slowly than James did.

An escape plan was slowly forming in James's head. He could see the means for it in his peripheral vision. The

## CHAPTER 27

best bit was, it didn't involve moving towards Harris, so the old man would be taken completely unawares.

'You know what?' he said, holding up his hands peacefully. 'You're right.' He took a step backwards.

'You're going nowhere,' Harris snapped.

'Fair enough. I don't intend to.' James leaned with one hand casually on the scaffold tower – and shoved with all his strength.

What happened next did not match the plans he had made.

The tower was meant to wobble, just enough to alarm Harris and take his mind off the gun, which James would then run forward and grab.

But the tower toppled against the next tower in line, which rammed into the next one – and so on, around the room like dominoes. James had set a chain reaction in motion as more and more scaffolding and bookshelves fell to the ground. The noise of tumbling wood and metal was deafening.

James only had eyes for Alice, still standing stunned and only just waking up to what was going on around her. He grabbed at her and pushed her to the floor with his body on top of her, protecting her.

The noise seemed to go on forever but was probably only a few seconds. At last, James dared to lift his head slightly. The room was devastated. Books, broken panes of glass and steel scaffolding lay on the floor everywhere. Two of the old dirty stained glass windows were broken because a bookshelf had flown through them.

And Harris? Where was the old man and the gun?

James leapt to his feet. There was the gun, lying on the floor. With that priority taken care of, James helped Alice up, still casting an eye around for Roger Harris.

'Are you all right? Are you hurt?'

'I'm fine,' she gasped. 'What happened?'

'Well, I've cleared the way for us!'

'If you say so. I'm certainly not going to let you shovel my driveway in winter. Where's Harris?'

James looked at the spot where a few minutes ago the fake lord had been standing. Now there was only a pile of books and overturned shelves, and a feeling like a heavy weight settled down in in the pit of his stomach. He fought his way around the table and started to pull away boards and books.

'Oh, my God! Oh, my God! James, what have you done?'

Alice came to help him clear away the debris. She saw the motionless body first. She lifted off a shelf and found the old man's head, his face smeared with blood.

James quickly felt for the artery in the old man's neck.

'Shit! I think he's dead. I can't feel his pulse.'

'Are you sure? Maybe you're not doing it right. Let me.' Alice hastily pushed James away from the body and felt for herself.

She stared up at James, distraught.

'James, you killed him!'

He swallowed against the same nausea rising up inside him as when he had clobbered the man on H.M.S. *Belfast* with an iron bar. This was ten times worse. He had actually caused a death.

## CHAPTER 27

'Give me a break! First of all, he was going to kill us. All right then, just me,' he added quickly as he saw Alice's eyebrow go up. 'And secondly, it was an accident. I didn't know this was going to happen!'

'No. Of course.' She stood up. 'James, what are we going to do about it?'

James chewed his lip.

'We're going to call the police. There's no need to bring you into this, but I ought to report myself. It's the law, and following the law is what makes us better than people like Johnson. We don't think we're above it.'

'Hey.' She slipped her hand into his. 'We face this together. And you're right, it was self-defence. Come on, let's get out of here.'

Alice started towards the door but James held her back, just a moment. He nodded at the book on the table.

'And what about that? When the police get here, this whole room will be a crime scene and everything in it will be examined.'

Alice stared at the book like it was a poisonous snake.

'Tear the page out,' she said.

'You're sure?'

'Tear it out!' she insisted. 'I … I don't care who I'm descended from. I have no intention of being Queen and I have no intention of embarrassing the one we have.'

James felt a freshly renewed burst of love for this amazing woman. He wanted to spend the rest of his life with her – and that could be severely buggered up if she suddenly became a member of the Royal Family.

'Your wish is my command!' he said.

It took a moment for him to tear the page out. He shut the book, then tossed it on to the floor along with all the other books he had accidentally brought down. There was nothing to show there had ever been anything special about it.

James folded the page and stuffed it into a pocket.

'And *now*, let's get out of here.'

Halfway down the corridor, they heard the first sound of a police siren. They looked at each other.

'That can't be for us already?' Alice said. James grunted.

'Only one way to find out.'

They ran down the big stairs to the ground floor. The sirens, which had been growing louder and louder, suddenly stopped. They peeked out of the window. Not one but two police cars had pulled up outside the gates. Officers were in the road outside, talking to each other.

As they watched, a TV news van pulled up to join them.

'How did they get here so soon?' Alice asked.

'I've no idea. Maybe a builder heard the scaffolding fall over. Maybe there's a burglar alarm. Well, it saves us time. Let's get this over with.'

James tugged at the front door, but it was still locked and there was no sign of any way to open it. He turned towards the window.

'Okay, we go out the way we came in …'

'Wait.' Alice put a hand on his arm to slow him down. 'Before we turn ourselves in, don't you think we should

## CHAPTER 27

get our story straight? Even without this bit of paper, they'll ask what we were doing here.'

James had to admit she was right.

'The best lies are the ones that tell as much truth as possible,' he decided eventually. 'We say Roger pretended to be George Anderson and hired me. We say the whole trail led here, he held us at gunpoint … but we say nothing about what happened to Annie's baby. This is where the trail went cold, and then Harris was tragically killed in an accident. Does that work?'

'It works for me,' she agreed.

'And me,' said an emotionless voice behind them. They spun around.

'In fact, I would find that almost convincing,' the voice went on.

Gun levelled, William Johnson emerged from a side passage.

# JACK

# CHAPTER 28

Alice recovered from their shock first.

'We heard you'd been fired.'

'That hardly matters. I swore to devote my life to the Royal Family. The fact they no longer appreciate my efforts does not release me from that vow. Come on now, and no more questions.'

Johnson waggled his gun and stepped back – a clear sign they should step through the door where he stood. They looked at each other, then held hands and did as Johnson wanted. The door led to a back passage into the depths of the building, and that ultimately led to a back door out to the street on the other side of the building.

'Keep going,' Johnson ordered.

They walked down the street for a short distance. Johnson was behind them, so they couldn't see what he was doing with the gun. Presumably, James thought, he was concealing it in a pocket. It was still too early for there to be many pedestrians about but even so James was pretty sure people would notice a gunman holding a couple hostage.

But they didn't go far.

'That black steel door on the other side of the road,' Johnson ordered. 'Stand next to it.'

They crossed the road. Now James could see the outline of the gun inside Johnson's coat. Johnson was much younger and fitter than Roger Harris had been. There would be no distracting or jumping him.

Johnson single-handedly worked a large, old fashioned mortice key into the lock of the steel door, and turned it, then stepped back.

'Open it,' he ordered James. 'Then get inside.'

James used both hands to pull the door open. The loud squeal of metal showed that no one had been this way for a long time. Inside was the top of an iron spiral staircase. They stepped in and Johnson operated the light switch with his free hand. Neon tubes flickered on. They were in a small cubicle with no other way out except the stairs.

'Close the door,' Johnson ordered.

'Where is this?' Alice asked as James obeyed.

'There are abandoned Underground stations all over London. Some were even closed before they went into operation. Now, downstairs.'

They trudged in single file down the stairs, James's mind spinning as he tried to think of a way out of this one. He couldn't. There was no chance of moving faster than Johnson, no scaffolding to provide a handy means of distraction ... nothing.

A small door at the foot of the stairs led out on to the platform. The lights were only just bright enough to show detail: the curved walls dwindling towards the dark tunnel at either end. Fighting to hide their trembling, Alice and James turned to face William Johnson.

Johnson smiled maliciously.

'Now. First of all, of course, I want the evidence you recovered from Dartmoor.'

## CHAPTER 28

'We didn't find anything in Dartmoor —' James began.

William moved faster than even James had believed possible. He lunged like a striking snake, lashing the side of James's head with the barrel of his pistol. James cried out and dropped to his knees, too stunned to stay upright. Through the haze in his brain he became aware he was clutching the side of his head, and could feel blood pouring through his fingers. He was vaguely aware that Alice had screamed his name. He stared with loathing up at Johnson through streaming eyes.

'You must have found something,' Johnson said calmly. 'I followed Harris because I knew that sooner or later you would report to him, but it was a surprise when he came to St Anna's because I also know there is not one shred of evidence linking it to Annie Crook, apart from Abberline's missing evidence, which you therefore must have found. So, where is it?'

'What's the point?' James gasped. 'You'll kill us anyway.'

'I will,' Johnson agreed. 'It boils down to, will I do it quickly or slowly? And will I torture one of you in front of the other until one of you tells me? But …' His eyes narrowed and his tone became more thoughtful. 'Back there, I heard you refer to "this bit of paper". What bit of paper was that?'

James just glared at him. His head and his eyes were clearing.

Johnson smiled thinly.

'Lady Alice. Search him and turn out his pockets.'

Alice didn't move. Johnson rolled his eyes and shot James in the arm.

The noise and James's bellow echoed up and down the platform, bouncing off the tiled walls. Pain roared inside James's head. It hurt more than he would ever have believed possible. He writhed on the floor, clutching his arm, eyes squeezed shut and teeth clenched against the agony.

'Lady Alice,' Johnson repeated. 'Search him and turn out his pockets. I want to see the lining showing so I know nothing is hidden in there.'

Fighting back sobs – of anger, not fear – Alice knelt and reluctantly went through James's pockets with trembling hands, trying to remember which one he had put the page in so she could miss it out. But Johnson was watching like a hawk and there was no hiding it. Eventually she had to produce the folded bit of paper, which she passed to Johnson. He opened it clumsily with his left hand, still keeping the gun trained on the pair of them.

Alice helped James into a sitting position as Johnson read, and pressed the hankie she had found in his pocket to his wound.

Johnson's mouth had dropped open.

'Good ... grief. This, I did *not* expect.' He stared at Alice. '*You* are the descendant of Annie Crook's little girl? Well, well.'

Abruptly his tone sounded less dazed.

'I will deal with this information my own way. The question still remains – where is the evidence from

## CHAPTER 28

Dartmoor? I could swear I looked everywhere and that foolish old man could still be alive if he had just told me.'

'Perhaps he took a dislike to you,' James muttered. 'I can't think why.'

'There's still plenty of places I could shoot you without killing you, Mr Kent.'

'You should learn to get your hands dirty,' Alice snapped. 'It was hidden in the coal cellar under the stone floor.'

'Ah ... very clever! Though by now you must have realised I have no hesitation getting my hands dirty when I need to.'

'But you don't need to,' James said. 'We took that page because Alice has no intention of claiming her title or doing anything to embarrass the Royal Family. Isn't that what you want? Now you can destroy it and no one will ever know.'

'No intention, Lady Alice? Why is that?' Johnson asked coldly. Neither of them believed this information would influence his decision, but Alice answered because of the simple human instinct that it was better to keep talking than to die.

'Well, maybe like you, I respect them too much to want to change them. Of course they make mistakes, but that's what makes them human—'

'Wrong!' Johnson bellowed. 'They *can't* make mistakes! They should be above the law! A shining example for the rest of us!'

'Well, something went wrong there, didn't it?' James sneered.

Red with anger, Johnson yelled at him.

'That's right! But I'm here to protect this stupid family from all dangers, and that includes itself!'

With a visible effort, Johnson brought himself back under control. He squinted down along the barrel at James's knees.

'So. The knees, the legs, the other arm … So much pain I could cause. For the last time: where is the evidence you took?'

James and Alice looked deep into each other's eyes. Then James answered firmly.

'Cause as much pain as you like. It won't change things. The file has been copied and distributed to every media outlet we could find.'

He and Johnson gazed steadily at each other. Johnson was obviously weighing up alternatives.

'That might be true. In that case there's nothing I can do to prevent the embarrassment it will cause the family – but without this bit of paper here, the storm will eventually pass because the last bit of the puzzle will be missing. There again, you might be lying, and however much pain I inflict there is always the possibility that you tell me a plausible lie … You might die before I establish the truth … It barely matters. You are amateurs, you have left a trail a mile wide. I can track back – I will find it eventually.'

Johnson switched his attention abruptly to Alice as he patted his pocket.

## CHAPTER 28

'Lady Alice, with this bit of paper, you are the rightful Queen of Great Britain. Without it, you are merely the descendant of Jack the Ripper. Can you live with that?'

Alice rolled her eyes in incredulity.

'Seriously? Of course I can.'

'I see.' Johnson paused just a moment longer. 'Then this conversation serves no further useful purpose.'

The shot caught Alice in the middle of the forehead. Her head jerked back as a dark hole appeared above her eyes, at exactly the same as a red mess blew from the back of her skull. She toppled to the cold stone floor like a puppet with its strings cut. The shot must have boomed and echoed but James never heard it because of his own scream, torn up out of him from the deepest depths of his being, scraping his throat raw.

*'No! No, Alice! No!'*

He flung himself on to her body, sobbing with the shock and horror. The face, so warm, the eyes, so alive – both were now just nothing, inanimate. Alice was gone. Blood flowed from the neat round wound in the front of her head and from the much larger wound at the back.

Utterly broken, James stared up at Johnson through eyes that streamed with tears of sorrow and rage.

'Why?' he choked. 'Why?'

'Come, come, James. You knew this was would happen. You and she are loose ends that I simply cannot allow —'

The red flower burst on to his chest at the same time as the shot echoed around the tunnel. Johnson staggered, and fell to his knees. His arms waved wildly to keep his balance.

'You ...', he gasped, gazing at something beyond James. His gun hand waved in circles as he tried to bring it round to aim.

Another shot caught him in the throat. Something red exploded from his neck and he fell over backwards.

James's senses had had too much. He couldn't take any more in. His brain was simply filtering out any new information. So he just stared dully at the man pacing down the platform, both arms extended in front of him, one holding his gun, the other some ID. James forced his eyes to move up to the man's face. Did he know it? There was some hint of familiarity but his brain was too numb to process the information.

'Sorry I wasn't here sooner.' The man knelt down by Alice and checked her pulse in her throat. 'Shit. I'm sorry.' He turned to Johnson's body and went through the same procedure.

Then he pulled a radio from his inside pocket and held it up to his mouth.

'Who the hell are you?' James croaked. The man glanced briefly at him before rattling instructions off into the radio.

'Miller, MI5.'

# CHAPTER 29

'Good evening. This is the BBC.

The funeral took place today of Lady Alice Gull, the daughter of the Duke of Cardiff, in St Paul's cathedral. After her family, the mourners were led by Her Majesty the Queen. The Prime Minister was also present.

Downing Street and Buckingham Palace have promised that a full statement will be made regarding Lady Alice and the Queen's former Security Counsel William Johnson. It is believed they were involved in what has become known as the Taxi Incident outside Buckingham Palace and also in the recent security alert at Windsor Castle.

In the House of Commons, the Leader of the Opposition has demanded a full investigation into how much of this was known to the Prime Minister, whose resignation was recently announced ...'

# JACK

# CHAPTER 30

It was a cold and rainy autumn day in London. The wind swept over the metropolis of millions. Very few tourists were out and about in this weather. Most of them enjoyed the museums or shopping.

Above Buckingham Palace, the royal standard blew and snapped in the wind and a few hundred tourists watched the changing of the guard in front of the royal residence. In one of the Palace's six hundred rooms, James Kent sat on a sofa, his arm in a sling. Opposite him, in armchairs, sat the Prime Minister and the Queen. Thomas Black sat and watched from a distance. On a small table in front of James stood his teacup, which he had just lifted to take a single sip.

'I would just like to reiterate that Her Majesty's government is deeply indebted to you, Mr Kent,' the Prime Minister was saying. 'You acted for the good of all the people when you decided not to make the case public.'

James glared coldly at him.

'How many times, Prime Minister? I didn't do it for the people or the country.'

It was probably more blunt than anything else anyone said to the Prime Minister's face, or in front of the Queen, but James was past caring.

The Prime Minister looked puzzled.

'Then who—'

'For me,' James snapped. 'I burned the file because I want to live free of fear. Look. One thing this whole matter has taught me is that people who look powerful and important, aren't. Very often there's someone behind them, using their name and their authority for their own purposes and never bothering to tell the people who are nominally in charge. It's everywhere, whether it's the White House, 10 Downing Street, or this palace. Ma'am, I am convinced that if you had known what Johnson was doing you would never have wanted such a bloodbath in your name, but could you actually have stopped it? So. I'm keeping quiet because you never know when another lunatic like William Johnson will come along and decide to take the law into his own hands again.'

He meant every word.

Keeping that file secret had been touch and go. Even after Miller had called an ambulance and he had been whisked off to hospital, he had been worrying about it. Supposing someone else got to it first?

As soon as he could get to a phone, James had called Uncle Howard to retrieve his car. He had taken it and the file back to Arundel, and it was in the back garden of James's uncle and aunt that the file had been ceremonially burned.

The Prime Minister looked shocked.

'I can assure, you, that will never happen again—'

'I don't see why not,' the Queen said unexpectedly. The three men in the room stared at her in surprise. 'It

## CHAPTER 30

happened once, after all. That means it can most certainly happen again.'

The Prime Minister immediately tried to assure her.

'And that is why, ma'am, I'm putting in place —'

She interrupted him as though he hadn't even spoken. James wondered if she enjoyed being the only person in the land who could do that and get away with it.

'Whatever your reason, Mr Kent,' she went on, 'your actions spared my family no little embarrassment, and I must thank you for that. Nonetheless, it is quite clear that a great deal was being done in my name about which I knew nothing and of which I would most certainly have been ashamed if I did know. And for that reason, I intend to make sure that the results of the enquiry are published, in full. There will be no cover-up. We have no file any more, but I think I owe that much at least to the memory of Alice.

'Thank you,' James said, taken aback by the honesty. He knew that for this woman, duty came first and foremost. Her own interests, even her own family's interests, came second. If she saw such truthfulness as being her duty then that was what would happen.

The Prime Minister looked shocked. But Thomas Black, James noticed, was completely impassive, apparently not disturbed at all. And then he wondered whether this actually would happen. Did even the Queen have that power if Thomas Black decided otherwise?

'By the way, Mr Kent, I have not yet expressed my condolences over what happened to Alice. I do so now. I only met her a few times at dinner events, but she was always very cheerful and friendly. A remarkable woman. I'm very sorry she passed away.'

The Queen spoke with her usual detachment, but James was sure he heard genuine sorrow in her voice.

After that it was just a few more pleasantries, and then James's time was up.

'Well, Mr Kent, I hope we meet again. Mr Black will show you out.' The Queen shook hands and disappeared into the next room, followed by the Prime Minister. Thomas Black was already standing by the door.

'If you would please follow me, Mr Kent?'

James smiled slightly. Here, he suspected, was a man of real power. He wondered what Thomas Black made of being treated like a butler. Maybe he considered it a price worth paying. James followed after him.

'What you were saying, Mr Kent, about there being someone always at work behind the scenes – that was very interesting.'

'Do you think so, Mr Black?' Together they reached the main staircase, which led down to the ground floor.

'Absolutely, Mr Kent. And not so wrong, either. But unlike you, I don't mind at all.'

'Oh, I don't think it's necessarily a bad thing, Mr Black. It all depends on how those people use their power.'

'Whatever you say.'

Silently they walked down the great marble staircase and out into a small courtyard. Outside the door stood a black Jaguar, one of the Palace's many official vehicles. Thomas Black opened the back door of the car and let James Kent in.

## CHAPTER 30

'Rest assured, Mr Kent, everything in Her Majesty's household is now in perfect order. Thank you for your assistance, but I don't believe we will require it again.'

'That makes me happier than you can possibly imagine, Mr Black.'

Black smiled thinly and slammed the door, then thumped on the roof as the signal for the driver to head off. The car drove out of the yard and turned left into Buckingham Palace Road. They passed the Queen Victoria Memorial and turned into the Mall. James twisted around in the back seat and looked out the window. Buckingham Palace became smaller and smaller as they drove on. Thoughtfully, he turned around again.

'Trafalgar Square, wasn't it, sir?' the driver asked.

'Yes, please. Only ... can we take a little detour?'

The man shrugged cheerfully.

'Of course! Where can I take you, sir?'

'To Highgate Cemetery.'

\*

Highgate lay just to the east of Hampstead. Drawing close to it, seeing the familiar landmarks appear, was a bittersweet experience. James remembered the beautiful evening on the Heath with Alice.

They drove on silently until they arrived at the entrance to the cemetery. The gatehouse looked like a small castle in its own right. James opened his door to get out. The driver wound down his window.

'Should I wait, sir?'

'No, thanks. I'll take a cab.'

James walked through the gatehouse and into the cemetery.

The old place had as many trees as it had graves. They gave shade in summer when the weather was fine, but now they only swayed wildly in the wind. Dead leaves and bits of grit swirled around James as he made his way to the place he had memorised.

The Victorians had made a fetish of being dead, he thought. The centuries-old gravestones and memorials were a silent competition in stone to see who could be bigger and better.

The one he was after was very simple, in polished red marble, and he soon found it standing at the head of the newly laid out grave.

The funeral had been the saddest day of his life. He hadn't wanted to go, despite Alice's father inviting him, because he didn't want to say goodbye. It would be admitting that Alice had gone away from him forever.

Since her death he had asked himself, again and again, whether it had been the right decision to destroy everything. But now he looked at the tombstone, he was sure Alice wouldn't have wanted it any other way.

Suddenly James noticed the single dark red rose lying in front of the stone. Next to it a polished stone held down a piece of paper. He picked it up and read:

> May your soul find peace, like all the other souls who have already died for truth.
> Sean Miller.

## CHAPTER 30

Surprised, he looked around. Miller had come to visit him in hospital. He had said he was quitting his job at MI5 and going to work as a cop in Cornwall. That had always been his dream, he had said, before finally saying goodbye to James.

James Kent thoughtfully left the court of the dead behind him and turned right. He plodded along without much thought for the next twenty minutes or so until he was at the top of Parliament Hill on the Heath. The wind had once again torn a gap in the cloud cover and the sun was shining through it. All of London shone before him in a golden glow for a few minutes.

Alice was right, James thought: this city was something extraordinary, because where else could you find such a mix of life and the world in such a small space?

*The End*

## Max McBridge

Ever since my first visit to London in 2000, I have been fascinated by its rich history, its progression and its advances. The mix of modern and traditional, and its international culture have always been astounding. Like many others, I am inspired by this open-hearted city and I would love to share it with you.

@MaxMcBridge

## McBridge Foundation

We are witnessing the ever-widening gap between those who can afford the rich opportunities of this great city and those who are increasingly left behind. The main objective of the Foundation is to bridge this gap by focusing on the prevention and relief of poverty. This also extends to the advancement of education, supporting arts and culture, and protecting the environment. The McBridge Foundation cooperates with charities and projects that provide efficient solutions for these pressing issues by giving grants to support their work.

*>> www.McBridge.uk<<*

Printed in Great Britain
by Amazon